D. HALE RAMBO

PRESSED

THE PLANAR PAGES

Cover Design by Fantastical Ink
The Planar Page Logos by Grace Lewis
Planar Pages by Rick Hertel

Fiercewood Press
401 Century Pkwy #1314
Allen, Texas 75013
United States
business@fiercewoodpress.com

Contents

FIONA WONDERED IF THERE were worse ways to spend one's evening than stalking the backwater floating isles of her home page, Restless Rise, waiting for the Painted Edge to show themselves. There were undoubtedly *different* ways, like crawling the pits of the page of earth, breaking under the weight of its immense gravity. Or searching the deep, dry deserts of Kerus without a splash of water or, worse yet, a safe pagemark to be found. But this truly had to take the cake. For one, it was raining. Not slightly. A downpour really. And two, she was pretending to be unseen, which was hard to do with a flirting faun alchemist and human pirate captain. After this stakeout Fiona vowed to treat herself to a warm bath with a cup of aggressively spiked coffee.

"Could you two please keep the romantics to a minimum?" Fiona waved her hand somewhat irritably at Gaili and Henrietta. "If I didn't need one of you to be the face and another to be the eyes, I would've left you adoring each other at home."

Gaili—blossom-pink curls, small black horns, and golden skin flashing in the soft moonlight—nodded quickly. "Sorry, Fi. We were talking about an upcoming trip and—"

"And I got carried away with it," Henrietta finished in her deep but charming tenor. Her peachy cheeks reddened with a slight blush. She straightened the cuffs of her shirt. Though usually brighter dressed, Henrietta was in dark-brown clothes fit for flitting through the darkness. She cleared her throat, barely audible against the noise of fat raindrops hitting the muddy ground. "I'll keep my thoughts to myself for the time being and focus. Apologies, mistress."

Fiona stifled a sigh and nodded. She had to admit she was a touch irritated through no fault of the lovebirds. The few weeks between stopping the Court of Copper from being torn inside out to this evening had been riddled with too many things outside her control.

No one had seen or heard from Sadie the shape-changing hag in all that time. Her home on Restless Rise had been emptied, servants dismissed (although with glowing recommendations so as not to be disgruntled), and path unfound. Though the search for the three missing crowns had to continue, Fiona hadn't the faintest idea of where to start with such a lead drying up. She could be anyone (well, human, faun, or centaur at least) and use them for anything. It made Fiona paranoid, not knowing if someone she was conversing with or passing on the street was Sadie. Mac had told her the only true way to know, without another fae-bond that would drain her, was by looking for the quirks pre-Inking faekin had. Mac, for example, needed to create a compulsion she channeled through her concoctions. In Sadie's case they took the form of her fascination with alliteration and contests. In the game of clues, this sign was a small one. And so Fiona strained to understand the intent in every meeting and encounter she had. It was exhausting.

The Order of Seven had asked Fiona for her eyes and ears outside of the page. She agreed, of course, but noted nothing out of the ordinary across the Book. The Travel Guild looked for Sadie as well, to no avail, but Fiona knew they wouldn't stop trying. Finding out one's dead sister was alive wasn't the sort of thing she expected Marcia, a Gilded leader and hidden hag herself, to give up.

Then the very public and very useless trial of the few captured Painted Edge members finally happened. The organization had stolen from the page of fire, almost destroying it; smuggled countless fire creatures out and tried to make illegal concoctions out of them; and then almost got away with it all, leaving the mess at the feet of the Travel Guild, the regulating force for most of the pages in the Book and overseers of the comings and goings of page turners.

And what did the smugglers get? Imprisonment in the Hinge, Guild headquarters. Removal from the public, yes, but they gave no further information about who started their organization or where the blasted airship they stole from Restless Rise was hiding. They insisted they took their orders anonymously, not meeting anyone else. And somehow anonymously all got the same exact blue-striped tattoo as well. Fiona shook her head thinking about their absurd answers again. Fiona had thought valuable information would've come from them—with the right pressure, of course—but Dodger had been able to gain nothing new, though his new promotion to Marbled at the Travel Guild had at least given Fiona a spot at the trial.

Denizens from the page of fire were there. She had tried talking to the few she saw, but they could give her no answers except that everything seemed to be, well, aflame. They hadn't been entirely clear and her Claire, language of the flame, was a tad poor. She wished Gaili could've been there with her flawless pronunciation to translate. The faun had fast become busy with not only her bustling shop but also with helping Fiona on the minor cases that new fame had sent her way, and with her burgeoning relationship with Henrietta and Matteo. It was Henrietta, visiting at their shared home once again, who came through with new information. Her associate smuggler who had been working with the Painted Edge had popped back up. Henrietta made some polite inquiries about work, suggesting that cocoa and coffee smuggling was no longer her main job, and procured an invitation to a Painted Edge recruitment meeting. Fiona had been most impressed with the captain's quick thinking. That the contact didn't know Henrietta was friends with an investigator Fiona counted as a massive win.

As she had come to learn, many people knew her face from the blasted *Card*, a news pamphlet printed and distributed all over the Book. Though requests for her to work on cases had gone up from the accidental promotion, so had her name and figure. She had to take to wearing her hair differently, more like the other human page turners of Rise, with her brown curls swept up into a bun and covered with elaborate fabric and netted cord. And her multi-pocketed, multi-page scarf had become more hidden as well, although not completely out of reach. It was becoming too well known. Sadie's questions about its abilities to reach the dark edge were never far from her mind. No, it had become time to keep it near but quiet, lest she be robbed of it again.

But it all meant she had to rely on friends, clever, loyal friends, to surveil with her. If she could catch the Painted

Edge out, then she would have at least one problematic entity in the Book dealt with and could close the case on them for good. And her friends had been great watchers, at least for the first few hours. But people got bored. That was the problem. And unlike Fiona, they didn't know how to self-entertain with curiosity.

"I find it odd that the PE would setup a hideout here to meet," Fiona murmured. She wrinkled her nose. "There are better, less populated places. Smallcrest for one, though it is at Plateau height, so too easily spotted perhaps." The Plateau, a massive flat land in the center of the world, rotated every season like clockwork. Surrounding this restless rise were more than a dozen floating islands at various elevation levels. Nothing too high above or too far below of course. Even the lowest floating islands stayed well above the thick clouds roiling below them all.

"It's so far away from a safe pagemark. Larrakane knows, rippers like them have used unsafe pagemarks before, but so routinely? And it is right on the edge of Woolring. I mean, wouldn't it be quite obvious to the sheep farmers when a group of people springs out of nowhere? There's only so many of them." She kept her eyes focused on the field in front of her. Mixed grasses and clumps of rock were most of what this land had to offer—though she suspected with this amount of rain it would offer even less to those who worked it for a while.

There was a scraggly tree every few feet or so and one dilapidated barn but not what one would call great cover. That they expected to have a meeting here and invited a new recruit meant they probably felt very safe here though. It made sense that whatever they came to talk about would be very juicy to hear.

"I don't know if anyone can see anything in this rain," Henrietta replied, pulling a lightly dripping curl of gray-tinged strawberry hair from her eyes. "We're lucky my dear Gaili's clever enough to pop a water canopy for us, or we'd be soaked through ourselves."

Gaili had devised a way to use a jar of trapped air from the winds of Mistral and oil from duck feathers (a creature too common to the Rise) to create an invisible, weightless canopy that repelled the rain. Well, for a time. Though the air was let out at a measured rate, the heaviness or longevity of the downpour could see it spent long before its hour of use. Gaili gripped the jar and the long-stemmed contraption she had built that attached to it with a steady tattooed hand. She kept her other firmly on the ground to hold her balance. Though her right hand had almost healed from the rapid aging it experienced dealing with Clara—it was only mildly wrinkled now—Gaili still favored her undamaged hand for precise work.

Fiona nodded. "That is fair. It's simply not the best plan I think." She pulled her cloak tighter against herself as the rain continued to pour around them. The water canopy carefully covered them from the deluge, but it did nothing for the cold. It should've been a warm summer night in Rise. Not this wet, cold mess that had been happening more frequently. It wasn't quite the season for rain, but the weather didn't seem to acknowledge that. Rise had reported to the Travel Guild much flooding and the beginning destruction of some crops because of all the rain. It was unfortunate that no one in the Book had the power to control the weather.

"There's not a lot of big thinkers in smuggling and thieving," Henrietta said, pulling out a small dark leather-bound flask.

"You have a leader who is the brains and then a bunch of arms to move goods about. Sure, you might come across a few with more lightning in their head than the rest, but when you find one, you get them closer to you."

"For better planning?"

"Easier to watch." Henrietta tipped her flask for a swig. "Larrakane bless, I'd settle for just a ship in Rise and one outside of it. I could run more coffee and cocoa than even the Queen's shippers. And if I could move *Big Betty* between the pages as they can, it would make all the difference. Completely change the game."

"Have you ever tried it?" Fiona had never thought to ask before.

"Of course, but it's not feasible. You'd have to have page turners to work the transport every time, and you lot can't stay away from Spine long enough to keep on the move. What's more, I don't know any ship that can make it through a page turn fast enough. They're big and bulky. And you'd have to make sure everyone was working together in congruence with the turn. Hard enough to get a crew working together just to sail the blasted thing. I trust mine to know what they're doing, but sailing across a page? That frightened even the heartiest of 'em."

"But if you couldn't get it in one go, how did you get *Big Betty* to Mistral at all?" Gaili asked, brow furrowing.

Henrietta snorted. "Bit by bit, 'course."

There was a crackle of thunder as the field and scraggly trees peeled away some distance from them to reveal a darkened forest. No light broke through the sky and the large trunks seemed to take up the entirety of the background. Fiona squinted. How deep in the forests of Spine were they coming from? A small group of people strode clustered together. The page closed up behind them. Fiona was startled to realize the group all had visible weapons that stood out in the soft moonlight. She had never seen so many, except for groups of jackets, and they kept theirs carefully concealed so as not to be out of place among people as they covered the pages. The Painted Edge weren't just smugglers and rippers. They were deadly.

"Looks like I'm up," Henrietta said, getting to her feet with a light groan. She patted Gaili's hand, readjusted her rapier at her belt so it was showing, and then slipped out of the shadows and toward the group with a confident swagger.

Fiona slunk back away from the area, tugging Gaili along with her. If the Painted Edge had any sense, they'd scout before conducting their clandestine meeting. She certainly had, walking the rundown barn in the distance that was probably where they'd huddle up to chat. Or perhaps the downpour of rain made them confident no one was lurking around. No one sensible *would* be outside in this mess.

They stopped when Fiona felt they were comfortably away to whisper. The figures in the distance moved, gathering as Henrietta approached. They had agreed that she would give Henrietta some time to initiate herself. If it seemed as if the group were going to travel, turn the page somewhere else, or anything beyond talk, Fiona would follow. There was no telling what the Painted Edge might do if they caught them. The whole organization was wrapped in shadow and secrecy. It was doubtful they'd be set free. Fighting their way out was not a strong suit of Fiona's. And no matter what her mother had said of her propensity to natter on like a daft hen, she doubted she could talk their way out of a situation with that many people.

"Gaili, what details can you make out?" The faun's eyes were much better in the darkness than her human ones.

"There are quite a few people, long-haired and darkly clothed," Gaili whispered. She shook her head. "They seem more ragged than I expected."

Fiona smirked. "I don't think most thieves carry on with the latest fashion while they sneak around."

"Still, they could have a little pride in their look. Matching cloaks for one," Gaili said, sniffing. Faekin did always think the other mortal beings in the Book could up their fashion game to match theirs.

Fiona didn't have the heart to tell her that no one could possibly beat the denizens of the Court of Copper when it came to fashion or their amazing abilities. The page was simply more advanced than the humans of Restless Rise or the anthropomorphized animals of Kerus. "Are there any smilodons or elephas?" Fiona couldn't imagine any of the peaceful sects of elephas being involved in the group, but without knowing their motives, she wouldn't count anyone out.

The faun shook her head. "Just humans as far as I can tell. You think it's to put Henrietta at ease?"

"More so anyone who may come upon them will have fewer questions, I think. This is far from a touristy area."

"They're moving into the barn with her." Gaili's voice pitched.

"That's our cue to follow." Fiona rose from the ground and brushed mud off her thick black wool stockings. She had been prepared to run, jaunt, or climb at a moment's notice. She would not walk away from this opportunity without knowing something valuable. If their lives were going to be at stake, it should count for something. "Remember, stay ten steps behind me and to the right. When I stop, make the noise." Though she didn't want to put Gaili in danger, she knew there was little chance the faun would leave her and Henrietta out here alone. Gaili could take care of herself and turn the page back to Spine if needed. It was Henrietta who was the sitting duck with the inability to leave this page should she have to.

Fiona silently strode from beneath the water canopy into the pouring rain. The sodding rain beat the muddy ground in a rhythmic pattern, helping cover her footsteps as a lucky bonus. She had traded her usual Kerus slippers for the knee-high boots of her kin that would make it easier to traverse the muddy ground. The woman on guard at the abandoned barn seemed rapt with attention. Unlucky for Fiona. With no close trees to slink behind and the short grass unable to hide her crouching form, Fiona stopped. She flapped her hand, giving Gaili's sure-sighted faekin eyes the signal.

A loud noise, like a wild creature, beckoned farther afield. Though Fiona had known Gaili was talented in linguistics, she hadn't imagined she could mimic the sounds of fire creatures as well as she did. The hissing and sputtering sounded very lifelike. But the guard's attention was captured. The woman raised her crossbow and stepped off in the direction of the noise.

With a brief glance in that direction, Fiona skirted toward the barn. Soft lantern lights glowed from the glassless windows. Approaching the wooden exterior, she crouched and made her way to the back of the building. So far so good. She craned her neck to peer into the barn.

As she suspected, most of the group were seated on rusted crates and stools. Some lounged on the dry packed earth. Henrietta stood nonchalantly in the back with her contact, as if she had no further questions and belonged there. She kept a loose hand on the hilt of her rapier and leaned in, grinning at whatever her contact was saying to her. Fiona was impressed with her ability to blend in so quickly with the group of rippers. Though she was by far the oldest there, she was clearly experienced. Eyes kept flicking toward the door as if they were waiting for someone. Some paced. Few were talking.

With the rain around her, Fiona couldn't make out a sound. She shivered, a cold breeze whipping her clammy face. She needed to be able to hear what they said. Reading lips would only take her so far, and if she was truly honest, the hard rain had become quite a distraction. The barn had three entrances. If she got to the other ground door, she could crack it open to hear while remaining outside.

Pressing her body against the rough wooden exterior, she slipped around the barn and cracked open the door. A flash of lightning drew her notice, and she stopped short. The guard from earlier, crossbow taut, was heading in her direction. With little thought, Fiona slid through the thin opening and closed the door quickly behind her. She would've liked to keep her quick escape route, but investigators couldn't be choosers. At least here she could hear the other room clearly without the rain muffling the sound, and wooden holes in the walls made for excellent spying. She sighed with relief, letting her eyes adjust to the dark. With her back against the door, she began pulling off her soaking-wet cloak. The scent of fresh ink wafted in the air. *Odd, that smell wasn't present earlier.*

As her vision adapted to the dim light, she noticed a shape crouched behind one of the large storage crates. Fiona froze, hands on buttons. A pair of wide golden eyes in a handsome tawny face stared back at her in shock.

The man was tall but bent awkwardly to fit his muscular form mostly behind the crate as he clutched several small pieces of parchment to his chest. His curly dark hair was long, as was the fashion, but pulled back at the neck. Though he wore knee-high boots like hers, his were better suited for an appointment at the palace than mucking about in the dark in a sheep field. His doublet matched his boots, with too much frill for this side of the page. He was no Travel Guild jacket, that was for sure. He did seem vaguely familiar in that position. Though he looked out of place here, he would fit in at court with the cut of his jaw, trimmed beard, and expressive tawny face. Could he possibly be a gentleman in service to a baron? Nothing made sense. Fiona found she was staring a tad too hard at his jawline. Her face warmed and she glanced away toward the door. Where had he come from?

"My luck runs over," he muttered and looked her up and down in one swift motion. "Well, at least you had the sense not to scream."

The voice held a tinge of accent that she couldn't place. Fiona pursed her lips at the man's insinuation, thoughts of his golden eyes pushed to the side. "Of course I didn't scream. Who in the dark edge are you?" Fiona whispered.

"I don't see how that's any of your business," he said tersely. "You can't stay. You'll get me caught." His rugged face creased as he frowned, showing him to be older than herself but not overly so.

Fiona blinked at the unexpected answer. "Are you—Who do you—"

He held up his hand. "I think it's best if you leave. You don't know what you're getting mixed up with, and I can't look out for you."

"Excuse me, but I have a very clear idea what I'm getting mixed up with," Fiona hissed. She crossed her arms and then uncrossed them, drops of water flinging out from her. The nerve of him. She needed to hear what was going on in the other room to make this not a wasted event, and here was Golden-Eyed Pompous to tell her she didn't know what she was doing? "You're the one who seems to be unread."

The man opened his mouth to speak but stilled as voices carried from outside the door. The guard and another person shouted to each other, words hard to understand with the drumming of the rain.

Swift as a cat, the man was up and on his feet. He wrapped his hand around Fiona's while the other held tightly to the parchments and pulled them both farther into the darkened room, swerving through stacked troughs and metal water buckets.

Fiona's heart stuttered as the smell of old books and crisp paper overwhelmed her senses. Was it the papers he clutched or him? His hand trembled. Nervous? Confused, Fiona didn't fight against him and instead crouched in the darkness, hidden by his form.

The sounds of the guard and whomever she was talking to faded away from the door. He immediately dropped his hand and stepped back.

Fiona kept bent to the ground and frowned at him. "You have quite the nerve." She tugged on her doublet, busy hands finding a purpose in the uncertainty of the moment. Why did he work to hide her? "You shouldn't accost someone simply because you can."

The man muttered something incomprehensible; his unusual accent deepened and rose swiftly from the floor. "Very well. Be their problem then. Not mine." He opened the door and slipped out, disappearing into the pouring rain without a backward glance.

Fiona bolted up. She pinched her lips together staring in the dim light at the door. She couldn't go after him. Though he was no jacket, it didn't mean he wasn't Painted Edge. He didn't hesitate to leave when hearing the guard. For all she knew he was someone within the smuggling ring spying on the other members. What had he been reading? It had preoccupied him so much when she first arrived that he hadn't noticed her immediately. Searching the area where they hid gave her nothing. But he had been bent behind the crate. Perhaps there. Fiona got down on the warm packed-dirt ground, soggy mud-stained leggings blissfully cushioning her knees, and felt around for anything that might tell her something. Her curiosity rewarded her. A single sheet of small parchment lay flat against the crate. She smiled and tucked it inside her overcoat to be read over with better lighting.

Well, now she needed another place to hide. Somewhere uncompromised. And quickly too. Henrietta had already been there for many minutes without someone watching her back. Scowling, Fiona listened at the door but, hearing nothing more than rain, quickly exited and strode away to the back. The only other place was up.

Fiona pressed herself to the wall and hurried to the stairs that led to the roof. She quickly climbed the ladder and lay flat on the roof, the rain soaking every inch of her. Cursing the golden-eyed man for her current predicament, she scooted along the rough roof until she found the loft hatch she had scouted earlier.

She had left the hatch open on purpose so it would be easy to tell if someone else had been there. It was still open, and she climbed down into the prickly rain-soaked hay. Here she could see the group downstairs through a wedge in the floor. It was not as easy or as comfortable as the previous location. She took a deep breath, pushing thoughts of the disagreeable man to the side, and focused on the group below. Many had piled their wet cloaks to the side and were clumping together and talking. He wasn't among them, but that didn't mean he wouldn't show up.

"How much longer do we truly need to wait?" one of the men sitting on an old milk crate grumbled.

"We wait for her as long as it takes," another gangly individual said. "I'm not making trouble."

"Not sure why we keep taking orders from her. She's newer than all of us," the milk crate man said. "I liked the upper-class one better. She was nice." A few others nodded in agreement. "If the boss says to listen to her, we listen to her." The gangly one crossed his arms and stood in front of the door as if to bar anyone leaving.

So there was a boss but then the mention of another person. A lieutenant of sorts? The gangly one spoke casually as if he talked to the boss normally enough. Which would mean known faces and not the anonymous directions the imprisoned Painted Edge smugglers held fast to.

The barn door opened again, sweeping the rain inside. A young, slight, brown-haired woman with tawny complexion sauntered into the center of the room. Eyes followed as the door shut. Her plain gray woolen dress matched most of the others, but there was no blending in. She looked at everyone in turn, pausing only briefly to lay eyes on Henrietta. "We have a slight change of direction, my friends. The main event is moving up a notch," she said, her working-class accent thick. She looked around the room with a raised eyebrow as if challenging for questions. Everyone looked at each other, but no one spoke a word. She settled on the balls of her feet. "We need to haul everything in the storeroom out tonight before we go. The other Dots will pick it up tomorrow for the setup."

Milk Crate crossed his arms. "We just got all the supplies in the storeroom two days ago."

Fiona flinched at the beatific smile the woman shone at the man. If it was genuine, she would've found the woman lovely, but there was something unnatural in it.

"Yes, and while that was a *great help*, they need to be moved back out tonight," the woman said.

"You couldn't have told us that then? Could've saved some time," Milk Crate said, staring back boldly. Whatever the others may have thought, he seemed to be over this particular person.

The woman moved to the man quicker than Fiona expected. Their faces were inches apart. She pressed her hand to his chest as if she was a tigress with claws. "Do you have a problem doing your part here?"

He flinched and took a step back, his face ashen. He dropped his arms. "No, no problems here."

"Then I *suggest* we stop chatting and get to work. The sooner we haul 'em up, the sooner you can all bolt back to your edge." She took a step back and clapped once at everyone. Swiftly like a choreographed step, people rose. Some got to work pulling up boards hidden in the packed dirt. The woman sauntered over to Henrietta. Fiona moved, straining to hear what they said, but the sudden increase in activity made it difficult.

Henrietta raised an eyebrow and nodded to what the brown-haired woman was saying. More than likely a question. Henrietta's contact started to speak, but the woman cut her off with a decisive slash of her hand through the air. It was clear to Fiona that the contact was scared of this brown-haired leader, but Henrietta seemed to relax even more. Oh, her card face was very good.

The brown-haired woman looked her up and down and then gave a curt shake of the head, pointing to the door. She said something, to which a brief flash of frustration crossed Henrietta's face, but it quickly dissipated. The captain shrugged and backed away to the door.

Fiona was surprised. She assumed that Henrietta, with her years of smuggling and ability to craft the best lies, would be accepted into the Painted Edge. It was unlikely this brown-haired woman even knew of Henrietta before this moment, so why was she rejected now when her contact had assured her they were looking for recruits? Fiona wondered how quickly she should follow and if she had enough time to reach the authorities and get them here before the group finished. What was in the basement, and just how long could it take with this many people?

The leader said something else to the contact after Henrietta had gone, and she nodded solemnly before joining the others. The leader turned to address the group. "That goes for the lot of you. Don't bring pulp to me unless they've been vetted. Listen to the format. Understand me?"

Many nodded as they continued to work, going down steps and hauling up boxes and bags. The brown-haired woman left swiftly, making Fiona sigh with relief that she hadn't departed quickly after Henrietta too. She'd be caught out in the open with her back to her. She listened carefully, but no sounds of shouting or fighting drifted up to her. She hoped Henrietta wouldn't go straight back to Gaili with the woman and guards out there.

Pressed between the guards and the group, Fiona stayed put and watched, trying to glean exactly what this big event was. If she couldn't figure that out specifically, at least she'd know what the Painted Edge were up to. She would then have a lead to share with Dodger. Crates were being pulled up from the basement with ropes and pulleys. Beyond that it looked like a large assortment of mundane gear. Nothing too impressive and nothing that would have any authority immediately charging them. They could be held on tattoo alone, but they were also page turners. They knew how to vanish somewhat quickly. Turning the page was never a blink of the eye and required concentration. But a hiding turner with a few precious minutes could get to another page before all of them were rounded up.

What was in the crates? Once they were gone, she could open them and possibly piece together all the contents. If they were going to move them out in the morning, she had to look in them tonight. Henrietta and Gaili knew she was independent and had sense. They wouldn't worry for a few hours, especially with what Henrietta heard.

Her legs stiffened as she lay unmoving in her squished position. As the Painted Edge left the barn, redressing for the unfit weather, she notated all their faces as best as she could.

Fiona strained to hear any names, but they did well not to address each other by much. Though they worked as a team, she got the sense that they didn't always do so. The chatter between them was one of familiarity but confusion in their task. They didn't seem to know what was in the crates or where they were going either. They worked with such focus that Fiona was quite sure whoever commanded them had made an example out of being curious. Not one of them opened a crate. It would take quite a feat for Fiona to remain so resolute. And what had the other group's name been? Dots? Without knowing the name of this group, it was hard to understand if there was a pattern. What was the structure of the Painted Edge that kept them so mobile and so well hidden?

Fiona itched to get down there and see what it was but willed herself to wait half an hour or so after the door had closed. When the time was up and she could be cautious no more, Fiona got up, groaning quietly to herself. She was not quite the young sprig anymore. This would be her thirtieth year and already she felt a little less eager to scale through windows and lay prone in prickly hay stacks—although, if her mother was to be believed, she was on death's door for as unmarried, unsociable, and unusual as she was.

Fiona shook her head of such thoughts and eased herself from the loft, through the now cleared night sky. The world was eerily silent as the rain had ceased soon after they left. The lanterns were gone, the moon clouded.

Mildew and damp earth mingled with the smell of sweat in the air. Fiona wrinkled her nose and felt the walls of the room she had been watching, taking the path she had mapped for herself. The large wooden crates had been stacked in the center, the mass of ropes, pulleys, and hooks next to them.

She skirted around the ropes, running her hands over them as she went to the crates. Their rough fibers were dry under her fingertips. They had not been used recently. Reaching into her sleeve, she tugged on her hidden multi-pocketed scarf to pull it partway out. She reached into a soft leather pocket and thought of her crowbar. In a moment it appeared beneath her fingers, and she slid it out before tucking the scarf back. The edge of the crate's rough wooden lid glided under her tapping fingers. She slid the crowbar in and shoved. Though she was thin, she placed every ounce of her weight on the bar to wedge the crate open. With a few tries, a solid crack announced the lid was freed. Fiona placed the crowbar gently on the ground and, wedging her fingers in tight, lifted the lid with a creak.

An enormous iron hook sat in the crate, nestled in fresh straw. No wonder it had taken so many to lift the crates out one at a time. It looked heavy indeed. She dug her hand inside, searching for anything else of note, but that's all there was among the straw.

She opened another crate, this one somewhat smaller. Tacked parchment hung from within the swinging lid as she pushed it back. It was small, quite like the ones the golden-eyed man had. *Interesting.* She pulled out her own identical parchment and held them side by side in the dim light. They looked exactly the same except for some portions of the writing. The language was completely unknown to her, but she could have Gaili and Henrietta take a look.

Thrusting her hands inside the crate, she felt several thick leather straps and buckles molded around something hard and metal. Was this a harness? Too small for a horse, but it had the shape. What were they doing with an iron hook, ropes, pulleys, and a harness? Hoisting something? Stealing something? Dare she light her lantern?

As if answering her desire, lantern light cascaded across the window, bearing the secrets of the open crates to any who could see. The soft amber glow threw shadows across the whole space, leaving places to hide but at the whim of the lantern holder.

Fiona dropped to the ground, stifling a groan as her body hit the warm earth. Someone had come back? It took them ages to leave; what could they possibly have forgotten? Perhaps it was the Dots group here to pick up early. If so, they needed to be caught. Fiona crawled to the nearest window and peeked out. Seeing no one, she pulled herself up and out quietly without hesitation. She could make it to the nearest guardhouse if she ran. The window of opportunity was open, and she wasn't likely to get the chance again.

"AND BY THE TIME the authorities would rouse from their bedside, everything was gone. I should've found a pagemark back to Spine immediately instead of relying on the closest Rise guards."

"Well, you had no idea they would move so fast. The woman said they'd get everything in the morning?" Gaili said, leaning over the scuffed wooden table in the kitchen. It was more Gaili's home workshop than kitchen really. Between baking, concocting, and the occasional experimentation, the entire room was hers to command. The countertops that once held a plethora of mismatched items now had stacked bowls, plates, and alchemical ingredients and seasonings somewhat labeled so as to not be accidentally swapped. The bricked fireplace that Fiona had installed when purchasing the old manor to modernize it now saw as much bread and cakes as it did potions and infusions. To Fiona's great relief, the daily smells were of good cheese, fresh coffee, and warm bread rather than the burning of forgotten experiments. Well, most days.

Gaili held a golden magnifying glass up against the lifted pearl-handled dagger. Careful not to touch it, she had it held aloft with a pair of tongs. She scratched notes for the umpteenth time in her journal, pert nose wriggling in concentration. Gaili had been working on the true effects and components of the dagger since they had gotten it from Sadie. When using the dagger, one saw visions of themselves in a variety of different moments. They all felt real and yet they weren't. Sometimes they were a memory of a previous moment but slightly different. Other times it was what was currently happening but from a different point of view. The blade itself was a vicious little thing Gaili had commented on. Eager to cut and slice through anything. It was all quite confusing, and Gaili was no closer to determining how it worked. She worried truly invasive tests would damage it forever, so she was careful. But still she had made time enough to study it and resupply Fiona with a new weapon, a slingshot, better suited to Fiona's tastes.

"That's what the leader said." Fiona tore a hunk of bread from the loaf platter, swiped it through the warmed olive oil thoughtfully set out, and bit into it. There had been something about the way the brown-haired woman spoke that had made her question the authenticity of the statement. Now she was sure the woman was lying. Fiona motioned with the bread. "I can't figure out why she'd lie though. If she's working for the Painted Edge and those are her associates, why not tell them the plan? Perhaps she doesn't trust them fully."

"All she said to me was I wouldn't do." Henrietta ripped a piece of bread in half, then drowned it in olive oil. "Wouldn't do. As if I was a piece of butcher's cut past my prime. Imagine the nerve of the woman. I've been in this business for twenty years." She stabbed out with the bread, making her point. "She was in the womb when I started with *Big Betty*. I know ports, caperers, officeholders, and more. *Wouldn't do.*" She snorted and sipped from the coffee cup Gaili placed in front of her.

Fiona inhaled deeply the heady aroma of her own cup, unsure how to make the captain feel better about the snub. The smell of rich coffee wiped away a little of the tiredness she felt, like a concoction any alchemist might whip up for a good amount of diamonnette paper, currency of the Book. But it was simply fresh beans from her home county in Rise, the perfect temperature of hot water, and having it served by Gaili. Coffee served by someone else somehow always tasted better than a cup you made yourself. The nutty chocolate scent made her think of the crisp, fresh paper smell from before. It hadn't lingered after the cursed man who messed up her initial plan had left.

He hadn't come back. Hadn't interacted with the Painted Edge at all. Why had he been there in the first place? She would've thought him a local curious about the random group of people, but his state of dress disagreed. If he was a member of the Painted Edge, he could've easily captured her. But he didn't. He spied in the same way that Fiona did. She hoped to meet him again soon and give him a piece of her mind for messing up her plan.

"There was something else," Fiona said, pulling out the parchment she had taken from the mysterious golden-eyed man. She hadn't mentioned him to them quite yet, not even sure what to say. "I saw a man there, skulking. Maybe Painted Edge, maybe an oddly placed courtier, but..." She handed the parchment to Gaili. "He dropped this. And it was identical in many ways to one I found in the crate." She pursed her lips and wrapped her hands around the coffee, thinking of all the evidence that had disappeared.

Gaili took hold of the parchment gingerly. "Oh! I don't recognize the language. Perhaps it's a code?" She handed the slip to Henrietta.

The captain wiped her calloused hands on a stained towel and took it. She pulled out spectacles and unfolded them with a shake to slip them on. "Hmm. This is no cant I've seen, but that doesn't mean I can't figure it out," she said proudly. She squinted at the paper, moving it closer. "The smuggler ledger was pretty commonplace. This one seems a bit more refined."

Fiona sighed. "So it will take a long time to break it?"

Henrietta laughed loudly, a grin back on her face. "Hardly. The thing about rippers and thieves is you want to make sure to change things up but still make instructions clear to those who need 'em. So with a little bit of work..." She looked around, but before she could ask for anything, Gaili placed quill, ink, and a blank parchment in front of her. Henrietta beamed up at her and patted her hand. "Thank you, dear." She began making quick notes on the provided parchment, jotting down shapes and figures.

Trying her best to follow, Fiona watched, silently sipping her coffee. She was eternally grateful to have met these two and to have earned their friendship. She hadn't always been easy to work with or be around. Perhaps she still wasn't much. But her adventures of late had taught her the value of being easy on herself, of letting her guard down and accepting the help of others. And perhaps being a little less pushy about her own help on them. Fiona supposed that when push came to shove, she was simply thankful no one had given up on her at her stubbornest.

Through watching Henrietta over the course of the late night, she found at last some semblance of a message taking shape. The captain supposed the cant to be meant for specific people within the Painted Edge. "Leaders most likely," she said, dipping her pen back into the ink. She paused and adjusted her glasses. "The ones you really have to watch out for." She pursed her lips, seemingly thinking of someone specific, but rushed on, "There's a bit missing I can't quite wrap my head around. And several pages that lead up to this I'm certain will make the context clearer, but..." Henrietta wrote out the last couple of words and tapped the paper before pushing it to Fiona.

Heed the red claw...the Guardian's wake.

When...is high, align the stone and Hazel's vine for...untold.

"The Guardian's wake." Fiona breathed, shaking her head. "I can't believe it. Are they truly trying to wake a Guardian?" She had suspected when Blaze flared back to life that someone would figure out there was a Guardian there. Though the Elder druid seemed to know of them, Fiona had thought it a coincidence of smugglers getting more than they bargained for when stealing the onyx gem that had contained Soots. But what if they knew what they were doing? What if they were looking for another Guardian?

"I don't believe she's with us, dear," Henrietta said to Gaili out of the corner of her mouth.

"No, no, I'm here," Fiona said, riveting her attention back to the duo. She inhaled coffee again and focused. "This changes everything. If the Painted Edge are looking for a Guardian, they must be stopped. There's nothing they could want one for that isn't destructive. We did get information though. They are planning something big, it's been moved up, and there's an actual chain of command. I need to send word to Dodger to put out feelers for this Dots team and give the faces for the Guild to learn. I may move in the shadows, but Dodger commands a small army now. If he finds any information in the whole of the Book, he'll let me know."

Gaili and Henrietta nodded. A look passed between them. Fiona, ignoring the tiny ping in her chest at the intimate gesture, got up from the workbench, draining her cup. She hadn't often been romantic in her lifetime. No one she had fancied in her early twenties would deal with her desire to work as she did. So her mother had warned her often. But seeing Gaili so much lately with Henrietta and Matteo had started to make her question if perhaps that might always be the case.

Henrietta cleared her throat. "Mistress, do you have a mind to speak with me on a...sensitive matter?"

Fiona raised an eyebrow. The captain was often enthusiasm itself, but her voice belied a more serious tone. What could be so serious that she wouldn't speak of it in front of Gaili? Fiona gestured for Henrietta to lead the way. The captain took up a lit candle and led through the gallery and into the chilly small office on the other side of the house. The darkness of Spine spilled through the murky windows but was pushed back by their light as they made their way to Fiona's desk. She sat and indicated for Henrietta to sit in the opposite chair, where most of her clients began. "What's wrong?"

"Oh," she began, pulling back her graying curly hair from her face, "nothing's the matter, beg your pardon, Mistress Thorne. I simply wanted to ask a favor."

She had often told Henrietta to stop being so formal, but Henrietta had her own manner, which Fiona found she couldn't quite dissuade. Once Henrietta had realized that Fiona was a page turner, she chose to address her with the light formality that their home page called for, but there were times she leaned into it unthinkingly. Fiona smiled wide trying to set the captain at ease. "There are a lot of things I would do for you. You've never asked much for all my requests."

"Never a spot of sunshine as warm as you are, mistress." Henrietta relaxed, leaning back in the wooden chair. "Well then, I'd be mightily obliged if you would allow me to escort you to your biannual page turner festivities at the summer solstice and introduce me to Queen Brilliance."

Fiona spluttered, "The Queen? Why would a pirate want to meet the Queen? Wouldn't you rather stay out of her line of sight?" She winced at her rather blunt words.

Henrietta waved her hand as if unoffended. "You can't move any further if you don't know who you're working against. I've learned that plenty times in my life. Larrakane bless, it's one of the reasons I learned to fly a ship as soon as I could get my legs under me. While my operations work to get around the absurd taxes and more that the Queen's levying on people's livelihoods, I can only do so much and keep a low profile."

Fiona remembered the concerns of her parents during her childhood on the grove island and its abundant cacao tree farms. Her parents' main complaint was the amount they had to yield to the earl of the island versus the amount they themselves got when they could be selling it for a higher profit. It took the entire farm working together and pulling in what they had to make enough for everyone, though she never quite thought of it that way as a child, running through the trees and living out her imagined fantasies unburdened by the responsibilities of such things. "I stay as far away from the politics of Queen Brilliance as I can." She gripped the arms of her chair remembering the vexing monarch. She had to formally introduce herself and make the pledge to the Queen for the first time at the age of sixteen. The Queen had barely given her a glance but seemed to be more interested in her at each meeting upon learning she had been one of the youngest to be inked. Fiona had more or less skipped visits as much as she could from then on.

"I understand that. Mind you I do. But if I can become a courtier, that will give me and mine the right openings to shake hands with the right palms. I could work my way in there the same way you nobles do it among yourselves."

"They do it," Fiona corrected her. She took a deep breath, calming herself down. "I avoid it."

With a smart nod, Henrietta continued, "Honest, I won't pretend what that Painted Edge woman said to me didn't stab deeper, because the area is already soft. This work is hard, smuggling. I'm not as young as I used to be. And perhaps it's time I stop flying around and getting into trouble before trouble stops me." The captain stood up abruptly as if simply thinking on it had her ready for action. She began pacing the length of the desk. "If I can work change from the inside, somewhat legitimately, then I could give *Big Betty* a rest. Or at least hand her over to someone who has the momentum to keep up with the times. If I can work my way into the court, I know I can succeed. I must try something different."

Fiona admired Henrietta. She didn't quite go in for the criminal kind, but Henrietta had a good heart. It was hard to see yourself at a certain age in a certain place and attempt change. Larrakane bless. Fiona sighed. She had hoped to make a quick exit of the dance after the trivial formality of renewing her fealty to the Queen.

The first human to be inked, almost two hundred years ago, had been Queen Pompania, and as she wanted to continue to rule even from her new home in Spine, she had set a firm structure in place, acknowledging the freedom of page turners while essentially buying their loyalty. This made it easier to account for them all and keep an eye out to ensure they were true to their word not to join forces for, say, Kerus and help the Emperor overthrow another page. Over the years, turners were barely called upon to do more than spy in other pages for the monarchs. But some royalty made that harder than was necessary.

How could she possibly gain a private audience with the Queen? She was nowhere near the peerage level to command attention. She had most purposefully stayed away from home as much as she could to dissuade such notions from her mother. "What about a letter of introduction? I have a favor due from a baron whom I can write something to."

The captain shook her head. "Getting in person, seeing people's faces, and remembering mine is what I need. A letter won't do, and truthfully, I could create that myself! Needs to be a proper introduction. And with your credibility now, it should go further."

Fiona rubbed her face. She would've preferred the letter. But there were other tokens of positivity if she stayed at the dance the entire time. She might find her skulking courtier. He would most certainly be in attendance if he regularly wore such attire. If she could corner him, she could get more information about the missing parchments. What if they detailed the whole of the Painted Edge's plan and sped up events? She needed to track him down, and this might be her best chance.

"You'll have your introduction, Henrietta. Not to the Queen, mind you, but even a baron will get you a foot into the court. I'll introduce you at the dance and give you some support. It would do better to start not too high anyways, otherwise the vultures will come quicker than you can handle."

"Aye, baron is noble enough for me. Fine amendment." Henrietta stuck out a hand. "You won't regret it."

Fiona didn't have the heart to disagree looking at Henrietta's weather-beaten bright-peach face and warm, wide grin. She shook her calloused hand. As much as she disliked saying yes, staying at the dance all night wouldn't kill her. She hoped.

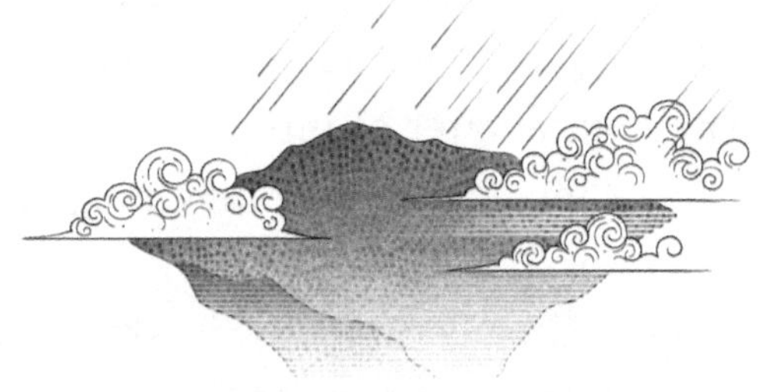

The joy of someone else making her morning meal was a feeling Fiona didn't realize she had been missing. Living in the manor alone for so long had dulled her to the small comforts of sharing a home. She felt a little lazy sitting on the floor pillows in her bedroom, soaking in the rising daylight of Spine, and letting her mind run across the events of yesterday with a veritable feast in front of her from Gaili. But her mind needed to tease out details she may have missed in order to decide how to best approach finding the mystery man and getting more information about the Painted Edge and their plans for a Guardian. She hated sitting and waiting to be told what to do. If there was something she could recall that she could dig into and could keep herself going, that would be better. Going enough to not let herself get anxious over having to stay in Rise soon for the festivities and see her increasingly worrying mother.

Though her mother's letters had been more frequent lately, they had been filled with such benign information that she supposed her to be gearing up for her daughter's visit. No doubt her mother would be happy to see her, but it would quickly dissolve into talks about her marriage prospects, her unfathomable career, and her fashion. Fiona was incredibly glad that her visit would be short-lived. Simply a few hours after she had put her bags down in the palace and then she could check it off her list for another year.

She took a sip of coffee, reveling in the small delight when the bell sounded throughout the upstairs parlor. The only people who would bother her at this hour of the morning were either in trouble or looking to cause it. She glanced out the window to see if she could assess which of the two it was.

An older woman, rich-brown complexion and taut face, stood on the doorstep. Fiona stopped and placed the coffee on the table gingerly. She hurried down the stairs, racing to get there before Gaili. Swallowing several times unconsciously, she took a deep breath to catch it and then opened the door.

Fiona's mother gazed upon her with a distinctive arched eyebrow. Brown and gray curls were tucked tightly beneath headgear, minus the few frizzled pieces that framed her face. Her dress had a ruffled neck, pinched waist, and ample skirts that gave her a sort of bell shape made her seen without having to say anything. Fiona wondered if she would fit through the slender door, but her mother breezed past her into the office.

"Well then. Format has it you can save a whole page, but you can't return a single letter?" Her mother took in the surroundings of the office in one decisive glance. From Fiona's view, she saw the unmatched cups stacked on the wood burning stove, the soot across the thick leather mat on the floor, and a nest of cobwebs, which she had thought quaint before but now seemed quite untidy.

"Hello, Mother," Fiona said and closed the door, trying not to slam it. Her mother's letters had sounded increasingly ordinary. A visit, however, was peculiar. What in the dark edge was going on?

Her mother strode away from the office and into the gallery as if commandeering the home.

Fiona followed behind, trying to think of what to say next that wouldn't immediately start a disagreement. "Perhaps you'd like to sit for a moment. I imagine the trip from New Rise was a bit bumpy." The district on Spine was the official pagemark to Restless Rise and watched over by the Travel Guild. It was some distance away from the turner district. Buying a manor here had been quite on purpose for Fiona.

"And as to that fact, I find it strange that you have answered your own door. Where are your servants? Can you not keep a household? Oh, why did you move all the way out to this confounded area? In New Rise there would be no such issue." Though most page turners were eccentric in one way or another, those who were human tended to cling tight to the rituals from their home page when becoming inked. This meant a host of servants, proper food and proper mealtimes, and the manners to go with them. Having been inked so young and in such a poor position back home, Fiona had never quite understood what all the fuss was about.

"And I wouldn't have to travel as far to see my one and only daughter," Lavinia continued, not waiting for Fiona to respond. "As much as she may ignore her aging mother."

Fiona winced. Well, she had opened the door, literally and metaphorically, for that one. She led her mother to a settee and sighed, indulging herself. No point in holding it back. "I don't have a staff because it's unnecessary, Mama. In my line of work, it's better to be on my own."

Her mother sniffed. "And I suppose you believe on your own you can do anything at all. Why, your sign doesn't even mention our family name. Singular identity. No time for anyone except yourself."

Fiona knew her mother found her priorities vexing, her choice of profession strange, and her continuing to be unmarried at almost thirty years, even as a page turner, truly too much to bear. But she had thought they were at least beyond discussing it and instead treating each other with mild pleasantries for short periods of time. What had spiked such a renewal of conversation?

Gaili waltzed into the room, full sky blue skirt swishing quietly along the floor and matching embroidered bodice, with a tray of refreshments and a big smile. Fiona was startled. How had the faun been so quick when she could barely catch up?

"Water, wine, bread, and cheese for you," she said, addressing Fiona. With a quick pivot she deposited the tray into Fiona's hands and made a small curtsy in front of Fiona's mother.

Fiona gripped the tray, trying to regain her footing.

Her mother cleared her throat. She inclined her head to Gaili and then stared at Fiona.

Knowing she was missing something, Fiona held out the refreshments to her mother. "Wine, Mama?"

"Your manners are lax. Probably this wild place you're forced to live." Sighing, her mother whispered, "You have to introduce us, Fiona."

"Oh, Mother, please let me do the honor of introducing you to Gaili Pannete. Gaili, this is my mother, Mistress Lavinia Thornbeard."

"You may rise, my dear," Lavinia said, inclining her head. "It is good to see that my daughter has at least one servant who understands the details of manners."

Unable to continue holding the tray without some measure of evidence at her frustration, Fiona set it on the sideboard. "She is not a servant, she is my friend. And a partner in Thorne Investigations. She's simply polite."

Lavinia pursed her lips.

"It is a pleasure to make your acquaintance, Mistress Thornbeard. Should you need anything, please allow me to acquire it for you," Gaili said, rising and lowering her head deferentially.

Fiona rolled her eyes. What in the dark edge was Gaili doing? She had gone from alchemist to steward in a matter of minutes. Perhaps her upbringing with so many academy leaders taught her more than just the right levels for concoctions. But it did buy Fiona time to get her head on straight. She did not want to fight with her mother. It always exhausted her and made her feel small. She straightened up. This was her house and the first time her mother had come to her in it. She would control this situation. "Thank you, Gaili. You are more than kind."

Gaili nodded and glided away, skirts whirling as she disappeared into the kitchen area with nary a clack of hooves.

"Her manner of dress is enviable. You should have her procure your clothes for next week's festivities. Especially in your audience with the Queen"

Handing her mother an unasked-for mug of water, Fiona poured herself a hefty glass of wine, not bothering to dilute it. She would need its full strength. "Are you worried I will present myself at the royal court in rags? I'll only see the Queen for a moment."

"There's no need to be hysterical, dear. It was only a suggestion."

Fiona bit down a retort and instead tried to understand why her mother had come. "I am going to be home for almost a week, Mama. I would've come to you as soon as I took lodgings at the palace."

"Can't a mother visit her daughter without reason?"

Fiona sat opposite her fingering the rim of the Copper-cut glass. "Of course you can. I'm glad you could come and see the manor and meet Gaili." She leaned forward. "If something were the matter, though, you would tell me?"

"Of course." Lavinia waved a glove irritably. "Forgive me for being sentimental in wanting to spend some time with my only daughter at her home for a short while." She rose unceremoniously. "Escort me to my rooms. Oh, I'm overcome from all this questioning."

Fiona gulped, almost choking on her wine. *Rooms?* Did her mother intend to stay with her and travel to the palace? Larrakane help her. "I—well..."

"Do you not have rooms enough for guests? What happens in this city, pray tell? In New Rise they have many large manors. Enough for the royal court itself to stay should they desire."

"No, no, of course I do," Fiona said, lying through her teeth. Room for a guest, yes. Room for her inquisitive and eyeing mother? Not as much. "I simply don't keep it ready for company on a whim."

"I see." Lavinia pressed her hand to her throat and nodded. "Your rooms will do for the few days." She picked up her skirt and made her way to the stairs ahead of Fiona.

A few days would feel a few years at this rate. She had hoped to spend more time on her cases before being forced to Rise. But she couldn't fathom doing that with her mother in tow. She sighed. Perhaps Dodger would find some breakthrough with the Painted Edge and she'd have to rush out to do something about it. Perhaps Larrakane herself would show up and cause a scene. One could only hope for divine intervention. There was no use trying to cause it.

I T ONLY TOOK HER mother one evening to completely overstay her welcome. Although she treated Gaili quite well, she lamented the lack of servants to a noisy degree and made Fiona run off her feet with requests. The blankets were dusty, the pillows too soft and then too hard. She required a bath, and then Fiona took too long to get it together so that she was too sleepy to use it. For a brief moment Fiona was happy, thinking she could take it herself, but as soon as she stepped in, the tinkle of a bell—one she was pretty sure she had hidden lest her mother get any ideas—rang from her bedroom and she had to hop back out again. She refused to let it bother her though.

Well, she tried.

Over the next few days, Fiona worked to try and uncover more from the parchment, but it was between moments of her mother instructing her on the latest court etiquette, dances, and which families to avoid due to scandal. As if she feared Fiona was so insulated on Spine as to not hear changes in her home page over the years (or be enamored by the dance manuals from the dancing masters like other lovers of art). Fiona had known Queen Brilliance to be fussy, but clearly that peculiarity had grown since she had last come to court.

With no news from Dodger and unable to slink off from her mother, Fiona acquiesced to her situation. Three things soon became clear to her: One, her mother still longed for her daughter to be married, by someone of her choosing, of course, as soon as possible. Two, she hadn't changed much at all, besides her ability to pinpoint exactly what would bother her daughter most in the moment. That had gotten eerily more accurate. And three, her mother was singularly focused on what would be a perfunctory audience with the Queen.

With Gaili in tow they had gone to more dressmakers than Fiona had visited in her entire life. The faun was enjoying the process, picking out bolts of brocade and silk fabrics, velvet trimming pieces, and more that were to be made into skirts and bodices in record time. Thank Larrakane for faekin dressmakers. Gaili's eye for detail included fashionable colors that enhanced Fiona's warm brown skin and delighted Lavinia to no end. The updated fashion on Rise, her mother alluded to often, was taken after the Queen's new style. Lace ruff-bands around the neck, stiff bonnets bordered in silk, satin, or velvet, and bell-shaped skirts to create an hourglass figure. Fresh clothing simply had to be embroidered with their family insignia, and exorbitant rush prices had to be accepted with little question. At first Fiona followed along to indulge her mother, but she continued because it was easier than arguing and, with her mother relaxed, she could pry. It was a tug-of-war of information, bit by bit, but ultimately she won.

"The court has taken an interest in us, has it?" Fiona said as they gathered the last remaining purchases and headed toward the hired carriage.

"Our history, yes. It's not so odd of course. All the houses are eventually recorded. As you are the first page turner in our family, we must get on the record. The royal historian seems to be updating the archives or what have you on Rise page turners. I had a long discussion with him at the end of the palace dinner the night before I arrived. Charming young man. Naturally he came to me when he couldn't get to you."

Fiona frowned. "He couldn't *get* to Spine?"

Lavinia rubbed her temple. "Dear, it is one thing to come here on holiday, but he's a member of the royal court! He must stay by the side of the Queen should he be needed."

"Naturally," Fiona said, not seeing anything natural about it. She started to say something only a tad biting but noticed her mother had fallen silent, head leaned against the pillowed interior of the carriage. Fiona reached over and squeezed her hand gently.

Her mother's eyes fluttered open. "With all the fuss made about you in the *Card*, more people, such as the upper nobles, will want to meet you. And by that extension, myself. We must make this perfect." Lavinia withdrew her hand and sat up straighter. "Don't slouch so, Fiona. You're not a commoner."

How in Larrakane's name her mother managed to wound her with four careless words at this stage in her life boggled her. She had spent literal years learning to work and walk among the nobles in her native page. Her mother had always assumed Fiona would marry well and they would rise from the cacao farmers they were to something just a might higher. Lavinia had gotten much more than she'd hoped for when Fiona had become inked at the age of fourteen.

Instead of musing down the lane of her mother's continued expectations, Fiona focused on the other half of her mother's sentence. She very much doubted the upper houses wanted to meet her, but she wouldn't mind being introduced.

Perhaps they would have problems that she could solve as an investigator. For a hefty fee, of course. This might be the only time she could work her way into getting an airship. A few more days and she would see her mother back home and go back to her own life. All she had to do was get through the festivities.

She stared out the window as the surroundings of the New Rise district winked by the speedy carriage. The light from the blue sky was blocked and unblocked over Fiona by the towering, teetering buildings that had been rustled up by the Schiflans who had migrated, some willingly and others as page turners. They managed to bring a bit of the Rise back to Spine. The royal residence had been built as tall as possible so that the highest chambers, fit for a monarch, could see much of the city from its view. Previous settlers stacked various brick and terra-cotta buildings on top of each other on the flat land that made up their district. It gave the sensation of being high above the clouds, much like in Rise, and the top floors went for quite the premium when purchased. In truth it made little sense as the manors, houses, and buildings truly in Rise were on the island grounds and the islands were the things that floated above the clouds, but humans were always set to go their own way.

The carriage stopped on the edge of a crowded square, letting them out. Fiona resolutely looked away from her mother and turned toward the Travel Guild booth. It wasn't hard to find. Banners hung from the official station with the Travel Guild insignia: an open book with various species footprints above it. With the new Guild Hall being built soon, Fiona hoped they'd redo the Guild symbol. It was not as refined as it could be, but it worked. Another banner waved in the air, this one of Rise with its clear symbology of the Plateau above a cloud. A Guild-run pagemark always let one know where one could travel to in a way that worked for everyone.

A cacophony of humans waited around the pagemark, jostling each other and their belongings. This district boasted the most humans one would ever see in Spine. While some of them were turners who didn't want to live in the turner district specifically, most of them were everyday laypeople from Rise who took a chance on a new life here. Though they may be farmers, crafters, shift workers, or even Travel Guild administrators, they lived quite well on Spine versus the Restless Rise page. The hand of the Queen was felt least here.

Human page turners lined up waiting their turn to travel to Rise. There were assigned time slots since there were so many people who needed to travel to the festival. Fiona led her mother and the porter with their trunks through the tightly packed area to the center. Some of the turners she recognized—general acquaintances over the years from turner training and the biannual fete. She nodded and smiled to a few, much to their surprise.

With the occasional murmur of agreement and interested sounds, she made it through the waiting period with her talkative mother unscathed till it was their turn to depart. Fiona, Lavinia, and their trunks got into the wooden lift that would take them up to one of the highest platforms. If they turned the page on the ground level, they could hit a floating isle when they turned. Going high meant they could turn the page safely within the air and control their landing. It was as targeted as one could get turning the page to and from Rise. People scared of heights didn't often travel back and forth. The lift was an inventive, and welcomed, gift to the Travel

Guild from the smilodon Emperor before he stopped being so polite.

They shrugged on their ornithopters, the many blades forcing them all to stand at designated spots, and pulled the rip cord. She grabbed hands with the bored-looking porter before gripping her mother's. They were shaking. "Mama, it'll be okay. I do this every day."

Her mother shook her head and stared resolutely forward, unwilling to talk. For once Fiona knew this wasn't about her. Her father had taught her the love of flying high across the land before she was inked. Her mother never joined them on trips, too focused on farming and managing the household. Fiona had always thought it was the inability to relax that kept her mother on the ground, but perhaps it was the lack of control so high up that had really weighed her down.

She gripped her mother's hand more securely and focused on minor things so as to not interrupt the leading turner who would be opening up Rise. Soon a persistent cold breeze blew across her face. The platform shimmered briefly and the world around her folded in on itself. The heavy smell of nervous bodies in Spine gave way to the fresh, clean scent of rain. She took a step toward the gray-clouded sky, turning from one page to the next. It looked exactly like the turning of a page in a book, where for a moment both worlds showed at the same time. It was silent beyond the whir of the ornithopter blades. Page turners knew to keep focused during a page turn, for a misalignment could prove fatal. Skimmers were warned not to interfere.

As if a reader decided to go back to the previous page, the world unfolded on itself. The shimmer disappeared. The view of the cloud-laden skies solidified around her. She let out a held breath. She pulled her mother closer as the awaiting airship, with its beautifully polished wooden planks and bright-blue hawk insignia, soared beneath them, right on time. The wind-whipped sails of blue and white were a stark contrast to the gloomy sky around them with its misty rain.

"And just like that, we're here," Fiona said. "They've truly made the journey as easy as clockwork."

Now it was her mother's turn to nod and murmur. Feeling she had done the best she could, Fiona landed lightly on the wide deck, tugging Lavinia with her. The trunks landed beside them, thudding softly as the balloons that slowed their descent deflated. The porter followed and quickly managed the belongings with care, hurrying off to places unknown. Fiona wondered what it was like before the page turners of yore had figured everything out. Her elderly, sweet, and gossipy neighbor Mistress Humbledraft used to be a spotter. One whose assignment was to find suitable pagemarks from one page to another page. She would know and undoubtedly be here as well. Perhaps the trick had been traveling with a bit less luggage.

"I don't know how you can stand it," her mother said, shrugging the ornithopter off and handing it to the nearest sailor.

He stared at it for a moment before nodding his head and walking away with it. *Smart man.*

"It does get easier over time, Mama." Fiona pulled off her own ornithopter before it could hamper her movements. Goodness knew her new dress was already doing well in that corner.

"Airships are much safer than those wretched things. Some of the earls have even purchased one for their houses. They must be a ghastly cost though." Her mother took a step and then faltered, holding on to the rail.

Fiona grabbed her waist, shifting some of her mother's weight to her own. "Why don't you settle in for the sail to the Plateau and I'll take care of everything here?"

Her mother nodded. "The lounge is suitable. I'll be there." Lavinia glanced around and then hurried after a group of ladies who looked far more agreeable than some of the other passengers.

Relaxed for a moment, Fiona watched as they speedily lifted higher in the air and away from the pagemark toward the Plateau. It would take a few hours to arrive, blessed as they were by speedy vehicles such as these. These airships were something of a marvel in Rise. Before the page was opened by the blessing of Larrakane, they'd all had to make do with bridges between the floating islands and temporary ones to the Plateau. It shifted every season without fail, giving the world the name written in pre-inked texts: Schiftland. Over time it became more commonly known as Schiflan. But it was the faekin from the Court of Copper who had given the page a name fit for a dramatis personae: Restless Rise. Temporary bridges were erected quickly after each seasonal shift. And far beneath the floating islands and the creamy white cloud barrier was endless water as far as the eye could see, providing no way to have permanent structures from below them.

Ornithopters had been handy but were expensive to maintain, relying on compounds that sourced from all over the page and could only fit a single person. Most had rented them as need be for travel from island to island. But when the Inking occurred, giving the world open travel to others, airships arrived at the same time. The newfangled airships, with their wide sails and roomy floors below deck, had brought Rise into a whole new era. Making it easier and easier to dock and undock them allowed a freedom of movement about the counties that only a page turner could truly understand.

Fiona had always suspected their invention had come from outside of the page. It was too coincidental. And while Copper and Kerus had something like it—sailing ships, they called them—they had no cause to ever have airships that flew the cloudy cotton skies. That the only other mortal pages in existence had something similar was her only clue that they were not native to the page. Well, the only other *known* mortal pages.

Her mind flashed back to the sodden earthy page she had glimpsed a month ago when Clara had torn a hole into Copper with the Seasonal Crowns. It had definitely been someplace different. Someplace new. Mac, her beloved friend and owner of her favorite tavern on Spine, knew nothing about it. She had conferred with her neighbor Mistress Humbledraft as well. Her golden years of spotting pagemarks and her thirst for knowledge had given her access to some very rare texts over the years. She even had an assistant, an old friend of Fiona's who crawled the stacks of the temple library in exchange for a spot of bother he had done to her earlier in the year. No one knew of any more pages than the seven.

If only she had grabbed a token of some sort in the struggle with Clara, but that had not been top of mind. She sighed, another mystery to add to her pile. What she wouldn't give for unlimited time and a lack of social responsibility to revel in it.

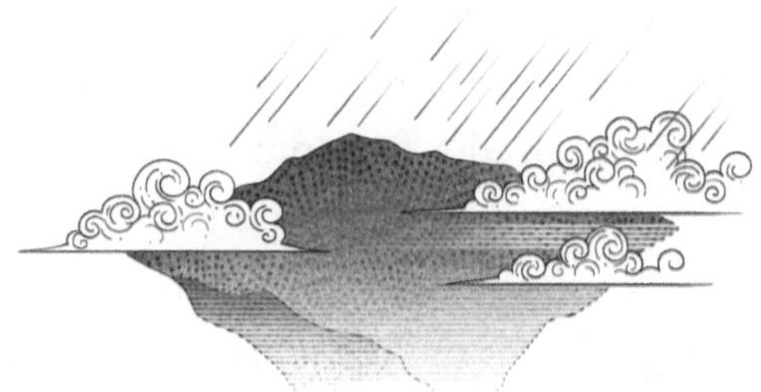

Fiona tugged on the lines of her plum satin skirt, trying to make her bum smaller. It was no use. The rolled-up padding at her waist was set there to make sure it wouldn't be. It was good luck she wouldn't need to shimmy through windows or run for her life this week. She wouldn't get far in this getup. Sometimes she missed the days when they used to be farmers of no consequence on a floating isle to the south of all the important people. Growing up running through the trees in a small home with her family and neighbors had made her carefree somewhat. It certainly had enamored her to plain woolen dresses.

Still, she didn't hate her entire person in the finery. Her thick brown curls had been pulled back from her forehead by one of the lady's maids assigned to this floor of page turners. Piled high with frizzed hair to the sides, it framed her long rich-brown face, giving it the illusion of being heart shaped.

"You do look lovely, dear," Lavinia said from behind her. She was still being dressed by the aforementioned lady's maid. Lavinia held her arms out and her head high for the maid to slip on a long farthingale over the bumroll already securely attached to her person. Then skirts, bodices, overskirts, and more that matched Fiona's slightly golden brocade. Her mother stood with a countenance of casual familiarity to the process. One might not have guessed her previous occupation.

"But do remember to take it slow and talk to the young turners of the various families you haven't yet met. You're not too old to move about in their circles."

Somehow open pages did not always mean open minds. How humans could keep the rules of propriety and impropriety as the most important thing in society was still most surprising to Fiona. Especially after living in Spine. Fiona turned away from the ornate framed mirror and smiled, for the lady's maid more than herself lest word get to anyone of their conversation. "I will endeavor to talk to as many people as you like. My escort shall ensure that, as it were. She's quite lively."

"Escort?" Lavinia stopped her lady's maid and strode over to Fiona. "You never mentioned already having an escort," she whispered.

She doubted her mother would've taken kindly to knowing she'd invited Henrietta, much less that she planned to introduce her to court. "Yes, she's a dear friend. You'll like her. She's a captain."

Lavinia's eyes brightened. "Oh, a captain. In the Queen's service? That's wonderful."

Fiona toyed with letting her mother continue down this line of thinking but discarded it. She didn't want to make things difficult for Henrietta or confuse the court. There were enough intricate social dynamics at court without having her mother going around discussing her daughter's connection with a Queen's captain. "She is not moored in Rise, and she is enamored with Gaili. They are quite the thing. So don't get any ideas."

Lavinia's shoulders sagged. "Well then, I hope she's lively enough to keep the right courtiers enthralled."

A swift memory of a certain courtier with dark curly hair and a prominent jawline brushed through Fiona's mind, but she flicked the image away. "That is our entire goal, Mother. I assure you."

Lavinia raised an eyebrow but said nothing as she returned to the awaiting maid.

Soon the time came to grab feather fans and amber bracelets and be escorted down to the banqueting hall of the palace. Rain poured frightfully outside, making the passageways that fed into the hallways and funneled toward the banqueting hall packed to the brim with guests. Many complained, but one could not control the rain. Thorn Palace was the only place the monarchs had resided for hundreds of years. Long before the Inking. There were ruins of arches and even a citadel of previous rulers throughout the Plateau, but the various historical wars had seen power concentrated in the great nation of Schiftland and in the power of the Bridewood family. That line continued to this day in Queen Brilliance.

Thorn was a sprawling complex of riches. There were many intricately designed buildings that connected together in various architectural styles of the different periods. It had been extensively expanded, renovated, and expanded again to include hundreds of staterooms, halls, and private, sometimes secretive, rooms for the royal family. The palace was situated on the banks of the River Tam in Old Schiftland, the oldest half of the Plateau. It was a grand statement to the human spirit and its long-standing perseverance. But what Fiona loved most about the palace were its beautiful courtyards and gardens. Oh, these spaces were the escape she always sought from the crush of bodies, the stares of the nobility, and the questions of others. Carefully arranged flowers and hedges made it easy to hide. She briefly considered making her way there now, perhaps not to be seen again until the dance commenced.

Lavinia nodded her head coolly toward Fiona, eyes pinched and focused as if hearing her daughter's innermost thoughts. It was not without a certain eyed warning toward the golden throne. Then she faded into a crowd of acquaintances she effusively welcomed. Well, at least she would be happy with her friends.

Fiona scanned the room to see if the captain's signature strawberry curls were anywhere, but they were currently missing. The familiar sighting of the Followers of Larrakane intrigued her. The insignia of Larrakane—black rings containing black circles—was prominent on their flowing cream robes. They pulled behind them a large golden statue of Larrakane, in her human form, through the halls toward the audience chamber. An offering to the Queen. One that reminded her who the true leader of the Book was but could also work as a gift. Clever. Though Fiona had only had one run-in with the Priestess Raina when searching for the fire page's missing artifact, she wished to know her better. Strange that she didn't accompany her Followers. Fiona would have to keep on the lookout for her fair olive complexion and sable hair among the crowd.

Fiona took her place in the queue to be announced to the Queen. She fiddled with the lace trim of her sleeves as she waited. The line moved quickly—no doubt easier to handle simple introductions than tiresome requests. Fiona kept her eyes flitting across the room to catch sight of any familiar faces.

There was a considerable number of courtiers on the right side of the hall. Deferential to the Queen but keeping to the side of upper nobility, they stood in groups. The barons stood together as one group with naught but their shades of gold and silver to tell them apart. The earls were more complex, their insignias marking them as different. House Hawkport had the blue hawk on each right shoulder, whether dress or cloak, making it stand out a bit less than the others. The two houses higher than Hawkport were situated more visible on the right side of their bodices or doublets. The next highest house could be so bold as to place their insignia over their heart on the right. And of course, the Queen's House Bridewood symbol, a many-branched tree, was not only worn on the front of garments or etched into the center of bodices, but the insignia was part of the official royal crest above the Queen's throne.

Queen Brilliance sat upon her seat, staring out into the sea of people as if she were the only raft in the room. The throne was quite beautiful and worthy of examination. Gold-painted peacock feathers spread behind it with small inset turquoise jewels. Pearls dotted the tips of the feathers, shimmering in the light. Queen Brilliance clashed with the throne, wearing as many shades of gold as could possibly exist in nature. Like all the monarchs after Queen Pompania, she was named not for her family but self-named. She was infatuated with lustrous material objects. It was an infantile display of control. Her ruling of brilliant or dull meant social life or social death. While her retinue wore entirely too many bright and glassy colors, those in the royal court who she deemed dull were forced to wear a measurable amount of drab and uncolored pieces. It was quite easy to tell the levels of courtier by the amount of gold they wore. Fiona's father had said she was the

Queen of brilliance, not the brilliant Queen, and there was a reason for that. She believed it very much.

Fiona would curtsy deferentially to the Queen, find Henrietta in the crowd, and introduce her, search for the mysterious barn courtier, and then begin the dance of pulling secrets. It looked to be a long evening ahead of her. Perhaps she should've eaten more at supper.

"May I have this dance, mistress of the page?" a baritone voice said behind her.

Gold flashed into her view and then she was standing face to face with her mystery man. His accent was so changed. He sounded like any other courtier around her. Although his hair was mostly covered by a hat of gold that matched his clothing, his attire was more or less black. She could see, in the abundant slow-burning candles of the court lighting, his hair was more reddish gold than dark brown. He wore the many-branched tree insignia of the Queen, Bridewood. *Well connected then.*

Fiona knew that etiquette and order of procession were of the utmost importance. Not following them would greatly upset her mother and, if the Queen bothered to notice, Her Majesty. But the dark edge swallow her whole before she put propriety before time with a willing suspect. He clearly recognized her from their run-in at the barn.

Fiona gave a small curtsy. "I would be honored, Sir..." She deliberately raised an eyebrow, awaiting his response to her overly polite reply.

The man smiled wide and led her away from the line of page turners and to the dance hall. The room was richly decorated with tapestry-adorned walls portraying royalty in various stages of fighting, conquering, and administering to the people. The tapestries floated from the high wide ceiling of the tall room, making the entire hall feel as if it was the most important part of the palace. For some, it was. Gold- and silver-trimmed courtiers danced to a lively tune around the hall while servants laden with platters of foods and glasses of wine ran to and fro. Laughter rang out from many a corner, rhythmically mixing with the thump of shoes across the timbered floor and the twang of instruments as the current dance came to a close.

Fiona edged close to the mystery man, subtly watching him. He kept eyes forward, face set in an air of open charm as he nodded to various people in the hall as they passed. He led her expertly toward the center crush as new music started, a lute echoing in the chamber. The dance began.

Fiona raised her chin high as they circled each other. She would not hide her frustration from him. Though it was unlikely he was part of the Painted Edge, she needed to be certain before she berated him for taking off with her evidence. "I do believe it is polite to give your dance partner a name. Unless you feel that doing so would be incriminating in some way," she said with light derision.

"'What's in a name? That which we call a rose by any other name would smell as sweet.'" He grinned as if they were sharing a joke. The playful façade didn't quite cover the strain in his voice. He was being cautious.

"Is that poetry? It seems rehearsed."

"More the daring words of an artistry that has taken the court's pleasure." He bowed as the dancers around them circled.

Fiona noticed the tilt of his head as he watched her beneath lashes. She smiled, prettily she hoped, to lure him in. "If a name is too much, perhaps a title then?"

He rose gracefully. "You may call me a collector of history."

Ah, the court historian. Unexpected. He had moved quickly. Meeting her in the barn, then calling on her mother to discuss her history. But why? How had he matched her face to her name? Probably the blasted *Card*. "I heard you were in the process of gathering page turner family histories."

"Yes." He turned, sweeping away from her in the dance.

Fiona moved to match him, falling in line with other couples to parade around the hall in dance. The music grew louder as they moved closer to the musicians. Fiona stepped nearer to him so as to not have to yell. "Do you often find you have to travel to the outer islands where people grew up? Talk to the neighbors to learn more about them?"

"No." He smirked as if toying with her. He raised his hand toward Fiona's. "I am simply a palace-bound courtier who *dabbles* in history. Nothing more."

Their fingertips touched. A small flicker of warmth surrounded her, like throwing a new log on an old flame. The feeling soon dissipated as she took a deep breath and a step forward in the dance. She frowned, refocusing on his face. Palace bound? So not a page turner then. Just because he was the court historian didn't mean he couldn't be part of the Painted Edge. She needed to press him, but knowing that he wasn't playing the part of a courtier meant caution. She didn't have friends inside the court who could protect her from a wrong movement. "What sort of things does a royal historian do then?"

"What did you say?" the historian asked with a frown. His hand dropped from hers, although they still paraded together.

She dropped her hand, too, confused. Did he not remember the dance? He did not look old enough to be forgetful or hard of hearing. Far from it truly. Her cheeks flushed with warmth and she glanced away. What in the dark edge was wrong with her? She cleared her throat before saying a little louder, "Do you maintain the archive? Search for information or *special findings*?" Fiona tried to keep her words obscured as the other couples enclosed them as they danced around the hall, but she raised an eyebrow at him.

The historian said nothing, inexplicably staring at Fiona as if she suddenly had two heads. Fiona glanced around her awkwardly to see if she was the product of his sudden feebleness or something else, but unfortunately he was still watching her, dancing etiquette done away with. It was only a touch worse than giving her nonanswers. She tried to think of what she said that could have confused him so but quickly came up with nothing.

They circled each other again, then separated to opposite corners against different partners. Fiona let out a soft curse under her breath. She was doing abominably. This shouldn't have been so difficult, but she needed to tread carefully. That must have been what was making it harder—the need to manage her words, her dance, her posture, all at once. Perhaps letting one go would help. She skipped to the historian as the rest of the partners did and took his warm, rough hand. Staring ahead, she said, "For a historian who doesn't travel often, you were quite away from the palace last night. I wonder, did you mean to be there?" Either he would deny it, or he would give her some long-winded answer. They always did.

"Yes," he said, posture stiff and eyes straight ahead.

Or back to terse answers then. Better than staring at her. Fiona sighed inwardly. He was giving nothing away. Maybe if she drew him out, his demeanor would break and she would get some insightful reaction out of him. "I wondered why you didn't arrive with the rest of them then. I thought I was supposed to report back to the boss about them. Didn't know they assigned two of us. Seems distrustful."

He snorted, the first break since they started around the hall, his face returning back to the grinning courtier who asked her to dance. "Don't pretend you're with them. You no more know those rippers than you know me."

Fiona glared at her dancer partner. "You speak in riddles as if they come naturally."

"I find that when one dances with an investigator, one should perhaps say less than they mean."

"So you do have something to hide." She smirked.

"I have a great many things to hide, yes. But apparently so do you." His jaw set, puzzled gaze turned suspicious.

"I have nothing to conceal," Fiona said, chin high. It was the oddest thing to say, considering he had been thoroughly giving her the runaround. "Why in the dark edge would I?"

"Because otherwise Larrakane is jesting with me." He shook his head, taking a step away. "And I haven't the energy for it."

She looked away from him, wishing this dance would end. Her mother was watching with a subtle frown on her face. Ah, not high up in the list of courtiers she was meant to be talking to then. That was more information than she had gotten from the man himself. Servants passed through the outskirts of the crowd holding trenchers and tankards on silver and gold platters. One of them caught her eye. He looked familiar, but she didn't know where she had met him from. Another caught her attention. Why were they so familiar? She didn't often come home, certainly not to the palace. The only place she saw many humans was rare trips to the New Rise district in Spine and on the stakeout earlier this week. But, of course. It struck her. They were some of the people she had seen at the barn. She counted three of them. Were they simply servants, or was there something more? Was tonight what they had been prepping for? There was the golden statue of Larrakane the Priestess had brought. Could that be what they were taking? But what would a present to the Queen have to do with finding a Guardian?

"You've missed a step." The historian's voice broke into her thoughts.

Fiona turned, pulled toward him. She tried to pull away, but he held tight to her hand.

He bent closer to her as they circled each other again. "If I let go, you'll simply run after them and cause a scene. They haven't done anything yet. Better to catch them in the act of something."

How dare he slander her like so. Talking to her as if she was a flighty thing. Fiona pulled her hand away. "I've never caused a scene that wasn't without benefit in my life!" She raised an eyebrow. "And how would you know what they are up to?" Did his coded papers tell more than the one Henrietta had deciphered? Oh, how she wished they were in a more private area so she could press him for answers without being watched.

"They've been here since this afternoon working with the other servants setting up. They don't seem like they're coordinating anything. They may be scouting, and I for one want to know what they are scouting for."

Though Fiona wanted to push back at him, she quelled her rebellious nature for a moment and focused on his words. He seemed to have been watching them for some time. So perhaps not only a historian but a spy of some sort? A Queen's spy, more than likely. She treaded lightly. "Are you going to stop them if needed? Or is your inaction part of your duties? It seems a big help to them to watch but do nothing."

"Help them?" The historian snorted impatiently. "I'm bloody trying to help you!" The dance ended as he shook his head. He took a deep breath, seemingly regaining his composure, and bowed to her as the other companions did.

Fiona strode off the dance floor, breaking away from the line and him without curtsying back. Several heads turned toward her as she hurried away, but she ignored them all. Help her? A veritable stranger who wouldn't even give a name and poked about suspiciously in the dark? Who took half her evidence, stole her best spot, and had the nerve to treat her as if she was in distress! Though he danced like a King, he spoke like a charlatan, through and through. She didn't need his help and certainly hadn't asked for it. She would get what she needed from the source. Fiona stalked toward an exit of the dance hall after one of the familiar servers. Beyond lay a darkened corridor that she wasted little time investigating.

Bright amber candlelight flickered as she tiptoed down the stone-floored passage. Her heavy skirts rustled against the woven rush mats, and Fiona bit back a groan at her inability to be quiet with so much fabric strapped to her. The passage turned right but ended in a set of wooden chairs with plush velvet cushions and a high table between. Candlelight danced on the lone scene. There was no one to be seen in the dead end. Where had the server gone?

"I'm not following," the historian whispered from behind her.

"It would be easier to believe if you actually weren't," she whispered hotly back without turning around. She pursed her lips and took a step toward the chairs, away from him.

He skirted around her with barely a breath in her direction and pressed his hand against the stone wall beside her, pushing two similar squares at the same time. The wall moved in and slid to the side. "Pretend I'm not even here," he said with an amused voice.

Ah, a hidden passage. She would've gotten there eventually. "I could do that easier if you would go away." She grabbed a candle from the high table to hide her momentary surprise before turning to face him. He seemed to be watching her every move, but she pretended not to notice. "But since you're insistent on being a blotter and following me, why don't you go first?" She wouldn't be tricked into heading into a darkened passage with someone on her tail.

He raised an eyebrow but ducked into the passage and hurried through. Fiona took a breath, a little surprised that he acquiesced so quickly, and then followed in. The stone façade door slid back silently behind her. Steep stairs downward greeted her flicking candlelight. Larrakane bless for the thin railing to help her down them in satin slippers. No dust lingered on the well-used servants corridor.

The historian moved silently down the stairs with sure steps. Fiona held on to the rail with one hand, skirt and candle in the other, and followed after. At the landing, unmoving candles ensconced on the wall illuminated a speared passageway. Which way did the server go? She took a step to the left, trying to discern any recent activity.

The historian cleared his throat.

"Yes?" Fiona whispered testily, turning back around.

"I've lived here for some time. That passage leads to royal chambers, which should be empty currently. But true servants would go through the other passages to the pantry and kitchens outside." He held his hands aloft, a small smile etched in his features. "But I'm not helping."

Fiona narrowed her eyes, assessing him. Either way could be a trap, but it seemed unlikely. He could have no way of knowing she'd run off after the Painted Edge servants. Could he? Fiona felt that small pull she always had when her instincts told her one thing but cold logic told her another. *Well then, this way will tell me if he's tricking me or truly helping me, won't it?* She indicated he should go first and then continued down the passage to the royal privy rooms.

Several doors marked the long stone hallway. Fiona handed the candle to the historian without a word and picked up the hem of her dress in order to make less noise over the loose rushes. She waved him forward again and slowed. Chatter came from one of the rooms. Making her way to the door, she pressed her ear to it, keeping one eye on the historian. The voices were too muffled to make out words. She turned the knob slowly, and it did her bidding. She would simply ease the door open to hear more clearly who was inside. If she recognized the voice of one of the Painted Edge members, they could ambush them.

The door swung open, pulling Fiona forward as she grasped the knob. A strong hand gripped her shoulder, tugging her through the now open door into an opulent sitting room. She fell to the elaborate woven rug, unable to catch or disentangle herself from the guard's grip. The room, brimming with courtiers attending to a small woman being dressed, fell into a hushed silence.

All gazes turned to Fiona, a mixture of shocked and curious expressions. Though her pale fawn skin reddened from a recent scrubbing almost obscured her identity, the small woman's narrowed eyes and pursed lips were instantly recognizable. Fiona's heart sank into her stomach.

"I do believe you don't belong here," said the woman with a tilt of her head. She snapped her fingers, and the room burst into activity.

Well, this was certainly one way to gain a private audience with the Queen.

THE BLOODY HISTORIAN WAS nowhere to be seen when Fiona was allowed to stand from the stone floor. Her silk stocking had torn where she had fallen, and she could feel her knee bruising immediately, but beyond that nothing else was hurt. The servant door had closed and there was now a guard in front of it as if Fiona might try to bolt. She relished the thought that they assumed her as an idiot. Perhaps acting like one would help.

"Many apologies, Your Majesty," Fiona said, stepping to the left of the Queen. She kneeled to the floor in slow motion and stared at it. "I was simply lost."

"Lost in the servants' passage? How odd." The Queen tsked. "Do you suppose me a simpleton?"

Fiona shook her head. "Of course not, Your Majesty." She glanced about the room, looking for any of the Painted Edge servers, but saw only a few maids, guards, and courtiers watching enthralled. There was a shift in the corner, and Fiona noticed a man in the shadows, neck ruffs almost as big as the Queen's. He watched her intently, making Fiona feel recognized.

Queen Brilliance stared at Fiona, lips pursed. "Perhaps you would like to tell me what you were doing then? No lies." The Queen turned as the maid pulled a silken skirt over her head. "Do not waste my time."

Fiona knew that some ears couldn't be trusted. Her recent case with one of the leaders of the Court of Copper proved that those in power were not always on the side of what was right. So she said, with as much truth as she could muster (a practice she'd happily honed over the years), "I was following your royal historian and he led me here."

She was met with silence. Fiona thought it best to answer only what was needed and so remained quiet, pushing down her desire to ask questions.

After a moment the Queen said brusquely, "My historian led you to my chambers, did he? Remarkable. Guard, did you see my historian?"

The guard by the servant door shook her head. Fiona pursed her lips to not say something unkind. Of course he was there, he was right next to her at the door. How could she have missed him?

"Guard says he wasn't there. Considering I should trust one of you, I'm sure you'll understand my choosing my most loyal guard over you." The Queen sighed. She looked at the jewelry laid out for her as if it was more important than Fiona or this conversation. "Perhaps you'll talk more truthfully with time to think about it. Take her to the hold and let her miss the festivities for a few days."

The guard grabbed Fiona's arm and pulled it roughly behind her back.

Fiona's breath hitched. "What I say is true. Please, Your Majesty." She darted a gaze around the room at the gawking audience. No one said a thing. Word of this would get around the court quickly. If she was taken away now, it would cause no short of worry with her mother and Henrietta. They would put turn stoppers on her and—she didn't want to think how long it would take to have another chance to plead her case. The Queen's pettiness might outlast her. It was all or nothing. "There were people, servants of the Painted Edge here. I followed one to see what they were up to, and your historian came along. He told me that they might come to court quarters."

Hushed murmuring quickly erupted in the chamber. Fiona winced that so many people seemed to speak and not so ignorantly, all at once. The Queen raised a hand, gold rings sparkling in the light. Silence fell. "The Painted Edge?"

Fiona nodded. She knew the leaders of the various pages had been warned of the organization. But news and rumors had started floating around about them as well. She was gambling on the Queen not being a supporter of them. "I am an investigator, Your Majesty. Investigator Fiona Thorne."

The Queen rolled her eyes and glanced back at her jewelry. A maid hurriedly picked up a piece and began clasping it around her neck. "I know who you are, Investigator *Thorne*. One does not stay Queen by ignoring society's outliers. Singular name to use outside of the page. It's what first caught my interest."

Unsure of whether that was positive or not, Fiona nodded and then let her gaze slide to the floor again. Being a simpleton wouldn't work any longer. Perhaps bargaining would. "I humbly ask that you allow me to search for them, for they could be up to anything. Spying, stealing secrets, or looking to heist valuables from you. For the Queen has the best jewels in the Book." She held her breath, hoping that the Queen wouldn't think her mocking. It was quite true, if one ignored that most of the gems had come from Cobbles.

Everyone seemed to hold their breath. The Queen waved her hand. "You may all leave. Except for you, my principal secretary," she called over her shoulder to the shadowed man.

There was a moment of confusion before the courtiers rose one by one and, openly watching and smirking at Fiona, left the room. The maids hurriedly followed with bowed heads. Once the door was closed, the Queen motioned to the other guard not holding Fiona. "Stand outside the door and make sure we are not disturbed."

The Queen sat slowly on the plush embroidered golden pillow within a wooden chair. It resembled a mock throne, albeit an awkward one. Both Fiona and the guard took a small step to keep the Queen on their right.

"I have been told of this Edge, though I must say if they come for my jewels, they will be quickly handled. But I have heard more of you. Unfashionable, unsparkling, but…" She paused and fingered a bauble on her bracelet and then smiled. "But valuable, it seems. I have an assignment for you, and if you desire, you can continue watching for this Painted Edge."

Fiona hesitated but kept her look lowered. She didn't want a task from the Queen. It would only slow her down or be a flippant errand. But she didn't dare refuse. Instead, she simply said, "Thank you, my Queen."

"Excellent," the Queen said as if she knew there was no other choice. "Tell me, do you know who the Guardian of Rise is?"

Fiona's head snapped up. She had only met one Guardian in her lifetime, and even that was purely by accident. "No."

Queen Brilliance leaned in, frizzy reddish-blonde hair waving about her face. "You *must* find me the Guardian of Rise."

"I have no powers to do so." How could she hope to find another one? Her reinforced gear for the fire page wasn't ready, so she hadn't had a chance to even visit Soots since the temperature within the fire page had increased.

"Find some."

She couldn't believe she was about to say no to the Queen, one foot from going to the dungeons, but she shook her head. "Truly, I think—"

"It doesn't matter what you think." The Queen rose, cutting her off. She nodded to the guard, who pulled Fiona roughly back a step. "Find them and bring them to me."

Fiona tried very hard in life not to agree to a case she couldn't solve. Oh, she had luck and favors to see her through most things. But what would a Guardian of Rise even be like? Elemental? Rock? A flying island? She would most certainly fail, and then she would be back in the mess she was in. She didn't doubt herself about finding items, but people, beings, had intelligence. And intelligence made for a more difficult case if there was no one to cooperate. It's not that she didn't want to delve into what a Guardian was and what they were guarding from. The way the Elder druid spoke, Fiona assumed that the elemental pages all had them. And that the Painted Edge was trading secretive notes back and forth about waking Guardians certainly meant she had to investigate the matter further. But a power like the Queen would want a specific result, not findings that could satisfy an investigator's curiosity or help the Guild take down a criminal organization. What would Queen Brilliance do with the Guardian?

"Tell me, how is your mother of late?" The Queen picked up her comb and idly passed it through her frizzy curls. "I heard she was having a bit of a bother and offended some of the courtiers. Very careless of her, don't you think? It would be terrible for her to lose rank. Where did you become inked? One of the farms on Grove Isle, yes? Perhaps she misses those long work days."

Fiona's mother's anxious nature these past few days rose to her mind. It was clear the Queen had already been working toward this goal before she arrived. She couldn't let her mother be hurt like that. "I will do what you ask."

"Brilliant." The Queen smiled as if she had bestowed a favor on Fiona. "I expect to be hearing from you soon." She turned deliberately away from Fiona, extending her hand to the shadowed man in elaborate doublet and ruff. He took it and escorted her out of the room without a backward glance.

The guard escorted her out and back to the banqueting hall. Fiona was fuming, curling her hands into fists within the folds of her skirt. If she could've gotten away from the guard without incident, she would have scurried off to the gardens as quickly as possible. Instead she let out a deep breath and watched her step, mind frantic with thoughts. Pressed into the service of the Queen was not what she had in mind for this week or this lifetime. How in the world would she fulfill this request? She didn't have favors enough to talk her way into something this large. And thinking on favors, someone owed her immensely. Did the historian know about the Queen's desire? Had he set her up to encounter the Queen in her chambers for this private talk? Why? Fiona swallowed hard as she reentered the hall.

"Gray skies, what's the matter, mistress?" The captain appeared at her side, resplendent in bright colors from head to toe. Her snug-fitting doublet of sky blue was embroidered with silver thread, and there were subtle compasses around the buttons down her middle. Her breeches and knee-high leather boots were perhaps the most fashionable Fiona had ever seen on Henrietta. And the sword at her side was more ornate than useful as it had been earlier in the week. She looked regal, fashionable, and as flamboyant as her personality was large. There was little doubt that the fauns had gotten a hand in the matter of her dress at court. Henrietta's warm fingers lightly gripped Fiona's sleeved elbow. "You look as if you've been flung right out of a maelstrom."

"Or into one," Fiona muttered. Fiona reached toward her neck only to encounter ruff. She forgot her scarf was tucked into her bodice. She missed the comfort of it. "I honestly don't know, Henrietta. My head is swimming."

"This way then," Henrietta said, escorting her to a sturdy chair outside the hall. She took glasses from a close servant and handed one to Fiona. "Drink deep. Wine helps all, I've found in my affairs." As if by example, she drained hers quickly.

Fiona did as told, letting the warm, sweet drink pour over the edge of her nerves, softening them. She closed her eyes for a brief second. "He's here, Henrietta. The courtier I spoke of. He seems to be the royal historian."

"Well, that's tidy. He's here and you're here. Get to work, I say." Henrietta smiled wide.

"But the Queen...she spoke to me." Fiona didn't want to worry her friend about exactly how she had gotten an audience with the Queen.

"She did?" Henrietta whispered, glancing back to the throne. The Queen was nowhere around. "I thought she was there just a moment ago."

Fiona laughed a little edgily. Some close to them moved away, glancing back at her. "If someone of her caliber can't disappear when it pleases her, there's no hope for me." She recounted the Queen's measured words to Henrietta. "It's clear she has had thoughts of my work. But the Guardian of Rise. This is a hard bind if ever there was one."

Henrietta nodded and leaned in to Fiona, placing a comforting hand on her shoulder. "It's not going to be easy, I know. But, Mistress Thorne, you're no unread turner. You've got ideas. All you need is a bit of time. But don't gnaw on that bone right now. There're others more pressing. Like the formidable woman who bears a striking resemblance to you baring down on us."

Lavinia was charging as politely as she could across the entry garden hall toward her reclining form. "Fiona," her mother hissed, "why are you sitting? You're meant to make your way into the Great Hall after being received by the Queen." She looked up, seemingly just now aware that Henrietta was standing close and listening to their conversation. She nudged Fiona with her hand and made wide eyes at Henrietta.

Fiona sighed. "Mother, please allow me the pleasure of introducing you to Henrietta Forestseeker. Henrietta, this is my mother, Mistress Lavinia Thornbeard."

"Pleased as a peach to make your acquaintance. The amazing and, dare I say, brilliant mother of my dear friend. You must be an absolute treasure to have parented such a woman." Henrietta gave a deep bow as if her mother were the Queen.

Lavinia, as many did, grinned at Henrietta and inclined her head. "I had heard you were to escort Fiona, but she failed to tell me how charming you were."

"She has a keen mind and I'm sure it was simply navigating through choppier cloud banks. I would be thrilled to escort you both inside, if I may be so bold."

For the first time in her life, Fiona saw her mother a bit speechless. She nodded her head and then frowned at Fiona.

Fiona read her meaning clear and stood on her feet. "I'm much better now, Henrietta. Thank you for the reprieve." She took a deep breath, concentrating on herself, and focused. She would introduce Henrietta as promised and then find the historian or the Painted Edge. She would investigate, she would listen, and she wouldn't be caught out again. She fanned her face and walked into the banqueting hall.

She quickly found the baron she wanted to introduce Henrietta to and made introductions. An old acquaintance from previous years who owed her a favor for a job well done. She made it clear that she had come calling and, after a few moments of conversation, left them to it. Henrietta was more than capable of taking the initiative.

Searching for the Painted Edge was more difficult than expected. She seemed to have lost all trace of them. The historian was much the same. No room held them, and no one seemed to remember seeing them. It was as if they had all vanished. Fiona had a suspicion that the two weren't a coincidence. Well, she would make sure at least one of them knew how she felt about it. She spent more time gleaning where the royal historian kept his papers, so to speak. Though it took her quite a long time away from the dwindling main activities, she struck gold with a servant who pinpointed the south side of the palace.

Fiona found the lower rooms rather easily enough. The few guards on patrol seemed to have a lax attitude to anyone going toward the dungeons—eyes pretending not to watch her, no doubt—and those who questioned her heard her desire for research papers as benign. Perhaps the mishap with the Queen had already reached the ears of those who needed to know that Fiona worked for her.

The wooden double door to the archives was locked, but it was little match for Fiona and the tools she kept within her scarf. It took longer to reach up the fastened puffed sleeve, pull the scarf out, and think of the tools she needed than to unlock the door. Once inside, she shut it quietly behind her and relocked it.

Silvery moonlight shone throughout the space from cut windows high up on the stone walls, throwing sharp rectangles of clear light across dozens of large, sturdy bookshelves. They lined the walls and stood in two rows in the center of the room, like soldiers at attention, facing the door. Low tables bookended the double doors and were tidy with sheaves of paper, the crisp smell of them permeating the air. Dozens of stacked scrolls tied with golden ribbons, inkpots, and quill pens aplenty crowded the tables as if they, too, wanted to be seen. Portraits hung high above the bookcases, but Fiona couldn't make out in the angled light exactly what they contained. In one corner sat a bulky object, hidden under blankets, and in the other two, arches led away from the chamber, one with a door and one without. It was eerily silent in the room, as if no sound could permeate its solemnity.

Fiona moved quietly between the bookshelves, looking at the titles. She would've preferred to light a candle so she didn't have to squint in the darkened areas, but without knowing if the historian was absent or merely sleeping, she didn't want to alert anyone of her presence. From what she could make out, one bookshelf held genealogy records, accounting of historical events, and history books on the various monarchs of Rise. Another shelf was more diverse with tomes from all over the Book. The collection within these walls could rival that of many a personal collector, including Mistress Humbledraft. That the historian kept his books in pristine condition, not a speck of dust or smell of mildew, told Fiona that although he may have underestimated her, he knew how to value the written word.

She headed back to the tables, still listening for movement from the other rooms. She examined one of the stacks of paper, pulling out sheets silently one by one. She paused when she saw her family name written in the human language of Schiflan and an accounting of her ancestors and their ancestors before them. It only went back the last two hundred years or so. Perhaps he did not care to track page turners back before the Inking, although she was curious herself.

There was a click in the lock of the double doors, and Fiona had just a moment to decide her course of action. By the clear surprise on his face, he hadn't expected that she would be standing in the center of the room, arms crossed, and staring thunderously at him as he came into the chamber.

"Oh, 'this passage leads to the royal chambers and this one to the kitchens— but I'm not helping,' you said. You were helping me. To the *dungeons*. How dare you trap me like that?"

Fiona barged toward him. "And do tell, where are the servants I had my eyes on?"

The historian slammed the door with some measure of strength and crossed the distance between them. "They bloody well got away."

She arched backward, meeting his golden eyes. "They wouldn't have if you hadn't pushed me into the lion's den."

"I was trying to keep you safe." He pushed past her to get farther into the room.

Fiona quickly stepped into his path. He wasn't getting away from her. "Safe from what? I'll have you know I investigate by myself regularly and I *don't* require protection."

He shook his head, looking up to the ceiling as if someone would come save him. "Blundering about a bit, I don't doubt. Like the last time—"

"The last time, you were the one who blundered into my carefully vetted space. Who knows what I missed while you were busy manhandling me."

The historian tugged on his beard, but a faint flush rose to his cheeks. "I was not manhandling. I was trying to keep us out of harm from your loud chattering." He rubbed his face roughly, a single golden ring flashing in the light. He sighed. "They know your face. If they had seen you following them in that dance hall, they would've known they weren't hidden and might've accosted you."

Stupid *Card*. She could've dealt with the situation, however. Fiona bristled. "Oh, and they don't know your face?" She crossed her arms, not giving way.

"No, they don't." He crossed his arms and raised an eyebrow.

"How good for them. I won't soon forget it."

The historian blanched. "Yes, well..." He trailed off, all bluster seemingly drained from him. He dropped his arms and turned away from Fiona, darting to a table. He began tidying up the already pristine space.

Fiona took a deep breath, momentarily confused by his response. He seemed so self-assured and then all of a sudden unnerved. Why? "If you had thought my face was known, you could've said something. Instead of handing me over to the Queen."

He lit a few candles and covered them with Copper-made colored glass. "She wanted an audience, and I thought it was best—" He whirled around as if reignited. "Oh, I don't know why I'm explaining myself to you."

"Well, someone owes me an explanation, and if you don't want me to be a thorn in your side, you might simply get on with it. With no riddles this time."

The historian looked at her, arms recrossed and unswaying. His face became impassive for a moment and then relaxed.

Fiona was immediately suspicious.

He gave a small bow. "Richard Mourninghide, Her Majesty's royal historian."

A name. A lot could be done with a name. Though she was curious why it wasn't Bridewood when he shared the Queen's crest. Fiona relaxed a fraction and inclined her head politely. "Why did you send me to the Queen?" Truly she wanted to see what he would say. If he knew about the Queen's desire, then perhaps it would confirm quite a bit.

Richard turned, shuffling through the stack of scrolls. "The Queen has of late grown worried about occurrences in the page. Then she deduced there was some sort of protector or Guardian that should exist here. She's mentioned a few things connected with your name. I have not found anything beyond myths, and she wanted you to take over the search."

Fiona was confident that she had only told a handful of people about her involvement with Soots and one of them was most definitely not the Queen of Rise. She supposed she shouldn't be surprised that the Elder would tell the other leaders, considering the druid clearly already knew of their existence. But that the Queen would tell her historian was another thing. It was odd, the Queen having a non-page turner spy, but since turners couldn't stay forever in Rise, perhaps there were more issues than she knew of here and he was telling the truth. "That is quite the task to entrust to a historian," Fiona said, walking slowly toward the tables. "One who dabbles in following suspicious persons as well."

"*Dabble* is perhaps a strong word. I do what I can." He shrugged.

Fiona didn't buy the nonchalance. "Your secrets are safe with me as long as you're not here to spy on me."

"If you're not with the Painted Edge, there's nothing to spy on," he said tersely, irritated again. "Look, if you stay out of my way, I'll stay out of yours. There's no reason for us to continue talking to each other. You've been assigned by the Queen herself, and I can get on with my own business elsewhere."

She started to agree but then stopped. He likely had valuable information in the form of the parchments he had hurried off with the other night. Allying herself with him would give her access to those and more if he had the ear of the Queen. Though she certainly wouldn't have thought about it in the past, trading information made investigating considerably faster. She ignored the niggling thought that suggested she simply wanted a reason to keep an eye on him. "Actually, if you can manage not to try and lead everything, working together could prove beneficial to both of us."

"Why in the name of Larrakane would we do that?" Richard leaned in, face bewildered.

His closeness warmed Fiona, and she pushed herself to not take a step back. "We're certainly doing some of the same work. I could help you with information that you may have a hard time obtaining, and, well, you could do the same for me."

Richard shook his head. "I know this page and the people in it thoroughly. Research does that to a person. I don't need your help here."

"I'm a page turner and you are not. There is much information outside the page that, put together, may help us both find what we're after. We are both after the same thing in the end. Are we not?"

He tugged on his beard gently. "And what would that be?"

"Oh, come now, Sir Mourninghide," Fiona said with surprising coyness. She didn't know why she was drawing him out. She most certainly wanted information he might gather, but she was usually more direct. But for some reason she didn't want to be the first to answer a question straight. "You owe me more than I owe you."

Richard sighed and rubbed his face. "To keep the page safe of course."

Something about the gesture, the fact that she rankled him, made Fiona smile. She caught herself and became more straight faced. She stuck out her hand. "Though you may not like my methods."

He looked at her hand for a moment and then shook it. "Nor mine. I'm not used to having an investigator in my path."

"And I'm not used to having a Queen's spy in mine, but the Book is thin, so they say." She reached for her throat, forgetting once again her scarf was in her sleeve, and dropped her hand. "You can start by telling me what you've found in the parchments that you took from the barn." She hadn't prepared to have her paper in reach so, with some reluctance, took a step back and ambled toward the bookshelves to fetch it out of her scarf as elegantly as she could without his seeing. "While I think I understand my portion of the coded instructions, your portions should prove illuminating." Stepping into the shadows, she removed the parchment from her scarf with only a little awkwardness. She turned back around and bumped immediately into Richard.

"What are you doing?"

"I'm trying to show you what I mean."

He motioned with his hand to her sleeve. "Literally up your sleeve then, eh?" He grinned, golden eyes flashing in the light. He looked slightly less cranky when he smiled.

Fiona ignored him and recited the words Henrietta had been able to deduce from the parchment. "What does your share say?"

His smile dropped and he pursed his lips. "I haven't been able to read them." He motioned to the table. "By all means, great investigator, try for yourself."

Fiona swallowed. She had watched Henrietta, yes, and understood a bit of what she had done, but she was no replacement for the woman's experience. But she desperately wanted to see what the other papers said. Perhaps she had been a fast learner. She nodded and marched to the table.

Richard pulled out two small slips of parchment identical to the one Fiona had.

She placed her own down and smoothed it out. The others looked like gibberish to her, but she would not be deterred. With no small measure of glee, she was relieved to find some of the words the same between her slip and the others. She looked up and found Richard sliding her ink, quill, and parchment with a focused face. Their tête-à-tête was truly ended now that there might be uncovered clues.

After some time working on the words she knew from the previous decoding, she guessed at a few others based on what Henrietta had done to tease them out before. With the right context, a deliberate message began to take shape, and after an hour or so she felt they had as much as they were going to gather.

...moon's...gaze, fix...torn earth.

...iron feather upon the island's breath.

Eyes naked...

Heed the red claw...the Guardian's wake.

When...is high, align the stone and Hazel's vine for...untold.

"Well, what do you suppose it to mean?" Richard set down a pewter mug of water beside her and sipped his own.

"I suppose anything really," Fiona said. She looked at the mug in a small measure of surprise before grabbing it. "It's clear that they intend on doing something with a Guardian. Waking it or finding one. But aligning the stone? Eyes naked? Perhaps when everyone is watching or somewhere everyone is watching. The island must be one of the islands in Rise." She drank the water, realizing she was quite parched.

"So you are sure it's the supposed Guardian of this page?" Richard began pacing the floor.

"I am. The Painted Edge that came in were all humans. Certainly, the hidden message favors the Schiflan language more than anything else. The instructions were left in such a way and in such a language that they would be able to decode easiest. Although very poetic." That the Queen and the Painted Edge were both looking for the Guardian of Rise made Fiona uneasy. She hoped they weren't looking for them together, but if so, the Queen wouldn't need her to do it. "What do you know of the Guardian here?"

His eyebrows rose. "You don't want to tackle the Painted Edge first?"

"*Someone* has put the Queen on my tail without warning, so what I'd like to do and what I need to do will be conflicting for a while."

He frowned but went to the door and locked it. Fiona glanced away as her face warmed. Her mother would be shocked to know Fiona was locked in a room with another unmarried person. But the act had also made her curious about why he kept it so locked.

Richard cleared his voice and waved for her to follow him. They traipsed through the initial library room of the archive toward the arches. Fiona glimpsed through the open arch to see a modest bedchamber before following dutifully behind through the now unlocked second arch. This chamber was smaller than the library room but held items as well as books and scrolls. Motes of dust flittered through the air, and she sneezed.

Richard rubbed his jaw, cheeks reddening. "Apologies for the lack of cleaning. I store items here but don't allow the servants within."

"Secret records?" Fiona said.

"Unique records that a persistent servant and a wet rag would give me a heart attack about." He smiled, a small, genuine smile. "I do try to strike a balance between madman historian and eccentric scholar."

Fiona smiled back. "The balance may be a bit tipped."

The tilted wooden table he led them to was covered in open books. Vibrantly inked drawings of majestic castles, knights with flowing banners high, lions and dragons and many other mythical pieces. On quite a few pages were islands floating against radiant skies and winged beasts flying to and from them.

"Myth is really all there is," Richard said pushing one of the tomes to her and watching her out of the corner of his eyes. "Historical accounts passed down from generation to generation verbally and then written the last few centuries, of course. Flying beasts who act as protectors to the islands."

Fiona had a head for historical facts. Though she wasn't formally educated—what farmer's child was, truly—she gobbled up stories and fables like other kids. She had never heard of specific beasts who protected the isles nor seen any such thing. Come to think of it, she couldn't count one flying beast that was native to the human page besides the birds. One would think there would be more with the floating islands that had split from the central plateau thousands of years ago. "Who wrote down these accounts? What families did these stories originate from?"

Richard raised an eyebrow. "Those are good questions."

"I have been known to have a few." Fiona crossed her arms. "Did Her Majesty not ask?"

"That she did not." He pulled another book forward, this one smaller with less detailed artwork within its pages. "Several prominent families have discussed the myths over time, as well as many from larger groups of people, before the unification of the islands. And the historians before me kept track of myths, fairy tales, and the like. Of course, the historians before me disagreed on what the beasts were protecting and what they looked like, so it's a bit muddled." He rubbed the back of his neck. "But that's as much as I could find."

Fiona nodded. "I can see why you've run into a dead end with our texts, but what of those outside the page?"

"Outside the page? Why would there be accounts of a Rise Guardian outside of the page?"

"I've noticed previously in historical texts, paintings, sketches that sort of thing, that elements of the pages bleed into others." She thought of a painting that Mistress Humbledraft had in her gallery that an artist in Copper painted before the pages opened. Didia talked of how the artist had dreamed of the scene of a mother crowned Queen, unknowing that almost that exact scene was happening in Restless Rise right after the Inking. "True they are rare finds, but they might have news of a Guardian as well."

"Well...I wouldn't have known." He tugged at his beard, stroking it. "But it seems that our *temporary* partnership is coming in handy already. It's *too bad* there's no actual Guardian to talk to from another page."

Fiona glanced at him under lowered eyelashes. Did he know about Soots or just what had been released by denizens of the fire page and the *Card*? "A shame," Fiona said lightly. Partnership didn't mean full trust. She wasn't a blotter. "I can continue from here looking into the bestial Guardian. This gives me a path to walk." Indeed, she would talk to the foremost expert on Guardians, Soots. Though the fire page was only accessible to fire elementals without the increased danger, she needed to talk to Soots directly. Perhaps Gaili was done improving her protection gear? Either way, she would have to figure it out now, and most urgently.

"And the Painted Edge?" Richard waved his hands in her face impatiently.

It was interesting how quickly he went from befuddled to commanding. Fiona couldn't tell which was his dominant personality or even if they were both his real one. Spies, like investigators, tended to play the field as they saw it. "I have no more pertinent information on them than you do at the moment, I'm afraid. But I intend to gain some back in Spine. I will share what I learn with you when I return."

His shoulders relaxed. "I suppose you won't tell me the details of how you'll be gaining information in Spine?"

"Let's simply say I have friends in high places. But not as high as yours." She winked.

Richard pressed his lips together as if trying to control himself. "Fair enough," he said in a strangled voice. He gestured for her to follow him out and escorted her back to the tall double doors of the archives. Unlocking them, he gave her a slight bow, "Till we meet again, Investigator Thorne."

Fiona inclined her head. "Till then, Sir Mourninghide."

He closed the door behind her with a click of the lock. Fiona tilted her head, listening for anything else, but all was silent. She couldn't even hear his booted feet retreating. Why did a historian need several locked doors and a soundproof chamber? What had she overlooked in there that warranted such security? She made a mental note to pay more attention when she came again. Curiosity set, she trudged down the hall to her rooms. She had quite a bit of work to do.

ALTHOUGH SHE HAD DIRECTION, she begrudgingly acknowledged that she also needed sleep, however short she could make it. The day had been long, and even though she hadn't wanted to say it to Richard, her leads in Spine regarding the Painted Edge were a tad dry. She needed a new plan, materials, and, ever cautious, to assess her mother's mood. She knew if she wanted to avoid a scene she should talk to her mother early in the morning rather than later about her disappearance the night before and in the future. She would need to be absent, carry her ornithopter, and unfortunately, not meet with the courtiers her mother had been quite insistent on. Though the last one didn't chafe Fiona personally, she knew her mother would be upset.

So, after a deep sleep and a quick change into appropriate clothes for the court, with wool stockings on instead of silk—the better for skulking—she took a deep breath and opened the door to their shared parlor rooms. Her surprise, however, couldn't be contained at the sight of Henrietta and Lavinia laughing over the morning meal. Cold meats from yesterday's mutton, butter, bread, and Fiona suspected wine more than beer spread between them like a sumptuous feast.

Henrietta seemed to be recounting one of her adventures in Mistral.

"I see I haven't been missed." Fiona picked a hunk of bread and slathered butter on it. She needed to fortify herself if her mother had become susceptible to Henrietta's penchant for booze at spirited hours.

As if reading her mind, Lavinia pursed her lips and raked her eyes over her daughter's mode of dress. "I distinctly remember not packing any wool stockings for you."

"It's good that I tended to my own bags before we left then." Fiona sat, happier to be reclining for this imminent argument than standing tired. "Lest I have nothing to run around in while I work my cases."

"You are not to be working this week, Fiona. You promised," her mother said. "You disappeared last night when I had just been discussing you to the baron of Heath."

"Yes, well, there may be more conversations I have to miss during our time here."

"I only asked for a few things, dear. Why can you not seem to keep to them? It's bad enough you ignored all my advice yesterday." Lavinia stood thoroughly preparing to reprimand her daughter. "But you left Henrietta to her own devices as well. I raised you better than to ignore a friend."

Properly reprimanded on an argument she couldn't refute, Fiona grabbed Henrietta's hand and squeezed it. "I am sorry. I didn't mean to leave you at loose ends. Were you able to discuss what you wanted with my contact?"

"No worries, mistress, it's as buttoned as can be. I got on quite nicely with him, and he introduced me to some of his friends and other guests at the party. Some are even staying at the inn I'm in. I was fine—"

"If you let her off the hook, she'll never learn," Lavinia interrupted. "You can't simply willy-nilly yourself away because you want to ignore your courtly duties during the festival!"

"I didn't willy-nilly myself away, Mother, I was on a case for the Queen!" Fiona shouted back.

Lavinia sat down like a soufflé collapsing into the chair. She grasped about for her cup. "The Queen? She asked you to do something for her?" She took a long draught from her wine.

Fiona hadn't wanted to share the information with her mother, but she had a habit of getting the best sort of rise out of her. She sighed. "Yes."

"Well, what is it about? What are we to do?"

"*We* are to do nothing." Fiona put her hand up, forestalling arguments. "No, this is my investigation. My work. Really, Mother, don't worry about it and leave it to me. Besides, you would be best kept away from knowing the peculiarities." *And best kept away from the Queen's eye to use against me.* "Maybe even go home? Since I won't be participating fully in the festivities, you may get bored sitting around in the chambers."

"Sit around? Oh, don't talk such nonsense. I have plenty of people to meet and friends to enjoy the days with. Why, do you think without you here I've whiled away my time alone? I know how to be an agreeable person to be around, Fiona. And the captain has been keeping me company this morning." Lavinia inclined her head toward Henrietta, smiling. She leaned into Fiona and whispered, "If you could be more amiable like Henrietta, then you wouldn't be so alone, my dear."

Though Fiona knew better, the soft words hit hard. She hadn't been feeling alone lately. That should've insulated her from the insult. But words were interesting in that way. They knew how to wriggle down to the heart where even one lied to oneself. Fiona rose with a tightened face and turned toward the door, having had enough morning chat with her mother for a lifetime. "Henrietta, would you like to join me on a jaunt back to Spine?"

Henrietta's face looked quite torn, and she shook her head ruefully. "Can't. Accepted an invite to go hunting with Baron Griffintail and Baron Skybash before luncheon. Out of all I met last evening, we had a smashing time together."

Fiona nodded understandably. Though disappointed, it was exactly what Henrietta needed for her first step. She turned to her mother with purpose. "I will be back before supper, so save me a seating." Without waiting for a reply, she walked out the door. She had more feelings than words and carried on in silent thought down the hallway. How could her mother not understand how her words landed? Could she truly be so unfeeling? She had always tried to be the best she could be at everything she did, but there was always some other rung for her to stretch to. Her mother wanting to see her married was just the latest one.

Fiona squared her shoulders and pushed familial thoughts away. She had given her mother enough information not to worry about her being missing, and that was all she needed to do. She had a date with the fire page to prepare for.

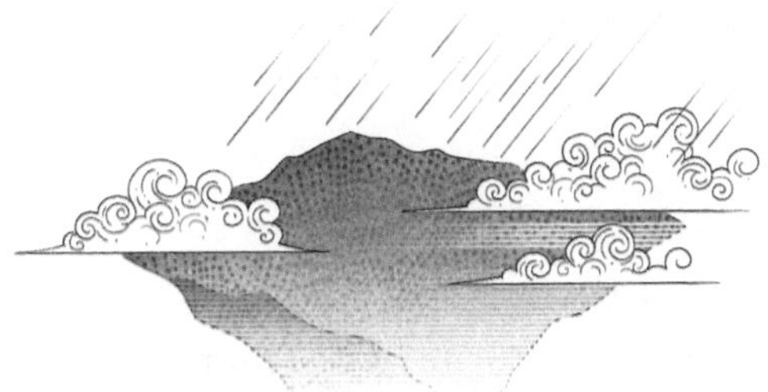

An airship ride and a few page turns later, Fiona was ready to tempt Larrakane's endurance and head into Blaze. Blessed Gaili had dropped everything she was working on to finish improving her gear in a rush. No one could work with intention quite like the faun could when it came to metalworking, alchemy, and simply the art of inventing. Though she tried to fuss over her, Fiona knew she only had so much time before she needed to be at the Great Hall again, and she darted off when Gaili finally took a breath.

The Travel Guild had temporarily closed all their outposts to Blaze in every page since it was unsafe for mortals to travel. This meant that instead of logging in at a stall and having to wait in what was typically a short queue, the pagemark in Rise she had chosen was practically deserted. She chose to turn in Rise instead of Spine because she wanted to be unnoticed. To that end she wore a heavy cloak over her black leather fire-resistant gear, braided her thick curls in a crown around her head to hide under the hood, and took the path least traveled around the outskirts of Heath. Though the floating island was mostly shrub and moorland, there were a few cities where people lived closer to the edge facing the Plateau. The island was rarely used to go to the fire page, although it was an excellent pagemark. The coarse grasses and flickers from the flame did not mix.

After watching the lone guard, bored and painting the lovely bell-shaped purple flowers that rippled across the landscape outside the pagemark, Fiona was assured he'd not notice her travel. Too intent on his brushstrokes.

Grabbing on to the sides of the cloak, she ran her fingers over the material. It was her bookmark to turn the page to Blaze, purchased like all the other elemental protection items in the artisan district on Spine. However, Gaili had lined the cloak with the chained metal she had made for Soots when they were but a flame sprite. Fiona hoped it would do the trick at improving the ability to withstand the hotter temperatures the page now had.

She focused on the elemental chapter and then the page itself. The tips of her fingers warmed, a new sensation, but she focused on connecting to Blaze with a rough jolt. Breathing slowly, she bound the heat that surrounded her to herself and blocked out the world of Rise.

Gray cloudy skies folded away from her and gave in to the roaring sound of a thousand flames. It was as if she opened the world to the sun itself. What had been intense heat was now a sundering of fire. Smoke billowed around her, obscuring her view. Her throat itched, her breath stolen by the flames, but the fire-breathing potion she drank quickly eased her pain. She thrust the unfamiliarity and the thought of fleeing clear danger into the back of her mind and took a step forward before she could change course.

The soft grass beneath her feet gave way to uneven rock and pebbles. The gray cloudy sky turned away, the page flipped completely to Blaze, and she was there. But *there* was unrecognizable. Before, this pagemark would've taken her to the Black Sand Desert, home to endless gritty ebony and jet grains of sand. But now…now there was nothing she could see beyond the gold and white flames.

Her senses tuned in to the fact that her body was warm but not uncomfortable. The chained metal must've been doing its job. She took a step forward, but fire shot up from the ground as if to block her path. She whipped off her dark-view goggles, unneeded with the brightness of the page. How was she going to get through to find Soots? Where was the Ashborn? For that matter, where even was she? All her knowledge of the page needed to be rearranged, redrawn. It would take spotters, those who found safe pagemarks between pages, years to traverse and detail this page again.

She wracked her brain trying to think of a plan as she took small steps. She was blocked every which way. Fiona threw up her hands, exasperated. Surely there had to be some way to find someone here who could get her to Soots or the Ashborn. She would have to be a bit more forward, it seemed.

She cupped her lips to her hands. "Hello!"

No reply.

"This is a bit unmanageable really. I thought I was always welcome," she yelled again. What was the equivalent of a formal introduction for the fire page? Perhaps something that would capture attention. Fiona carefully reached into her cloak to the scarf wrapped lovingly again around her neck and chest. She pulled out her rope and shot it into the air. It immediately caught fire, but the hue was blue, not orange. Though it went far up it, burned through quickly and scattered ashes back down on her. She waited another minute, but no one came to see who sent up the blue color. She cupped her mouth once again. "Really, Soots! You're supposed to be the whole page. Where are you!?"

The obsidian ground beneath her feet shifted, and she stumbled, falling onto her back. The flames were quickly speeding past her and she rose, ground seat and all, higher up into the sky. She gasped as she got above the flames. Rows of lava stretched out before her like fences one might see on a farm. Spiral towers punctuated each row. And at the head of them all was a massive, and quite active, volcano.

"Who are you?" a voice, like a warm crackling fire said through the flames.

Echoes of the question surrounded Fiona on her platform. She winced as the heat rose and sat up into a more dignified position. "I am Fiona Thorne. Do you not remember me?"

"A Fiona?" the fires emanated the question. "A Fiona is a thing we have seen before." There was a pause and then a burst of lava from the volcano rang out, "But what is that to us? Why have you come into our domain uninvited?"

Fiona frowned. She hadn't expected Soots not to remember her. Indeed, if they didn't, there wasn't much hope of getting answers from them and they might consider her an interloper. "I wanted to visit. It has been a while since I last saw you. When you were a small flame sprite." She rubbed her neck, sweat starting to drip from her. She shouldn't have been feeling the heat with her protective gear on, but it was slowly intensifying. How much longer could she stay here? She needed—wanted, truly—Soots to remember her. "You came and stayed with me for a while. You ate so many of my books and papers, remember?" She pushed back tendrils of hair that stuck to her sweaty forehead. Would Soots remember?

Small tremors vibrated through the area. Fire rose and danced closer toward Fiona and the volcano. There was such an intense heat that Fiona could barely pick up the thread of curiosity mingled with it, but the feeling was there. With curiosity came a desire for answers. Fiona knew well enough how curiosity could be fed. She had answers in spades. "I called you Soots and so did Gaili, the faun with the pink hair? She created a metallic suit for you so we could travel together. We went to the page of air first, a beautiful place, if I do say so myself. You learned from the cloud people, the cirelles, and helped them restart their furnace."

As she talked, there was a shift in the temperature. Not something one would call a cool breeze, but the heat lessened around her considerably. Perhaps all Soots needed was to know how much their friendship meant to her.

"And we went to Cobbles, where you tried to protect me. You protected me so many times. Without you I wouldn't have learned to lean in to people who care for me. We got on so well together that I still miss you, even now. You are my friend. You will always be my friend, whether you're an important Guardian or a flame sprite dancing by my side."

A figure began to pour from the lava, chameleoning among the impressively changed landscape. Face as tall as the palace tower, chest as wide as the city gates, and their body riddled with letters of Claire wrapped around their bright-orange rib cage. A large ebony gem hung in their center, like a brick supporting the bones of the creature's chest. The figure's soft features began taking on more of a humanoid shape. Long limbs extruded from the fire into condensed white-hot molten rock. It was a familiar shape, even without a mirror to compare herself with.

The volcano shifted as well, becoming a stately seat of blackened rock and obsidian jewels that twinkled in the fiery light. The figure sat and the volcano burst. It spewed forth fire and lava, molten rock pouring across the creature's shoulders like a heavy velvet shawl. The lava poured from their shawl to the rows leading away deep into the fire that Fiona now hovered high above.

The figure's head tilted as they regarded Fiona. Where there was nothing around the humanoid face, curls burst out as sprays of lava, creating ringlets Fiona knew she could never achieve with her curls and coils. The face split, showing a white-hot glow. Fiona realized it was a smile.

"So you've come at last, little one." Soots waved their molten rocky hand idly from the chair. The stone of Fiona's flew closer away from the flames and over the lava rows to them.

"Well, I was expecting some sort of invitation." Fiona thrust her hands on her hips and grinned. "But it seems you've been a mite busy. Redecorating, are you?"

"I thought some structure was needed." Soots held out their hands. Fiona's rock flew gently toward it until she was in their palm. "Pockets for each of the denizens to live as they please. Better pockets for them to mix."

Fiona raised an eyebrow. "Encouraging fraternizing among the hotheads?"

"The Ashborn suggested a way to maintain diplomatic relations." Soots's mountainous shoulders seemed to shrug as if this was a concept above their head.

"I am glad they are well. Are they leading you, or are you leading them?"

"It is a mutual arrangement at this time." There was a tickle in the air, a quiver of rippling smoke that Fiona took as Soots's laughing. She supposed that the Ashborn was probably more than happy to have someone to confer with who would not immediately forget like the salamanders or start a fight like the other elementals. "The Ashborn remains on Radiance Peak, their domain untouched."

"I am sure they appreciate the consideration from you."

Soots inclined their head in the way of Fiona, not acknowledging a guess. "But, more importantly, I am happy you have come. I have missed you."

"And I you," Fiona said thickly, warmed by her friend's words. "I would've been sooner, but the rearranging has made it a bit difficult for mortals to enter, you know."

"I thought you warm-blooded loved warmth?"

"Yes, but not quite so much of it." Fiona reclined, back aching looking up at Soots's enormous face.

From this distance she saw the spires that punctuated each row looked like teeth still and figured she was somewhere around the original Obsidian's Tooth. The spotters would truly have their work cut out for them finding pagemarks here again. Perhaps the job would best be left to the fire page turners for the quickest mapping. She'd have to advise Dodger when she saw him. Thinking of Dodger reminded her of the Travel Guild's previous desire. "Soots, do you think you'll allow Travel Guild outposts in Blaze now?"

"Of course."

Fiona raised an eyebrow. "You seem so sure. Why? The Ashborn was most against it."

"It is what must be done. Ever-Burning Blaze deserves the protection they will bring. That is all that needs to be understood."

Blaze wasn't the only thing needing protection. Fiona let out a deep breath. "Soots, I need your help."

"I will give you all that I can. We are friends and I only survived because of you."

All other thoughts flew out of her head. Had the Painted Edge been trying to kill them? "How do you know they were trying to get rid of you instead of kidnap you?"

"Ever-Burning Blaze would be unprotected without me," Soots stated in Fiona's matter-of-fact cadence.

Fiona shook her head at the mimicry. "Would it have died if you had stayed in Spine and the Blackstone remained hidden?"

"Dying, but not dead. Ripped, but not torn," Soots said back in their own tone.

"What does that mean?" Fiona wiped her face with a gloved hand. "What are you guarding against? Are there other Guardians like you? How did you come to be? Oh, I have so many questions and no one seems to know anything, or if they do, they won't say. There seems to be some sworn secrecy. Are you beholden to the same tight-lippedness?"

There was silence. Fiona watched the face of Soots, the rocky exterior smoothed in an image not entirely unlike her own. Thinking, perhaps.

Fiona continued, "I assume Larrakane, perhaps, has tasked you with guarding this place. But how can we prepare or guard ourselves if not everyone is told what the trouble might be?" Fiona reached out from the small rock she was on to touch Soots's palm. It was like touching the kettle when it had been left too long, and she pulled back, holding her hand.

Soots made a sound like a tsk and rose Fiona higher to their eyes. "I am tasked with maintaining the balance of Blaze, as are my elemental brethren. We are the source of power for the page and embody all elements of the page itself. We are the page, and we cannot leave it."

"But you did. You did leave." Fiona rubbed her forehead, brow furrowed. They had been broken from the Blackstone, and as such their connection was strained. If a Guardian left a page, the entire thing would start to fall apart. "Do you know if there are Guardians for the mortal chapter?"

The gargantuan Soots rested their loose hand on their face, mimicking Fiona's movements. "There must be. A Guardian keeps the balance. But they are not my brethren, and therefore I cannot name them. Though I will add it to my list. As I have been away from my page I have many questions of the Book. Many...thoughts."

Fiona grinned. "Your time with me has made you curious, has it?"

"Indeed, you have taught me to question."

"Well, I certainly hope you get your answers." Fiona huffed. "Perhaps they will align with my questions as well."

"The druids of the Book have been most helpful," Soots said. "Why not ask them directly?"

The druids! "How come you to know of the druids?"

"The druids have come often to care for me. I have not needed much, but I have asked many questions."

"The Elder has been all riddles with me. And unfortunately, Soots, I am not a page Guardian, so I think my leeway for questions is a bit lower than yours. Is there anything you know that could help me with them?"

There was silence but no movement from Soots. It was hard to read the side of a volcano, no matter how humanoid and chiseled they seemed. But there was a moment when she swore Soots raised what could be considered an eyebrow. "Tell the Elder, and only the Elder, that your friend and theirs Glowkindle sends regards. For I only name my brethren and my brethren can only name me."

Fiona nodded. "Glowkindle. That's quite a lovely name."

"Indeed. But nothing can touch Soots."

Fiona grinned. "No nothing."

"Perhaps you now take a lesson from me. Those who push to protect others are the ones who need answers the most. Be fire, be flame, be all-consuming."

Soots was right, Fiona had been tiptoeing around with the Elder druid, wary of angering or isolating the leader. But if she was to help people, she would need to be in the light, not in the dark. She sighed. She had been here long enough. "No time like the present. Thank you for the advice."

"Anytime, little one." Soots set her back down, on the top of one of the toothy spires. "And remember you are always welcome to turn the page to my hearth."

Fiona pressed her hand to her heart and waved goodbye. With a last look around at the shifting landscape of Blaze, Fiona turned back to Spine, preparing for a very stubborn discussion. No one made demands on the druids. But Fiona Thorne wasn't someone who was afraid to go first.

THAT SOOTS HAD CALLED them the druids of the Book was not lost on Fiona. She had always known them to stay in their corner of Spine, Forest's Edge, and not travel too much. They were page turners after all. No page turner could be gone from Spine for long, three days at the most. But where she had supposed the druids to all live in Spine, she had never wondered if there were more druids in other pages. She had never heard of them, but if there was a secret—because clearly there were always secrets in the world—then why wouldn't a druid network across the Book simply be another to add to the list? It was getting rather too long for Fiona's taste, but she was working hard to trim it down.

It was early evening now, the sky of Spine beginning to darken by the time she came back from Blaze. She noted with a mixture of relief and amusement that turning the page from Soots's hearth led her only half an hour outside her end of the massive city. *Door to door, eh, Glowkindle?* She tramped through the forest clearing to the road and into the turner district. She needed to catch a carriage speedily to Forest's Edge before she was late for supper back in Rise. Luckily the human district was separated from Forest's Edge only by the district resembling the page of earth, Little Cobbles. It wasn't uncommon for a turner to zigzag back and forth across Spine to get from one page to another hurriedly. It was faster to come back home than to travel across any of the pages. Not always safer though.

That the page-like districts were at the south of the city and the turner district was at the north was no coincidence. Although many unread page turners wanted to stay in places that reminded them of their native page and were known pagemarks that made travel back to them easy, a large handful did not. Dusty page turners who had seen the Book in many ways and were a bit tired of it all—retirees, though one could never actually retire from being a page turner—tended to work in the north away from the ever-growing population of skimmers who traveled in.

The northwest boasted of rows and rows of farmland to feed the city. To the east were the Rocky Bluffs, cliffs that housed the massive lake that was secretly fed directly from the page of water itself capped off the north—a secret Fiona had discovered in her usual manner of listening more than she talked around important people. The water flowed into a river that stopped at the temple district and through aqueducts (a proud product of Kerus) down into each and every district. It was a well-built system to keep the city running with light oversight by the Travel Guild and labor by the dusty page turners.

As the carriage coach trundled along the streets, shouts of workers, hoof beats of the horses, and a mingled mess of smells from baked bread to heavy perfume rushed in one window and out the other. Fiona was squashed between a few fauns and a lone ursidon as she didn't want to wait for an emptier carriage. The fauns dressed in the topmost fashion of the current season—velvets and silks a bit unnaturally clean in the city—were clearly heading to the theater within the Arches. The ursidon kept their furry bear head down, sketching a well-drawn interwoven circle on a bit of parchment. It was a symbol Fiona had seen only once or twice and always on a ursidon, but before she could snoop any further he got off at the dwindling closing market. Fiona sighed and repositioned herself with the additional room. She directed the driver to Little Cobbles hoping there would be no questions. She needed quiet to think of how she was going to ignite her way into answers with the Elder.

The Elder was one of the kindest people Fiona had ever spent time with in Spine. She had been surprised by the Elder when she first met them. Where she expected a stuffy or conspiring leader like the ones of her page, she instead found a warm and welcoming person who truly wanted her to succeed. This is what surprised her most about their previous quiet on the subject of Guardians. They seemed to understand when to speak and when to be quiet. When to show up in the middle of the forest with a pot of coffee and rapt attention. And, unfortunately, when to not be nosy and keep to their own affairs. A trait Fiona thought people put too much emphasis on.

She had done a fair job for them when they wanted her to look into some ill-natured smuggling happening in Spine. That job had quickly rolled into discovering the Painted Edge and more. Perhaps if she pressed on the fact that she was more useful let in on a plan than on the outskirts of one, she could get more answers from the druid. No, not perhaps—she would. Druids thought of time and priority a bit differently than others. She would make giving her answers a priority the Elder couldn't refuse.

The carriage rolled to a stop, the horses snorting and stamping their feet as if to say they too wanted to wander into the forest. Fiona alighted and paid the cheery driver. Once they had departed and she was quite alone in front of the rocky district, she turned about and started to head toward the druid's forest.

The stone streets gave way to nature much quicker than previously before. Often she felt as if the forest was more alive than anything else in Spine. It seemed to shift or change with some inner desire. A protective barrier, Fiona was sure it was meant to be. Squirrels crinkled through the nested branches and leaves of the trees; bees buzzed from some unseen hive. A bounty of delight and sounds swelled in the space—perhaps a gift from Larrakane to the page turners she bonded to the place. A token of pleasure to be gotten nowhere else.

Fiona mused as she strode the dirt path through the cedar-heavy forest, the scent encasing her in a gentle swell. She tugged off her cloak and wrapped her scarf lightly around her neck. She was known to the druids and she would not hide herself. Arriving at the wooden building, a cocoon-like structure naturally grown from the forest floor, she took a deep breath and knocked on the carved wooden door.

She waited, rocking back and forth on her heels, but no one came to open it. Pulling out her pocket watch told her she only had a few hours before she would be very late for supper. Being reprimanded by her mother a second time would be a fate worse than having to come back again another day, but only just. Perhaps she could simply make her way in from the forest.

Or perhaps she could get lost for days tramping through the trees that way.

The sound of hooves alerted her that someone else had arrived, and right to the druid's doorstep. A fae woman, small in stature with ochre skin like earthen clay and downy ears sat atop a beautiful chestnut horse. Her bodice and skirt seemed plain, even if the colors were vibrant creams and bright red, like apples by the bushel. But when she moved to dismount, Fiona noticed decorated golden lace edging on her ruff around the neck and sleeve cuffs of her linen shirt. Large cherry beads hung from her neck and gently swayed as she stopped. Her eyes grew wide and the subtle golden tattoos around her eyes and cheeks glimmered. "Well, hello there."

Fiona inclined her head politely to the stranger. There was something slightly familiar about her. She must've seen her around Spine before. But the fae wasn't a druid, not with those clothes. Perhaps she was here for a meeting as well. "Hello. I've rapped a few times but no one has come to answer."

The fae wrinkled her nose and tilted her head, staring at Fiona. "You're Fiona Thorne, aren't you?" The fae smiled big. "It's quite nice to meet you. I've heard so much about you." She swung herself from the horse and lowered down to the ground.

Pushing down her surprised reaction, Fiona nodded. There was no use trying to deny it. She obviously recognized her from her scarf and picture. "Do you have an appointment with the druids?"

"I do indeed," the fae said, patting down her horse. She nuzzled its head before whispering to it. It cantered off to the edge of the forest. She turned to face Fiona. "Let's see if we can't get their attention then." She strode to the door and knocked loudly in rhythmic succession.

Before Fiona could tell if the knocks were a known pattern or simply quick, the door unlocked, a soft click that had Fiona raising her eyebrow when a young brown-skinned woman opened the door. She was human but with the flyaway loose curls and crinkled green-and-gold garb that said she was more druid than Schiflan. Were the druids able to escape from obligations like the page turner festival with the Queen? Fiona held back a tinge of laughter; of course they were.

The druid woman smiled at the fae and opened the door wide without a word.

A well-known visitor then. Interesting. Fiona stepped forward, filling the space the fae vacated, and relaxed her stance, telling herself to be at ease. "How do you do? Apologies for the unannounced visit, but it is imperative I see the Elder at once."

The woman smiled regretfully and shook her head. "I'm sorry. The Elder is very busy and cannot be bothered at this time."

Fiona pressed her lips together but inclined her head politely. She wasn't going to make an appointment and come back, not when she was almost through the door. "Please tell them Fiona Thorne needs to speak with them urgently. It is important to..." She stopped, glancing at the fae who was watching her. Oh, what could she pass on that would make it clear without alerting others? "To our mutual goals."

Wide confused eyes took her in, and the human woman said, "I'll deliver your message, but it may be some time before there is an answer."

Fiona nodded, not wanting to press the girl, but she couldn't help tugging at her scarf. How long would it take?

"She can come with me if that is fine with you," the fae said.

Though it was a polite phrase, there was a hint of command in it. Who was this fae to carry such influence within the druid camp? And she was going to see the Elder? Fiona tensed as she glanced between them both.

The woman quickly bowed her head and opened the door for Fiona to enter.

With a small amount of surprise, Fiona hurried over the entryway before anyone could change their mind. "Thank you."

The fae smiled, her downy ears perking up. "Think nothing of it."

The door closed softly behind them. The druid beckoned them forward into the sunny pavilion. "Please, follow my path."

Through the entrance pavilion, many paths crisscrossed in a pattern that usually had Fiona somewhat confused, but she noticed that the interwoven design was more reminiscent of the drawing the ursidon had been sketching on the carriage. Had it always been that way? What could they possibly have in common? Tucking the mounting questions away, she dutifully followed step by step after her guide and the fae, as was the proper manners of the druids' den.

The chosen path led away from the actual forest. She was surprised. The Elder's office and home was within a clearing in the opposite direction, but they were heading to a small hut, its walls thick tree trunks bursting from the ground. A roof of nettle clung to the top of the trunks, making it seem as if a bird put the hut together. The woman inclined her head toward the building and then continued on the path, leaving her and the fae alone. Fiona glanced back. Druids weren't the trapping sort, right? She shook her head, throwing away her fancifulness and said, "I can wait out here until you are done."

"Nonsense." She waved the words away and approached the open door. "If you're here to see—" She paused and tilted her head. "—the *Elder*, then it must be important. Come on."

Inside were bookshelves sprouting from the walls. Dozens of books and trinkets were nestled between rough ledges and pops of leaves. A small desk, perhaps the only outside item of furniture she had ever seen in the grove, sat to one side. It seemed to belong more in the Court of Copper with its innate swirls etched around the border and its bright-blue design. It reminded her a little of the Thread, the inn and tavern that Mac owned. Sitting at the desk, scratching away with quill and ink, was the Elder.

The Elder was, to Fiona's now experienced eye, more fae than usual. While in the past she had thought the Elder to have both human and fae ancestries, after her bonding with Mac and time spent in the Court, Fiona was certain they were wholly fae. Their skin was a warm golden brown, much like an acorn. Quite different than the majority of fae but no closer to Fiona's own warm brown human skin tone. And with no tattoos to speak of, which rang as odd to her. Their hair was pine green and often tucked behind their overly large wilting ears. They wore human work clothes: brown working pants and cheery sky-blue linen shirts that matched the forestry world around them. Though it had been a couple of months since Fiona had last seen them in person, they were still intriguing as always. There was something about them that made Fiona want to ask the most impertinent questions. But she had more manners than that.

One of the Elder's wilted ears perked up as they entered, but there was no other sign of acknowledgment. They seemed to be bent over a rather thick book, scrawling in bouncy measured strokes. At the end of a line, they sat their quill down and, before Fiona knew it, were on the balls of their feet in front of them with a surprised look on their perfectly pretty golden-brown face. "Oh, dear Fiona, how the time has flown since our last chat. I am sorry you find me so occupied at the moment."

"Good evening, Elder. I'm sorry for interrupting. I ran into your guest, and she was gracious in letting me accompany her."

"She said it was important for your mutual goals. Why have her wait outside in the dirt when she could follow me in?" the fae said, arms crossed, standing in the doorway.

The Elder looked at them both and clasped their hands together. "Fiona, I am sure you won't mind if we take our meeting *first*." They motioned to the woman.

There was strain there, a hit of the word that Fiona found she never heard the Elder use before. Either the fae was even more important than she seemed, or something was amiss. If the druid could put off what Fiona had unexpectedly come to tell them, she supposed she had no choice. "I can wait to talk to you, Elder. Of course."

The fae moved forward, leaning over Fiona from behind. "I am sure the investigator wouldn't have stopped by unannounced if it wasn't for the protection of the pages. I will meet with your druids and discuss farm supplies until you are free."

The Elder visibly relaxed and nodded. "Thank you."

The fae smiled. "Pomp and formality never quite suited us." She nodded toward them both, gave Fiona a small wink, and strode out the door, calling over her shoulder, "I'll be back."

Fiona glanced after the fae woman, still trying to place her. "Who is she?"

The Elder grinned at Fiona. "An old friend. Please sit." They motioned to a chair with one hand while simultaneously pushing the book they had been writing in farther to the back of their desk with the other.

Fiona leaned over to glance at the book the Elder had been writing in as she sat down.

The Elder leaned with her, obscuring her view. "How goes your investigation of the Painted Edge? I heard that the few who were captured didn't provide much information."

Fiona took the offered seat. "Heard from whom?"

The druid looked surprised at her question but gestured to the outside world. "Word does get around in Spine."

"Yes, well, that's why I've come to you. I believe the Painted Edge is searching for the Guardian of Rise."

The druid stepped back, eyes widening. "How? Why?"

Fiona raised an eyebrow, the only indication of her surprise at the Elder's reaction. "They met in Rise recently and seem to be planning some event in connection with the Guardian." She recounted what she had learned from the parchments she had deciphered, but there was no flicker of recognition from the druid in her words. She sighed. She had been hoping the druid knew exactly what it all meant.

The druid, hands distractedly rubbing the edges of the desk, frowned. "They must never find the Guardian. Nothing they could want with one can amount to any good."

"I am agreed. But they aren't the only ones searching now. The Queen has put me up to finding the Guardian of Rise as well," Fiona said, thankful she could tell the truth to the Elder instead of having to lie, "and Queen Brilliance does tend to get her way."

The Elder shook their head with a jerk. "You must put her off at once."

She gaped at them. "But I can't."

"You are a page turner," the Elder said forcibly. "You don't answer to Brilliance or any other leader outside of Larrakane. It would be better that the investigation cease immediately."

"For however much I am a turner, she still has the power to make my life miserable. To make my mother's life miserable." Fiona sighed heavily. "Or would the druids help her?"

"We could take her in here, of course, but our attention is on Spine."

Fiona snorted. Her mother live with the druids instead of her home? Not likely. "My mother isn't the kind to make herself uncomfortable for anyone. And she couldn't stay forever. Surely you must see I have to handle the Queen with delicate care for more than myself."

The Elder nodded, brow furrowed. "And she must know about Guardians and the Painted Edge and other dangers that may come her way. How I wish the Binder had thought—but of course he had to tell the other leaders."

Of course the Elder and the Binder would share information. They weren't against each other, as Fiona had thought before she got to know the druid. Though the Elder said it as a statement, their tone seemed remorseful. But why? Why not have the leaders of the pages be on their guard? Why not Fiona? "I know I'm not the Queen or a leader in Spine, but am I not trustworthy enough to be told what is going on? You speak of me so highly to your friend, and yet you don't think I'm accomplished at handling complex situations?"

The druid reached out, grasping Fiona's hands in their warm ones. "Of course, you have proven yourself more than once. It is not lack of trust that binds my lips, dear Fiona. It is care."

Fiona pulled her hands back from the druid and crossed her arms. She tipped her chin up, leaning back in the chair. "Insensible. If you care about the Book, you would be willing to gather more people to help you protect it. Not blocking those who want to make it safe and work alongside you." Fiona got up to pace the small hut. "If you can't tell me what you and the leaders so secretly discuss, you can at least advise me. The quicker I appease the Queen, the faster I'll be able to focus on what truly matters, like the Painted Edge." She uncrossed her arms, sighing. "If I don't find the Guardian, the Queen will simply send someone else. I'm already her second choice. But if I can find this Guardian first, I can get her to stop looking, perhaps even hide their existence further. This is the only way I can save them from Queen Brilliance and ensure my mother will be safe from her wrath."

The druid glanced back at the thick book they had been scrawling in when Fiona arrived.

Fiona followed their gaze, but the cover was nondescript. What could possibly be contained in it to draw their attention?

The Elder shook their head, blocking the book once more. They frowned. "I am so sorry I can't share more with you."

She sighed and rubbed her pained neck. She was disappointed. She thought the druid believed in her more than this. But if she truly didn't have the measure to be seen as valuable, even after all her work with them, perhaps they would prefer the word of someone more powerful than she. "Glowkindle sends their regards, from one friend to another."

The druid eyed her with more suspicion than Fiona had ever believed them capable. They turned to the desk, blocking her out. "Do *not* speak that name out loud here."

Fiona scrubbed a hand over her face. Perhaps she had bargained wrong with giving the message. "Soots told me their real name very deliberately. But no caution to not use it."

"There is power in words." Shoulders hunched, the druid turned toward Fiona once more with an ashen face. They bent their tall form down to her, face inches away from her own, and said quietly, "Heed me true, Fiona, for however you feel about me withholding information. A name can tell you more than it should, and true words can give power where it shouldn't. Do not bandy Soots's name about outside of Blaze."

There was something there, worry or perhaps fear, in the Elder's eyes. Though they didn't touch her, Fiona felt as if she was locked in their grip. She nodded. "I believe you. I won't again."

The Elder's shoulders relaxed, and they bounced back from her, warm air filling the gap. "Thank you." Their downy ears perked up, one lifting high as if to listen outside, but it wilted down again just as quickly. They nodded slowly to themselves. "As always you have managed to surprise me, but I believe I have recovered enough to advise you now. At least a little." They ran their fingers across the spines of books on one of the many shelves in the small hut. "In truth, though you may think this a ploy, I know very little about the Guardian of Rise." They tapped on a thin book and pulled it out, showing the cover to Fiona.

The words were in a language unknown to her, but she nodded, no longer feeling charitable about what she could or could not understand. She acknowledged she was upset with the druid but pushed her feelings down and simply said, "Any lead is helpful."

The druid opened the book on the desk, not bothering to move the thicker one, and flipped through the pages. "From what I was told, you have beasts in your midst. This is all the record I have of them. They do not interact with those of Soots's nature, so I don't have any firsthand knowledge." They tapped the page to a snippet of a poem set against a painted backdrop of human knights on horseback, banners flying in the wind.

> *In days of old, when kings alone did reign,*
> *With hearts of courage, not of those of feign,*
> *Three golden beasts in fields of red*
> *Upon the banners they were spread.*
> *Whispers carried through the wood*
> *Of creatures proud where once they stood.*
> *In sunlit glades, their forms did shine,*
> *Symbols of a royal line.*

Fiona's hand flew to her mouth and her eyes widened. "So not only do we have a beast hidden somewhere within our page, but we have three?" A beast, mythical as it may be, was more or less what Richard had found.

"Beasts unnamed. And upon the banners they were spread." The Elder paused and raised a downy ear. Brow knit, they said, "There is power in words and names, my dear. Less in titles, I believe. Your page is thicker with them than the other mortals. But a beast. Where would one even hide such a thing?" They shut the book with a raised eyebrow and took a step back. They began busying themselves with putting the thin volume back on its shelf, seeming to deem their advisement done.

Fiona repeated the words of the poem and the druid's proclamation to herself to tear apart later. "Thank you, Elder."

The druid nodded with a small, distracted smile. They glanced back to the thick book on the desk.

Fiona swallowed. The druid had never made her feel so in the way before. "I will leave you to it then."

"If you need me, please do come back," the Elder said dismissively, already back at the desk and dipping their quill in ink.

Fiona said nothing but closed the door. She found her way out of the druids' camp on her own, feeling somewhat on the precipice between frustration and anger. Did the Elder think that all leaders in the Book would forget about Soots as a Guardian, or Guardians in general? How long would they try to hide them?

She walked on from Forest's Edge toward New Rise, lost in her own thoughts. If she were a leader, like the Elder, who would know their secrets? The other leaders of Spine, no doubt. She had spent more years learning as much as she could about the leaders of her chained city. And had only recently gotten acquainted with the Elder and Priestess Raina. While she held fast to the notion that Marcia would come through on her payment for an introduction to the Binder, she didn't know when. And she hadn't felt the need to press it quite yet. Those were the only leaders she knew of in Spine, but she was fast coming to terms with the fact that what she knew could fit at the bottom of a coffee mug.

Perhaps the leaders of the Book as well then. But no, if that was true, Queen Brilliance would already be well aware of

Rise's Guardian and wouldn't need Fiona to find out. But was Queen Brilliance the only leader in Rise? Truly her advisors did more leading day to day in Rise and made more decisions than the Queen alone. There were few of them on her privy council, her mother had stated, but they were prominent members and five of them were of the peerage. Perhaps she should be talking to them about a Rise Guardian instead of outsiders to the page. Perhaps they would even know about the beasts.

Fiona reached for her scarf and twisted it. Of course, the creatures could even be with one of their families. There was power in words and less in titles, the Elder had said. Most of the peerage took their names from ongoing cultural changes, marriages, alliances, and the like, and some of them had begun quite soon after the Inking, when the Guardians were created. And the heraldic banners of her page depicted changes in symbols, always. The poem had said the three beasts were spread upon the banner. So the Guardian could be connected to a family with a beast in their name. It was the most logical explanation.

On the privy council sat three important families with beasts or beast-like words in their name: Earl Hawkport, Baron Griffintail, and Baron Dragonkeep. Where names had frequently changed hundreds and hundreds of years ago, now they stagnated to preserve legacy and, most importantly, inheritance. Fiona smiled at the thought. People really did like to show off and be clever. Perhaps staying at the palace longer wouldn't be a waste of time after all.

IN A MATTER OF an hour, she was back on her way through gray skies to the palace. Lavinia waited for her, coffee in one hand and a thick letter in the other. Her attire was more elaborate than usual, crisp white neck ruff dangerously close to wagon-wheel size. Fiona held back a grimace at what supper would be like if her mom was putting so much effort into blending in with the royal court.

"Where have you been?" Lavinia said as soon as Fiona walked through the door of their shared rooms.

"I did tell you I would be working on my new case." Fiona tried to slip past her mother.

Lavinia moved with the swiftness of a lioness about to pounce on her cub. "Yes, but you also said you'd be on time for supper. It is nearly fifteen minutes till."

"Fifteen minutes till is still fifteen minutes spared, Mother." Fiona picked the cup of cold coffee from her mother's hand and downed it, giving herself a moment to dampen her irritation. "Is that a letter for me?"

Lavinia handed it over slowly, watching with barely contained interest. "It's from the Travel Guild. They sent a messenger here directly for you."

Dodger must've finally gotten some information! Fiona eagerly tore into the gold wax seal.

From the Desk of Marcius Festinius Cervidus

Fi,

This is not what I thought you meant when you said travel the Book and work with you. For one, you're the only one doing the traveling. It's as if you have a perpetual lure for clues the way the PE landed on your doorstep. Either way, I have no new information about their current work, but I do know about their past heist.

We've worked out that they tried to steal a variety of airships, not simply the one they made off with. Some broke apart during the page turn. Pieces have littered various known and unknown pagemarks. But it seems they finally gave up on taking it as a whole item and instead took it piece by piece. So, while we were all wasting our time trying to figure out how they got it in one go, they were apparently planning something new.

I will send jackets to investigate. I know there's no stopping you. Please let me know what you find. Perhaps a souvenir as well.

Always, Dodger

Piece by piece then? They would have to know how to put it back together. And the only ones who knew airships were the Hawkports. Interesting. Fiona pursed her lips, rereading the letter. She supposed she could nose around the Hawkport facilities. Find out if anyone who would have the knowledge has been missing. If everyone's accounted for, then that may mean someone still around helped the Painted Edge and may know where they are hiding. But how to get there and back again without being watched? The facilities had to be heavily guarded. Airships were expensive.

"You know, *if* you are going to continue working for the Queen, you're going to have to learn to be in multiple places at once, dear," Lavinia broke in, glancing at the letter. "What would I have done if she wanted an update from you?"

"I have no intention of continuing to work for the Queen after this." Fiona folded the letter and tucked it into her scarf. "Where is Henrietta?" It would be good to confer with her on this new development immediately. She wanted to tell her all about the beasts on banners too. No doubt she would have ideas on how to proceed.

"She had an appointment to make and took her leave. And don't try to change the subject. We need to stay on Queen Brilliance's good side, Fiona. Working for her keeps us in her favor." Lavinia clasped her hands together.

There was something about her mother's voice, the way it cracked perhaps, that made Fiona peer at her with renewed focus. For all Lavinia's faults, she never seemed truly worried. It was usually a show to produce guilt in her daughter, and Fiona had hardened herself to it over the years. But her mannerisms didn't seem false. "Is there some reason we would be out of favor?"

Lavinia shook her head and picked up her own coffee cup. "Of course not. I've done nothing worthy of reproach, and it seems even your peculiar profession has become advantageous to her. But you must keep her thinking positive. And we should talk to others of the nobility. Make acquaintances."

Blessed be, I may be able to satisfy my mother's desires for once. "Suppose I speak to someone important? I could do both at once if that would make you happy. Like Lord Hawkport or Baron Dragonkeep. They are in the Queen's privy council."

Lavinia narrowed her gaze. "*You* want to make acquaintances with House Hawkport and House Dragonkeep? Why are you following my advice suddenly? What was in that letter?"

Larrakane help her, even when she was agreeable she was under suspicion. She couldn't very well say she needed to investigate their families. She tried to think of another tactic. "It would greatly benefit me to get better acquainted with someone as important as House Hawkport and avail myself to them. Show them how capable I am. That the mentions of me in the *Card* were correct."

Lavinia sipped her coffee and then gave a short nod. "I agree."

"You do?" Fiona said, surprised at her quickness.

"Yes, it will fall that the rest of the peerage will want to know you as well if the Hawkports engage you."

"Well, you have been making fine suggestions and I should follow them," Fiona said. And because she couldn't help herself, she continued on, "Well, some of them. Shall I introduce myself at supper?" Tired as she was, she couldn't pass up an opportunity to get ahead with the investigation.

Lavinia shook her head. "One doesn't simply introduce themselves to an upper noble, my dear." She finished her coffee and stood. "We start with the fringe rabble and work our way up gradually. Change and we'll go downstairs. They'll be suppering in the Banqueting House, no doubt, with so many people."

"But I've already changed." Fiona resisted the urge to smooth down the soft satin lavender bodice and kirtle she had changed into on the airship. It was the only thing they had picked out that she could see herself wearing again.

"Too gentle. We need to suggest you're in the Queen's favor without suggesting you're above any who actually are. All of the upper nobles will have heard about you working for the Queen by now, I'm sure. A touch of sparkle will go a long way."

Fiona pursed her lips but said nothing. She was quite sure that no one save the historian would have any idea she was working for the Queen. It was a request with more secrecy than most. Why would the Queen explain it to them?

Lavinia dipped into her room and out again in a flash with a closed velvet box. She smiled, a mischievous grin that lit her face and cast away years of frowning in Fiona's general direction. Her mother hadn't smiled much like that since Fiona's father passed away.

"What's all this?" Fiona said, unable to contain a smile herself.

"Simply a little something I've kept for a rainy day. I had hoped to give it to you on your marriage day but, well, never mind." She opened the case revealing a gold chain necklace. The gold pendant was oval with their house color, an emerald, set inside. Three tiny pearls hung from the bottom. "It's small, I know. I wanted to have another made with a cameo of you and your father, but I—well, I took some liberties here."

For once feeling quite speechless, Fiona turned around and let her mother hang the pendant around her neck. It sat warm against her skin. She moved it to lay over her bodice where it winked at her in the mirror. "It's perfect, Mama."

"Yes, well. I do know what I'm doing." Lavinia laughed quietly. "And now you look elevated."

Fiona turned away from the mirror, letting the warmth stay with her for as long as it could. "Let's head down, shall we?"

Through the busy passageways, down stairs, and through the Low Gallery they went. Portraits hung on the wall of royals and courtiers, some with glancing familiarity, although Fiona couldn't explain why any of them looked familiar to her beyond having seen one or two at the dance the night before. Statues and tapestries depicted landscape scenes of the banks of the River Tam that separated the Plateau in two, vividly wrought in thick threading. Some of the works were livelier than others—an essence of the Court of Copper artists, no doubt. Fiona noted that most of the newer artwork was from outside the page. It seemed the Queen would not be like the royals of old and completely ignore the work and connection of the other mortal pages. Surprising for what Fiona knew of her.

Lavinia seemed to be in her element as they traipsed to supper. Though it was raining once again, keeping everyone indoors, it was as if the seas of people parted at Lavinia's wishes. First she introduced Fiona to all her friends who were mingling around the Low Gallery and through wooden terraces, asking who was still in the Great Hall, the Banqueting House, or had moved on to the gardens. She worked with ease between various groups, complimenting, connecting, and smiling. Though Fiona wanted to stop repeating the same conversations over and over of how she was getting on as a page turner, how they were getting on together, and oh, how good it was to see her mother after so much time in Spine, she started to understand the lay of the courtier land that her mother called House Fringe. These were people who were there because, like her, someone in their family had been inked and raised them to a gentle station. The more page turners, the higher they were within this level of peerage. All the way to a gentlewoman who seemed to understand what Lavinia desired (and from Fiona's vantage seemed to owe Lavinia a favor) and introduced her and her mother to a cousin, Mr. John Hawkport the lawyer, nephew of Lord Hawkport.

The Hawkports had only one page turner in the whole family but had been granted an earldom since the beginning of the Inking. Many believed it was due to their impressive fleet of airships that had been commanded by the monarchs since then. In exchange for their use, if not their secrets of creation, the Hawkports had been given the two smallest counties, Shade and Smallcrest. Lords, farmers, traders, laborers, peasants, and serfs combined, the house boasted only three percent of the entire population of Rise. But many continued to labor for the Hawkports since the beginning even as many of the lower class from other counties were flocking to the Plateau and paying labor. The Hawkports had not let the Inking change how they conducted their business too quickly. They were the least historied and noble of the five earls, but Fiona wouldn't have thought that by the preening and mannerisms of most of the family.

After the introduction, Lavinia and Fiona made their way to the tail end of a table where the cousin, John, and other like guests dined. Judges, scholars, merchants, and other professional families made up the bulk of this corner of the hall. The flickering light from the candles and torches ensconced around the walls illuminated the bustling hall, softening it a bit into an intimate setting. Aromas of roasting meats and spices from the lower counties floated on the air. Fiona's mouth watered.

Lavinia allowed her chair to be pulled out by a servant before sitting and smiling at the table as if being across from her daughter was the best seat in all of the palace. Fiona sat on the other side of John and gave him a gentle but pointed greeting as if happy happenstance had seated them together. Servants moved almost invisibly to set out plates and utensils, the clattering distracting Fiona. She glanced about the hall, her gaze resting on the Queen and a few of the earls on a raised dais at a high table where they could be seen. She needed to know exactly who was who so she didn't look foolish when talking to John about his own uncle.

Amid gossiping guests, laughter, and toasts ringing out sat Richard Mourninghide looking utterly out of place. His dark-wine doublet fit his broad shoulders much too snugly, and he kept trying to loosen the small white ruff about his neck. He looked up as if feeling her gaze, and before Fiona could do more than raise an eyebrow, he was up and out of his chair heading toward her.

Fiona set her glass down a bit too hard on the table. She was glad that the rising music of the musicians had started to fill the air, and no one noticed the sound. Her stomach fluttered and she winced. If Richard came over, he would say the wrong thing and her mother would pounce on it like a salamander with fresh food. She quickly looked around to see a rather garishly dressed man looking at the table. She gave him a small smile and he fell for the invitation, making his way to the empty seat beside her. Before he could fill it, however, Richard placed a hand on the table and slid into the seat. The garish man was rebuffed.

Richard inclined his head toward Fiona. "It is a pleasure to make your acquaintance again, Mistress Thornbeard."

Fiona inclined her head in return and glanced at her mother to see if she took notice. Their eyes locked; Lavinia's held questions, but she said nothing. Well then, polite mannerisms and an explanation would be needed so that her mother didn't turn his words into a tizzy later. Fiona cleared her throat. "Yes, dancing last night was most enjoyable. A pity you had a headache afterward. The music was quite grand, Sir Mourninghide."

He nodded, examining up his wine glass. "Yes, too much gravy at supper. I will try to be less indulgent next time."

Happy that Richard seemed to pick up on her cue to lie, she smiled. "And you remember my mother, Mistress Lavinia Thornbeard."

Lavinia's eyes narrowed briefly but she kept her face smooth. "I don't believe we've had the pleasure. How do you do?"

"Mother, this is Sir Richard, the royal historian."

"Ah, so you're the keeper of the royal library." Lavinia clasped her hand to her chest. "Very good to meet you. I have heard you are asking questions about page turner history. Should you ever need to discuss our family tree, I am happy to oblige."

Fiona frowned. "Mother, haven't you already discussed our family tree with the historian?"

Lavinia's features tensed. "I have yet to make his acquaintance, and I believe I would remember if I had. Such a good-looking young man." She waved her arm wide as if bestowing a queenly compliment on Richard and then glanced edgily at Fiona. "You must be mistaken, dear. Now"—she turned to John—"do tell me, what is it that you do? Working must make a splendid use of your time."

Was her mother deliberately lying to her, or had she truly forgotten she had already spoken to the man? Fiona squinted watching her.

"You haven't touched your cup, Mistress Thornbeard. The wine is most delightful, although I can't determine its vintage. Perhaps you will have more information?" Richard lifted the glass to his lips but raised a subtle eyebrow.

Questioning her about what she may have learned already, was he? He wasn't a patient man. She sipped at her wine. "No, much too muddled. I would have to drink the entire bottle to really determine more."

"A pity this bottle is half full then. Perhaps you'll have the chance later or at a more suitable time."

She started to answer but gasped in pain as her mother kicked her underneath the table. Fiona looked up sharply, but her mother was listening intensely to John going on about his law work and how trade was growing quite rapidly these days. Fiona rubbed her shin with her other leg and twisted out of her mother's reach.

"Are you alright?" Richard said, eyes narrowed.

"Simply hit my ankle on the table leg." She smiled brushing it off. She knew she should be talking to John as well, but she didn't need to start immediately. The first course hadn't even arrived yet. Regardless, she turned toward the lawyer and tilted her head as if she had been listening all the while.

"And of course, I work out of the Smallcrest estate most of the time. The grounds are simply breathtaking, with rolling lawns and a lovely rose garden. My family has owned the estate for generations, you know."

"The land itself is more important than who currently possesses it, don't you think?" Richard interjected rudely.

Lavinia darted a look to Richard but quickly turned it into a tinkle of laughter. "How wise. Of course, as a historian I would think you'd agree with Mr. Hawkport. Tracking genealogy and generations as part of your work. It's most noble of you."

Richard rubbed the side of his face, fingers scratching through his neat beard. "Yes, well, the work can be rewarding. Illuminating, even, with the right context."

"And what context would that be? A nobleman, a laborer, or even an outsider to the page? Which makes our history more intriguing?" Fiona said, leaning toward Richard.

He straightened, turning completely toward her. "I don't see much difference between a nobleman or a laborer anymore in that regard. History is still the work we've done, the mistakes we've made. We should learn from them. And we do in time. An outsider, though, they would put our history in a completely different perspective."

"Yes, I agree," Fiona said, warming up to the subject. "The different pages, in the mortal chapter at least, seemed to start much the same as each other. But various difficulties, a war or enterprising youth turned leader, sent them down quite different paths."

"Like untamed fire. Each splintering and splintering until they are but shades of each other." Richard nodded. He took a sip of his wine and gazed at her. "But do you think, Mistress Thornbeard, Larrakane did it on purpose or for experimentation? The thrill of change perhaps?"

Fiona met his gaze, a surge of excitement striking through her. "I've often been of the mind it was on purpose. A deliberate plan enacted for, oh, who knows why in her infinite wisdom. But with absolute care."

"I can agree with that. The planning that is. But absolute care," Richard repeated, frowning, "that I cannot give her credit for. More careless than a mortal, that one is."

"But—" Fiona started, poised to disagree heartily with him.

"I do think we've gotten a bit off the topic," Lavinia interrupted. She motioned and smiled at John. "You were talking about the Smallcrest estate. I want to hear it. No offense, dear Fiona, but I think theoretical conversation should be best *left* for the dessert course."

Fiona took a deep breath, pulling herself away from Richard and back toward John. She had quite gotten entranced in the conversation, but unfortunately her mother was right. She needed to focus on talking with Hawkport lest she lose the chance to make an immediate impression and thus make headway. She had time later for waxing theological with Richard when she updated him. "Yes, the rose garden sounds thrilling." Even to herself she sounded strained and tried to mask it by picking up her spoon and focusing on the second course of stew that had arrived by stealthy servant.

"The roses were planted before the Inking and haven't changed one jot, if you can believe it. As I was saying, the house itself dates back to the thirteenth century and has a fascinating history—"

"Many old structures have equally fascinating histories; one estate is much like another," Richard muttered into his wine cup.

Fiona glanced at him and subtly shook her head. She didn't understand why the subject bothered him so, but now was not the time to get in an uproar about the peerage being materialistic. "I am intrigued about the architecture of that period. Each county seems to have a different style from before the Inking, as if they deliberately competed with each other."

John straightened his velvet sleeve, sitting up taller. "Yes, well, there are these beautiful vaulted ceilings and arched passageways. If you're very interested, I could show you around." He smiled wide at her. "With your mother, of course."

Fiona swallowed an exclamation and nodded slowly. That he was inviting her so soon was questionable. He seemed keen to know her. Too keen. She bit her lip, pushing her Sadie-fed paranoia back down. It was more likely that he was a nice man who enjoyed having a person interested in him. As if in agreement, her mother grinned, looking as though she had just been served the best present in the world.

"Oh, we would be delighted to accompany you on a tour." Lavinia sipped her soup.

"I've heard Smallcrest also houses your family's fine airships," Fiona said. If she could get a personal invite in, it would save her time trying to scout the place herself.

"Well, one of the manufacturing bays and several warehouses. The work is split across Smallcrest and Shade. Are you interested in airships?" John directed the question at Fiona with wide, eager eyes.

"Yes, quite." She was being only a little truthful. She was curious about them mostly. No one could reproduce a Hawkport airship. They seemed to hold the secret of their creation close to heart. No one could build them, so they had quite the monopoly. Secretly she believed they must have some inner working that came from outside the page. Probably from the Court of Copper. Anything that seemed a smidge advanced usually came from a faekin there, whether they claimed it or not. As long as it wasn't gotten in a bind, then it was above board enough that no one questioned it much. "I would love to see them up close. If they aren't too far from the estate."

"Not at all." John shook his head, blond locks of hair going wild. He placed a hand on her chair. "We can accomplish it all. How does tomorrow work for you?"

"That works fine," Fiona said, leaning away. She glanced at Richard, who sat overly interested in his recent acquisition of a pheasant-filled plate. Now he had nothing to say, apparently. It irked her. "That's very kind of you, Mr. Hawkport. I'm looking forward to it."

John nodded and picked up his glass, leaving his other hand resting on Fiona's chair.

Fiona hoped his interest was one of pure novelty, the investigator part of her or the page turner piece perhaps. She had to be careful here and tomorrow. There were things she could learn, like if the Hawkports had massive beasts hidden away in their airship warehouse or on their estate. Or even if they had any links to the history of such Guardians. She wanted to investigate without being caught or her mother noticing. But more pressing, she wanted to follow this trail without ending up courting a Hawkport. If she could do all that without accidentally becoming engaged tomorrow, she would be thrilled.

Richard cleared his throat and rose from the table. "If you will all excuse me, I have an important matter to look into before tonight's masque." Without waiting for any replies, he strode purposefully away from the table.

Fiona swiftly stood up, hoping to catch him.

"Fiona, where are you going?" her mother hissed. She exchanged a shocked expression for a smile to John, but it didn't quite reach her eyes.

"I need to ask a quick question of the historian," Fiona said over her shoulder. She hoped to be able to explain her peculiarity away as the nature of her living on Spine to whomever needed the excuse. She caught up with Richard outside the banqueting hall. "Sir Mourninghide, a word."

Richard stopped but didn't turn around, as if engrossed with the elaborate hallway. "Yes?"

Fiona frowned. She stopped, letting a servant pass her into the hall. Why did he sound so terse with her again? "I had a question for you about some members of the privy council."

His shoulders rose and he sighed. "And?"

"I would truly love not to talk to your backside." People milled around, so she lowered her voice. "Have I offended you?"

He turned slowly and clasped his hands together. "No."

Fiona nodded. "Good, because I haven't done anything to offend you, so it would be entirely rude on your part to treat me as such."

"Blasted woman, what did you want?" He tugged at his trimmed beard.

She bit back her smirk at him losing his one-word streak. "I've gotten some information that makes me believe the Guardian may be connected to a family on the privy council. Do you know Baron Griffintail or Baron Dragonkeep, by any chance?"

Richard shrugged. "I don't keep close companions with the Queen's council, though I've heard of them certainly." He glanced around and moved closer to her. "Why do you suppose they know about the Guardian?"

Fiona clasped her hands, barely containing her excitement. "Beasts, Sir Mourninghide. Beasts in connection with the family's name."

His brow furrowed for a moment and then relaxed. He looked thoughtful. "Clever," he muttered. "Well, it's a good enough theory anyways. Dig in to it."

She was surprised that he didn't think her theory idiotic. "You agree with me then?"

"What? Oh, yes." He glanced around and then gently gripped her sleeve, pulling her farther away from the hall entrance. "Why not add Bearspear to the list?"

"They don't sit on the privy council."

"Yes, but they hold a county, and a county holds many a thing."

Fiona nodded in accord; she hadn't thought of it quite like that. There could be no harm in investigating everyone who might match. Perhaps a Guardian-connected family wouldn't want the exposure of being on the privy council.

"Is that why you were talking to Hawkport?" Richard gestured in the direction of the Banqueting Hall.

She tilted her head. "Of course." What other purpose would there be for suddenly ingratiating herself with them?

"It rather seemed you were courting him a bit just then. He is an attractive man, so I understand the interest." Richard waved his hand as if dismissing his words, but the light tone was not on his face.

"I most certainly am not," Fiona said, dropping her courtly pretense and crossing her arms. She glared at him. "I haven't the inclination or the time to think of marriage." Of course he would think the same as all Schiflans on this matter: she was too old to continue being unwed, page turner or not. For some reason she had thought him less fanciful than that.

"Don't get your arms all twisted up. Simply with your mother and you, why, you basically had poor Mr. Hawkport penned. He's quite the catch, I'm sure, if you can ignore that big nose of his and his propensity to blather on."

"He seems rather nice actually. Not grumpy or terse," Fiona said, feeling flushed.

"So you do have an interest," Richard said, raising an eyebrow at her.

"I didn't say that," Fiona hissed, annoyed. He was pushing her to advocate for someone she didn't even care about. Why was he being so ridiculous? They had much more to talk about than marriage. She dropped her arms. "This is a stupid conversation to be having. I am waiting to hear back from my contact. I suppose I'll inform you of something, whether Guardian or Painted Edge, tomorrow."

Richard looked at her, but Fiona couldn't read his face. It seemed as if he was trying to read her mind.

He nodded toward her dress. "Beautiful color on you," he said and abruptly walked away.

She stood there for a moment, warmth melting away as she watched him disappear into the crowd of people. He was incredibly odd. Always tugging his beard and drawing attention to his jaw. Why was he so terse? He wore the Queen's insignia again, but Fiona hadn't seen him talk to anyone but herself. Did he have friends in the royal court or family? She hadn't done much research into this supposed ally. Perhaps she ought to be more thorough before trading all her information. Just because she wanted to trust him didn't mean she should.

She quickly strode back into the hall and sat down to finish her meal, ignoring the reproachful look from her mother. Between bites she discussed more of John's interests in horseback riding, falconry, and attending his local debating club. Her mother leaned back, seemingly pleased with how the conversation was going, and ate slowly, barely adding in her thoughts. Happy to have eased her mother's suspicions, Fiona turned the conversation, with some careful steering, toward the privy council.

"And do you know any of the privy council personally?" she asked.

"Beyond my uncle Henry, I've known Baron Griffintail since I was a boy—well before he was Griffintail even. His husband and he combined names. A bit avant-garde, but the Queen allowed it. Besides that, Lord Mossbard I know of. Highly respectable man, but I haven't gotten his eye. Not yet. I am working on it though," he said, quickly turning back to her. Good gracious, his nose really was big.

"Of course. I'm sure it's just a matter of time till you have his notice. What of the others?"

He beamed at her, then pressed his hand to the back of her chair. "Yes, well, the archbishop of Three Churches seat has been empty since Archbishop—I mean, Priestess Raina was inked, of course. But you probably know her as you're both...well, page turners."

It wasn't a small group who met around the water well, for Larrakane's sake. "Yes, I do."

He nodded, satisfied. He picked up his glass but stalled. "Oh, there was an old chap, Baron Lionheart. Quite frightfully old really. He stayed in his rooms a bit, but Uncle Henry talks about him still, so he must not have departed this mortal coil yet." He laughed.

Fiona smiled at his attempt at humor and tried to get it to reach her eyes. So there was one more beast name to account for then. "Do you know where I could find him?"

His brow wrinkled. "Afraid not, although even he must come out for the celebrations this week. You'll probably see him at the outdoor events festival at least. The privy council sit with the Queen to preside over sport and the like."

She nodded. "I wouldn't miss it for the world." It would be good to interview as many as she could, and if they were all conglomerating, so much the better for her.

"I'm glad to hear you say that," Lavinia said, suddenly interested again. "I'm sure Captain Henrietta would want to enjoy the festival as well?"

Fiona fought back her desire to question her mother's newfound interest in Henrietta. Though the captain and

Lavinia were both human women around the same age, they couldn't have been more different. What could they possibly get on about? She would ask Henrietta herself. "Yes, I must speak with her then, perhaps tonight." Fiona reasoned Henrietta would also be the best person to look into Richard and see if he was a trustworthy spy or one she had better feed only certain details to. "In fact, I think I may send her a note and rest before tonight's masque."

"Yes, get plenty of rest now, for tomorrow shall be quite an outing," her mother said, smiling. She rose and kissed Fiona on her cheek. "And I'm sure tonight will simply be a lovely precursor."

Fiona's face warmed; her mother had never shown such affection in public before. She must really be too close to John Hawkport for comfort. She would have to feign a headache to avoid her mother getting them to dance together all night during the masquerade. She bid them both goodbye, truly meaning good night, and escaped to her room. While her mother may be preparing for a delightful courting, Fiona needed all the rest and preparation she could get for vigorous sleuthing.

AFTER SENDING HER SHORT letter to the inn Henrietta was staying at via a quick Hawkport courier—running the airships meant the ability to run the mail and goods throughout the page—Fiona arrived with her mother in tow on Smallcrest. John met them with a smile and not a small bit of flourish at the large four-wheeled coach, elaborately decorated with the blue-winged Hawkport crest. The wooden borders of the coach were carved with enough artisan flair to rival what could be produced in Copper. Fiona pressed her lips together, unsure of herself upon seeing it. It was fit for important guests, that was clear. Whether John had brought it to show off the status of his family to her or he was simply accustomed to such wealth in general made her rethink how to approach the day's outing. Just as swirling as Fiona's thoughts were on what it meant, her mother's thoughts were much simpler. Lavinia beamed at the sight of it and exclaimed to Fiona that she could get used to this sort of life.

John took them first to the Hawkport facilities. They were much larger than she had expected. The area they arrived in was clearly the dock: wooden pillars raised high into the sky and platform-like shelves allowing more than one airship to land upon it. Open areas scattered with parts of airships were easy to see from their entrance. Maintenance workers cleaned parts, fixed pieces, or carried crates to and from the large warehouses. The smell of metal and wood mixed with hints of polish, making Fiona wrinkle her nose. A racket of sounds greeted them as they got closer to one of the buildings. Workers yelled back and forth to each other, as casual as could be, although some straightened up seeing the coach pull up and them alight.

"Let's try not to purchase an airship while we're here," Fiona whispered lightly to her mother.

Lavinia's eyes widened. "Is that an option?"

The coach door opened, and the driver presented a gloved hand to Fiona to help her out.

Lavinia moved forward, taking his hand instead. "If you're considering investing in one, there are smaller models now that may work for skimming! Henrietta was telling me all about them."

Fiona rolled her eyes privately in the coach, wishing she hadn't said anything at all, and allowed herself to be helped down. The volume of her dress, style chosen by her mother before she could even wake properly, was crushed between the doorframe, but the gloved driver seemed to have more experience than her. She set foot to ground without looking completely out of place, though she felt it entirely.

"Are you looking for an airship?" John asked, offering his arm.

Fiona hesitated, then took it, reasoning it was easier to do so than offend him out here in the open. "It seems I might be."

"Well, we have to head to the newer ones then." He smiled down at her. "I haven't told anyone we are coming, so…" He placed a finger to his mouth, then winked.

"Oh, I'm very good at keeping a secret," Fiona said, laughing at how true that was. Now she just needed to figure out how she could scurry off for a deep look around without causing questions.

Lavinia made a small noise, letting Fiona know she understood what she meant and was less than amused. Fiona turned to her mother and winked, tickled for a moment that her mother wouldn't say anything too reproachful in front of John. Fun aside, she started to truly pay attention when they entered the most populated area.

She noted the workers and layout of the woodworking area as she walked beside him. Many laborers were bent over pieces of wood, shaping and polishing them. Wood shavings littered the ground, piling up around the workers' booted feet. Others sawed away at large chunks, hacking them into smaller bits to be pieced together, presumably for the airships' hulls. Foremen in this room walked around inspecting finished parts and organizing them into piles for crating.

"You'll find Hawkport's has just the right amount of sparkle for a family airship. It's not unlike a house coach, just with more room," John said, beaming as he led her farther into the warehouse. Guards posted at the entrance and walking throughout the hallway were plentiful. Though they tipped hats to John, they didn't move to greet the entourage.

"Of course," Fiona said, eyeing the rooms as they passed. A large glow dominated one, a hot forge going with the clang of hammers on anvils ringing from within. Another room was quieter, softer even. Walls were covered in beautiful drawings of airships moving about the page. Was this a room for inspiration or a room for design? There was only one person within, a thin woman bent over a drafting table, clearly painting.

"And of course, our captains are certified to take you everywhere. Simply another member of staff. How many staff do you have, Mistress Thornbeard?"

"None at the moment," Fiona said absentmindedly, watching through the doorway of a large room. Rows of workers were bent over various pieces of fabric stitching. Satins and velvets and plainer fabrics, too, were each married to their partner. Embroiderers worked in stiff-backed chairs stitching family colors and crests into decorative elements that would, more than likely, fly on the sails of the airships, adorn the seats, or cover the private family compartments. Overall, everyone was doing their own separate job. A foreman stood watch over them, going from row to row. While she had expected a sort of carriage repair shop, she was intrigued that there was more to it than that. It seemed a very organized and detailed operation with everyone doing their part.

John interrupted her thoughts with a surprised murmur, "None?"

Lavinia jumped in, "She means in Spine, of course. As she must stay there. I have more and will be the one using the airship. Though she will be getting more staff in the future, should the right circumstance come along."

"Oh, of course, of course. Dear Bunny doesn't tell us much about being a turner."

Fiona turned her attention back to him away from the focused workers at the odd name. "Bunny?"

John gently took Fiona's arm and pulled her away from the room and toward a flight of stairs. "Oh, our family name for our cousin, Sedhare. She's always bouncing back and forth. Being a page turner must be a lot like that for you too."

"Oh, it's much the same from one turner to another." Though she didn't completely agree with what she was saying, she didn't want to waste time talking about something so benign. She turned the topic as they climbed the stairs: "Do you see a lot of your extended family?"

"We often meet for supper at Shade Manor. My parents reside in Smallcrest Manor with me and other cousins, as it's large enough to accommodate us all, of course." John brushed a piece of invisible dirt off his gold-and-red-striped doublet.

"Of course," Fiona said lightly, trying to ignore his preening. How to segue to beasts? If the Hawkports kept them, they would need plenty of food. "Do you hunt?" They got to the landing with Lavinia right on their heels. Up here was a more formal setting of a few intriguing, closed offices and a large chamber at the end of the hall.

John led her toward the chamber. "Just as a means of training the hawks. If you're interested in hunting, my uncle is an avid hunter. He often goes out for weeks at a time to our family house in the forest and brings back a massive stag."

A less-than-known forest house? This was promising from a Guardian perspective. Fiona wrinkled her nose as if confused. "All alone? He must have a strong demeanor if he can take down a stag by himself."

"Well, I wouldn't say all alone." John laughed, smiling down at her as he edged closer. "He has his older son and my father to go with often. They used to take Grandpapa, but he's passed on."

Before Fiona could ask more, John blushed and made a low bow to someone behind her. Fiona whirled around to face this newcomer who could make John bow. Lord Hawkport. The man was similar to John, if wide to his thin. He wore a thickly textured doublet of gold brocade, elaborately embroidered and padded, and a large, starched pearl-white ruff around his neck, ornamenting his long, well-groomed beard. His hat was almost as tall as his ruff wide and adorned with bright-blue feathers from a bird—Fiona was sure in her guess—that was not native to the page. Lord Henry Hawkport no doubt. She bowed quickly to hide her surprise at finding him here. John introduced herself and her mother with a slight tremble in his voice. So he was unaware as well that his uncle would be showing himself.

"Mistress Thornbeard, how lovely to make your acquaintance." He beamed at her as she rose and then fiddled with one of his many overly large gold rings. He leaned in. "You are the talk of the royal court, my dear."

Fiona objected to his conspiratorial tone, but as the milk had come to the cat, she smiled. "I haven't the foggiest idea why that would be. But I hope it is a positive conversation."

"Quite, yes, dear." He tilted his head, assessing her, and then with a raised eyebrow strode away from them into the larger chamber. "I heard you talking to my dear nephew about hunting. Are you a bow and stable hunter?"

Unable to prove it true should she be asked, she shook her head. "I don't often have to ride a horse or wield a bow at home."

"No? Pity. I was thinking of hosting a small party at Shade Manor after the outdoor events this evening and having some sort of sport as entertainment. If not hunting, we will have to find some other way to enjoy ourselves." He smiled and narrowed his gaze at Fiona. "Perhaps you and your mother would join us?"

From a gentlewoman's standpoint, that was a more than gracious invitation. That an earl, no matter who they were to others with their title, would invite her family anywhere was just short of a miracle. But when it came to veiled words Fiona was no blotter. Hawkport wanted something from her or wanted her for something, she was sure. But the best way to find out was to go along and have her guard up. She glanced at her mother, who was smiling up at Hawkport like he was the sun and it had been a long, cloudy life. How in the world was she going to protect her mother? There was a small jab to her side as her mother elbowed her. Fiona leaned out of her reach but nodded, realizing she hadn't answered back. "That would be lovely. Thank you for the invitation."

"Yes, Lord Hawkport." Lavinia bowed deeper. "A most welcome one."

Lord Hawkport guffawed and waved the compliment away. "We have a box for the festival. Come and sit with us there. John says you are interested in airships. We have a beauty docked at Thorn Palace that we use for daily travel. We can take you directly from the festival to Shade Manor that way." He clapped John on the back. "Why don't we show them the newer versions?"

Lavinia sighed happily and squeezed Fiona's hand without saying a word.

Fiona barely registered the gesture. There was no breaking away to look for secrets now that the earl was with them. He seemed to have his eyes directly trained on her. What could he possibly want? Perhaps it was simply business. A purchase of an airship. But John hadn't told him they were coming. He was just as surprised as she was. Had Lord Hawkport come for her? That he was paying particular attention to her and her mother boded good and bad. He might be curious about Fiona for her sake, or for marriage to his nephew, which would mean he'd dig into her background and past. Or he might be curious as to why the Queen would hire an outside investigator, for she was sure if anyone knew of the Queen's request, it would be those on the privy council.

Perhaps it was more than that. The people at the facility seemed to be highly focused on their individual work. There were quite a number of people there but stationed so very separately. And with so many guards posted at each room, it was doubtful that they traveled too freely between their area of work and where they probably put on their uniforms. They wouldn't be able to tell anyone how the airship was built. From all the rooms she saw, there was no assembly room. Someone must have the know-how, but the Hawkports kept it a tight secret. If a person here had been helping the Painted Edge, they would have to have an overview of all the pieces and how they fit together. A floor worker wouldn't be able to do that, so it must be a Hawkport specifically. But why would they work with the Painted Edge? What could they possibly be getting out of it? Until she understood everything, she needed to be careful, and she needed to protect her mother.

John suggested he get them refreshments while his uncle took over the tour for the moment. Fiona asked a few suitable questions as they continued. Mostly to please her mother. But remained carefully neutral talking to Lord Hawkport. Though she wanted to press on where pieces were stored, how the assemblage came together, and so on, more important people than her had already tried to wring secrets out of them and failed.

John returned with cold refreshments, which delighted her mother. Ice was not often gotten outside of palace meals. Only from Copper, of course. When he tried to talk of the future to Fiona, plans she might have, plans he certainly wanted to discuss at length, she avoided the subject. She discussed her life on Spine openly, hoping to make it clear that she truly loved her city and, if there were any doubts, how it wasn't the best place for a noble. She kept a respectable distance from him as they continued throughout the remainder of the facility, politely rebuffing his proffered arm and glancing at his uncle as if he were the cause. Though John seemed to be taking her distance in stride, her mother was not.

"Dear Fiona," her mother called, entwining her arm in hers. She inclined her head, smiling, at John and Lord Hawkport while pulling Fiona away toward the carriage. She whispered hotly, "What, in Larrakane's grace, are you doing?"

"I am being polite, Mama," Fiona whispered back. Of course, if her mother knew she was investigating the Hawkports, this might be more than a simply whispered reprimand. She didn't want to encourage her, but as the footman assisted her into the carriage, the door to the carriage closed with John sitting up front, leaving her and her mother alone. Fiona groaned internally.

"Talk yourself up, child. You are not without valuable qualities a person would want in a partner," Lavinia said. "And I can tell that you are instead trying to talk young John here out of liking you very much."

"He shouldn't put any hopes on me. I am bound to Spine." And he may be a criminal in a family of criminals, or even worse, nobles with the real power of a Guardian. There were so many reasons truly.

"That may be, but it doesn't mean you can't have a fulfilling life in Spine with someone who loves you and children and a life to look after."

Fiona scowled. "I already have a life to look after."

"Not this again. Fiona, you will not confine yourself to spinsterhood for the love of a…career as an investigator! Perhaps if you worked with the Travel Guild more, it would hold some prestige, but as it is—"

"Is that all you care about? Prestige? There is a whole Book out there that doesn't give a wit who we are."

"After everything I've given up, everything I've worked for in my life, do not begrudge me the things I desire."

"You were a cacao farmer, Mother. I don't believe it was *you* who paid for this desirable placement."

Lavinia's mouth fell open and she turned away, shielding her face with a readily produced lace handkerchief. She pulled her arm away from her daughter and moved to the other side of the carriage.

Fiona tensed, turning to glare at the countryside. How dare her mother be upset at her. She was the one who should be mad! Her mother worked hard to make Fiona feel insignificant, not doing enough, not following the preferred path. And she had the gall to say she had given everything up. She wasn't the one who had to leave home at fourteen. Nor the one to be alone without a soul to call on until Mac and Dodger came along. Fiona pulled her multipocketed scarf from her dress sleeve, uncaring what her mother thought of her peculiar habits. She reached into a soft linen pocket and pulled out a fan, waving it to cool her flushed face.

"You still have that?" Lavinia said through a strained voice, motioning to the scarf.

"Of course," Fiona said snippily. "Father gave it to me. I wouldn't give it away for the world."

Though her face was taut, Lavinia nodded. "He was so happy to have gotten it for you. I didn't understand what it was for, but he seemed so proud of himself." Her face cracked into a smile, and she twisted the lace handkerchief in her hand as she stared out the window.

Fiona slowed her fanning. "Do you know where he got it? It's quite special."

Lavinia shook her head. "Your father often went to Middle Market without me. Such a long trip."

Fiona pursed her lips. He loved to fly with his ornithopter. It was probably a chance to get away from his cares and be free a little.

"I would stay home with you and all of us hands would work and watch you at the same time. You were so into everything. I couldn't turn around for one second without you off somewhere you weren't supposed to be."

"I'm sure that annoyed you to no end." Fiona swallowed and stared out the window again.

Lavinia tsked. "Annoy me? Oh, don't talk such nonsense."

Fiona frowned, confused at her mother.

The carriage stopped, and before she could ask more questions, Lavinia wiped her hands and leaned out the window. "Gracious, such a magnanimous estate."

Nestled among rolling green hills, the manor sat atop the largest one in the distance. Fiona didn't have to pretend to be impressed when the coach rolled to a stop at the entrance. Smallcrest Manor was notable.

"I think I'll stay in the carriage for a bit," her mother said lightly, pulling at her handkerchief. "Why don't you enjoy yourself? I shall be quite alright here for the moment and then will join you shortly."

Seeing her mother's face wrinkled and pinched, Fiona bit back a quip on propriety. It would make it easier to look around without having to hide it from her as well. Though if she wasn't inside within half an hour, she would have to make sure she came and took some refreshment.

John escorted her from the coach personally this time and, after a brief explanation about her mother, led her toward the manor. They walked through the stone path, flanked on either side by rows of rose hedges, to the front entry of the estate.

"Of course I would have had the driver take us here but wanted to give you a view of the roses. So pristine and perfect."

Fiona dipped her head, hiding her expression. "Thank you for the consideration." She glanced around, taking in the grandeur of it all. "This *is* a beautiful estate."

"We have my ancestors to thank." He stood up taller. "But I do manage the upkeep of all our properties. Well, with the steward."

Of course he didn't actually do any of the work. There weren't many servants outside of the manor, tending to things. They were too much alone. Fiona quickened her pace toward the manor's open door.

Once inside, she let her inner skimmer free, staring at every arched window, mammoth stone fireplace, or painted ceiling she could find. The main building hulked between two towering square keeps on either side. When there was a stairwell she headed into it before being called back or cut off by John, who politely rebuffed her. Any door that seemed unguarded she opened, looking in before John could quickly discuss it. She glimpsed his office for a moment before he told her there was nothing architecturally interesting in there. He strode instead to another wing of the estate. This was an additional wing for the family with over fifteen bedchambers and sitting rooms. In contrast to the main building's older grandeur, she felt a softness to the family wing, even if she didn't make it past the first floor of the ornate woodwork staircase. It truly was a pre-Inking manor, so rare to still have completely in use. The people of Schiflan seemed to pull bits and pieces from the other pages over time, making the architecture quite a bit different on many islands. But this place stood as a reversal to all that.

The manor bustled with servants, so many Fiona once again thanked her stars she could manage without staff. They were everywhere doing a bit of everything. No family seemed to be home at the moment, however. Fiona asked questions, trying to learn names and positions as well as she could to see who always had access to the airship facilities. It seemed Lord Henry Hawkport, his sons, and John's father were the ones more active in the day-to-day management of the facilities. That they didn't delegate daily work to anyone lower in the family struck Fiona as a tad odd. Earls acting as merchants in trade? No other lofty family would even think of it.

She learned that the main family took up residence at the Shade estate because it was much larger and newer. Many of them, if not all, were at Thorn Palace for the week of festivities and so would be out of the house. That explained why the servants were cleaning so much without them. It reasoned to stand that if there was a hidden secret, such as beasts that lived around the estate, one of the servants would most definitely know. But how to keep a secret with so many people? Fiona reasoned it couldn't be completely possible. It would have to be off manor. Which meant the care and feeding had to be within someone's books. Could she get into John's office without him noticing?

"Do you suppose we might have some refreshments?" she said to John after the thorough and—she had to admit—wonderful tour.

"Of course. The steward has told me he's seated your mother in the library. We can join her and take coffee there."

Fiona took a deep breath upon hearing her mother was back in attendance. She'd have to extract herself carefully. As they rounded the path toward the library, she forced a pained expression. "If I may be excused one moment." She picked up her skirts and looked thoughtfully around.

John, taking the hint, directed her toward a privy. She headed in that direction, but as soon as she was out of sight, she doubled back to the office. The servants had been cleaning this way earlier. With some luck, they were nowhere to be seen. She slid into the office and closed the door silently behind her.

Large windows looked out toward the green on one side of the room. A desk and bookcases balanced the room on the opposite side. She scoured the bookcases, noting that although the leather-bound books looked very respectable on the shelves, they were all mostly unread and unopened. She frowned at John's lack of reading but moved on, finding no other information. A tall, ornate copper-handed wooden clock ticked loudly as she scampered toward the desk and its beckoning stacks of papers. She scanned quickly through the bits and pieces of parchment. Here was paltry correspondence of daily matters and the running of the estate. She glanced toward the windows, sunlight streaming into the room and directly over her. She ducked down below the desk, the smell of recently oiled wood clinging to her nostrils, and went through each of the drawers. List of servants, schedules, and John's own personal diary of events. Nothing seemed to be amiss. Perhaps there was information too valuable to be kept in the office desk? He had no other places to keep files in the room. Where were his contracts, his important documents?

Fiona jerked from the desk when she heard the clack of footsteps outside the door. She quickly closed the drawers and moved to the opposite side of the entry door; should it open, she would be obscured for a moment. She waited, blood pounding in her ears at the worst situation to be caught in, but the footsteps moved on and faded. She let out a quiet sigh of relief. While she may have been able to explain it away, she would've most certainly been cut off from directly investigating Hawkport's connection to the Painted Edge airships. And direct investigation was the hardest to get.

Staring at the desk from this side of the room, Fiona noticed a misalignment in the wooden wall. Why would that be?

Locking the door now so she had some sort of warning if someone entered, Fiona strode to the wall and ran her hands across it. The plaster covering the stone walls was clearly slit in two with a small door on it, meant to be concealed. It wouldn't have been as easy to see if it had been newly put in, but it was clear this was part of the original wall. Probably a happenstance of the house over the few hundred years. Fiona pressed her hand to the door and it popped in. She wiggled it, sliding it to the side, where it disappeared into the wall.

Inside was a small cubby with stacks of files. Contracts and documents! Fiona smiled, happy to not have given up so easily in her search. She quickly thumbed through them. Many were for the management of the facilities, of a town house on the Plateau near the palace, and one for the management of the airships for the Queen. As John had said, he kept administration of all the properties for the family, but there was nothing about the supposed hunting house in the woods. Hidden from the Queen then?

Crushed between files were blueprints, sketches, and detailed descriptions of a new airship facility. While this may have been something for a rival of Hawkport, it was nothing to her. She sighed and folded everything back up when a thick document slipped from between the pages. In bold gold letters from the Queen's own hand, she saw a rejection to the new facility being built. Odd that the Queen herself would reject anything, especially against the Hawkport family, given their standing in the royal court.

Putting everything back in as neatly as she could, she felt a thicker folio at the back of the cubby. She had almost missed it as it blended in with the dark walls. Fiona quickly eased it out, listening for any sounds of would-be discovery. There was a lock on it with a keyhole. What would need such security even in his own home? And where was the key!? She hadn't found one in his office. Where would someone like John keep it?

She glanced about the room and her eyes settled on the shelf of unread books. Quickly she searched through them until she came to one that had been cracked open. Pulling it out, she triumphantly found nestled in its page an iron key. Pity for him he didn't read more.

Fiona's elation quickly skyrocketed upon unlocking the folio. There were several internal reports of stolen parts filed by foremen of the Shade and Smallcrest facilities. Further in was a full report made out to the Queen about an intact missing airship. The report was signed by Lord Henry Hawkport. Fiona frowned. It was Lord Hawkport who had reported a whole airship stolen? Interesting. If he reported it directly, it must've been to cover up the fact that he had given it to the Painted Edge. Did John know? Or was he simply an "as you say" person to his uncle's machinations?

The doorknob rattled. Fiona bit back a sound as the noise startled her, and hastily she placed everything back into the folio and into the cubby. The iron key would simply have to live with it as well, as there was no time to put it back into the book. She hurriedly pressed herself against the wall behind the door, tucking in her skirts and mashing down the rounded hips of her dress as much as she could.

There was a click as a key unlocked the door and it swung open. A servant entered, heading straight for the fireplace at the end of the room with a bucket and stiff broom. As silently as she could, Fiona lifted her skirts, slid around the door and out into the hallway. She wished that she was wearing her normal slippers, her feet clicking as she headed away from the office. She didn't look back as she descended the staircase and made her way back to the library.

She took a small stop outside, composing herself before entering, face full of smiles. "Apologies for the long wait."

John crinkled his nose as if he didn't want to think about what could've kept her so long, "Yes, well, I was showing your mother some of our most valued paintings. The brush strokes of this one are marvelous. Don't you agree?" He gestured to the airship painting in front of him.

It was marvelous in the way that a child's finger painting could be considered cute by a parent. There was too much paint on the canvas for her liking, though the sails of the ship were rendered nicely. And the blue Hawkport insignia was too big upon the ship. But she nodded and smiled. "I do, I do! It's a wonder your family can make so many airships at a time for the Queen. Have you thought about opening other facilities?"

"We have." He stopped, seeming to think better of explaining so much as he glanced at her mother and back to her. "All in due time, of course."

So he wasn't inclined to be forthright? That was fair, but she needed more. "Where would you open a new one? I should think any proposed area would be very happy to have it with new jobs and such."

John scratched his nose. "Er, well, that is still part of the discussion. Closed discussion, as my uncle likes to say."

"I see," Fiona said. She leaned toward John and batted her eyes, feeling a little ridiculous. She would rather use her brain than her scrap of charm, but she didn't want to come off as too knowledgeable. "I suppose I'll just have to wait like everyone else to see what you clever Hawkports do next. Perhaps I'll wait to purchase in case the Queen's approval..." She trailed off, knowing that many people loved to finish a sentence.

"I should think you won't have long to wait if *that's* any deciding factor," John whispered.

"Oh, why?"

"There was a small matter of who owned the land, but that will all be cleared up soon."

Fiona furrowed her brows, not having to pretend to be confused, and prodded for more information. "I'm not following."

John patted her hand. "Never you mind. Your path is clear, and that's all you need to know. Shall we return to Thorn to change before luncheon?"

Fiona nodded. Who owned the land that Hawkport wanted, and how was it being cleared up? Perhaps it truly had to do with airships, an easier place to hide activities. Or maybe the land held something powerful, like the Guardian. Lord Henry Hawkport was working with the Painted Edge. The Painted Edge was looking for a Guardian. They need not be disconnected. She needed more than suspicion here though. Her evidence in regard to the Guardian was practically all conjecture. Perhaps talking to the other beast-named suspects would give her more information or bring them into the light.

Lavinia cleared her throat and roused Fiona from her thoughts. *Ah, yes. Entertaining a possible suitor.* Fiona cast desperately about for something that would quickly end the day so she could go and have a think. When in doubt, too much information would do.

"Do you know, I believe I need the privy again."

LAVINIA SAID ABSOLUTELY NOTHING on the airship ride back to the palace, which suited Fiona fine. While she knew her mother was upset with her for her behavior with John, she couldn't have done more without getting into a sticky situation. If only she could be open with her mother, tell her about the investigation—but no. She didn't want her to worry about the Queen or the Hawkports. Better to let that sit with herself and her friends.

They entered their rooms and were both delighted to find Captain Henrietta waiting inside. Though Fiona knew where her pleasure from seeing the captain came from, she wondered again about her mother's fascination with her.

"Captain Henrietta! How darling of you to come back for the outdoor events. I hope we weren't interrupting anything important."

Henrietta inclined her head, graying strawberry curls waving. "Never too busy to see a friend, Lavinia."

Lavinia clapped her hands together, beaming. Fiona opened her mouth like a caught fish and then closed it again, unsure of how to approach this newfound friendship. She pinched the bridge of her nose and said, "I'll just get ready for the luncheon."

"Er, before you leave," Henrietta broke in quickly, "I have that pamphlet you requested. It should prove useful."

Fiona grinned at Henrietta's light subterfuge. "Help me change? The dresses one must wear at court are exceedingly complicated."

"They have lady's maids for that, Fiona," her mother said, exasperated.

"And I'm sure they take twice as long as me doing it with the help of Captain Henrietta. I am independent and dress myself every day, you know. Simply in straightforward attire."

"Yes, yes, don't remind me," her mother said, rubbing her temple. "Well, for propriety's sake, leave your door cracked please. If you're caught half nude with an unmarried person, I won't be able to live the scandal down."

Henrietta nodded and bowed to Lavinia, who waved at the both of them, seemingly exhausted.

Henrietta gestured for Fiona to go in first and then closed the door softly. "I don't suppose you really wanted this information written down?"

"No, but quick lie all the same," Fiona said, heading to the bureau at the edge of the room. "What did you find out about Sir Mourninghide?"

Henrietta turned away from Fiona, allowing her privacy. "Your royal historian is relatively unknown around here. Either people don't bother with him, or he doesn't talk much. The facts and details are sparse."

"By the skills of his dancing I would've thought he had plenty of practice with the courtiers."

"No one remembers much about him except bits and pieces. I did, however, find out that he has no relatives currently. He had family, but they've passed on."

To have all his family gone so soon must've been hard on him. "Married?" Fiona pulled on the farthingale her mother had suggested earlier. "Or confirmed bachelor?"

"Widowed, it seems."

"Makes sense. He certainly knows how to argue with someone. But nothing else?"

"Well, the dust seems to be gathered in people's memories about him, but there's enough there to suppose he's physically around a bit."

"Well then." Fiona pursed her lips. If he was hiding something of his past, he had done a good job of it. "What do you think?"

"He's a damn good spy." Henrietta nodded. "People know just enough about him to get used to him. His position at the palace is boring enough to be ignored. But he can be relatively everywhere and ask questions. He doesn't seem to be known outside of the page though. None of my rippers have even seen his likeness."

Fiona raised an eyebrow at the assertion that his job was boring but said nothing. "So I can trust him?"

"As far as your intuition allows," Henrietta said. "How fare you with the, er, protector finding?"

"Not well." Fiona huffed as she put on the final pieces of her dress. "I found nothing solid about a Guardian at the Hawkport's on Smallcrest beyond some issue leasing a new facility with the Queen. I should check out their other grounds, but that is no small feat. You can turn around now, Henrietta, thank you."

Henrietta sat in a spartan chair and rubbed her chin. "Anyone else on your list?"

"House Griffintail, Dragonkeep, Bearspear, and Lionheart." Fiona sighed. It was a short list but anyplace to start meant she could at least start.

"Well, Griffintail you can cross off your list right there. Other half is a faun, so they haven't been Griffintails that long."

"Really?" Fiona said, raising an eyebrow. "I haven't met them yet, but Mr. John Hawkport did mention they took each other's names. Well, that removes one. I am going to make a point of talking to Dragonkeep today."

"Why not check out their history with the historian? Seems you could get quite a bit of information that way before being direct with them."

"I suppose that's true," Fiona said, tamping down the excitement at talking to Richard again. Why she should feel excitement, she didn't know. "But he'll probably anger me and then I'll say something mean and it will go nowhere." She grabbed her pocket watch and hung it from her belt.

"Sometimes that's the best place." Henrietta grinned, leaning back into the chair. "Are you sure you're not"—she tapped her lips—"sweet on him?"

"Me, no, why would I be?" She only liked riling him up to get his false veneer to crack. But after this case with the Queen, she'd go home and not think about him again, she was sure.

"Seems your type. Learned, mysterious. Can hold his own in a conversation with you apparently."

"Oh, Henrietta." Fiona rolled her eyes. "I have no type."

"We all do, mistress. We all do." Henrietta smiled wistfully.

"Your time with Gaili and Matteo is going well, it seems then," Fiona said as a change of subject away from herself.

"Aye, I've had adventure before, but those two. They keep me on my toes. We may be the same age by standard Book time, but they've had more life than I could fit into a thimble." Henrietta shook her head. "Matteo has the mind of a devil, creative and bold with enough sense to say what he means at the best of times. Gaili is, of course..." Henrietta waved her hand as if it was a ship on light seas. "She never ceases to amaze me. When I told her I was thinking of a change, she suggested I should find something to branch out on. One of their Copper sayings. Working my way through Rise has been...interesting."

Fiona inclined her head at the change in tone. "Too much hobnobbing already got you down?"

"No, no, that's not it. I'm certainly making progress with Baron Skybash. He's an amiable fellow, if a bit routine. Wants to hunt, eat, drink, and then repeat the same thing tomorrow. We are shipping off again to Four Hills today. Supposed to be better game there."

"Does Baron Skybash have an airship of his own?" Fiona asked, eyes narrowing. After her Hawkport-filled morning, she started to suspect that more of the peerage were riding in their own style.

Henrietta's eyes lit up. "Oh yes, and she is a beauty. Don't tell *Big Betty*, but she's a runner after my own heart. Ship's got more curves and compartments than I could've imagined. He's even let me sail it a few times."

Fiona clasped her hands together and walked the length of the room. That Henrietta could get on with anyone Fiona had no doubt. But that she flew his ship was a bit surprising. He should have his own personal captain, and as far as she could see, most captains didn't like to share. She bit her lip, rounding back to her friend. "I suppose if you're enjoying yourself and getting what you need out of the connection, there's no issue. But be careful. Nobles are not usually as close to their label as they seem."

"Of course, of course," Henrietta said, nodding her head insistently. "But there's certainly been quite a bit of eating and talking about nothing to last for a while. No wonder no one's getting anything done. They all go so slow."

"If anyone can spur on the likes of the royal court, I have no doubt it's you, friend." Fiona held out her hand to help the captain up.

Henrietta clasped it amiably and rose with a light groan. "Don't spread that around though. I'm trying to seem aloof."

The idea of someone like Henrietta appearing aloof made Fiona laugh. "Well, I will take your advice and seek out Richard. Are you sure you don't have time to come with me and meet him in person?"

Henrietta hesitated, then shook her head. "Really should get on to my meet with the baron. But I will be back for the festival."

Fiona rubbed her neck. "Of course. And then another supper. My mother somehow procured seats with the Hawkport family." Fiona quickly recounted what she learned about the Hawkports and the stolen airship from Rise. "So, while that seems pointed enough, their connection with beasts is only conjecture."

"I'll keep my ear on them as well then. I'm sure the lower peerage would like a chance to rail against them to a newcomer."

"Fingers crossed we get a solid lead by the end of the night." They were halfway through the festivities for the page turners. Soon everyone would be gone back to their normal days and the Queen would come calling for answers. With a feeling of dreaded eagerness, Fiona departed from the chambers and headed toward the palace archives.

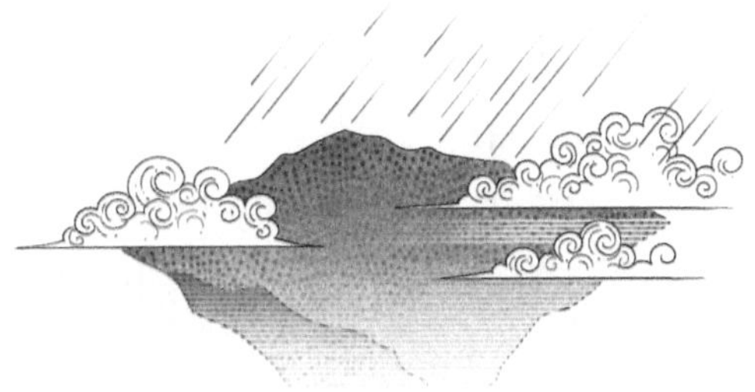

Fiona knocked for the third time on the historian's door. She couldn't hear him through the thick wood, but a guard said he had gone in not an hour ago. She pulled lock-picking tools from her scarf and opened the door easily. It was all quiet. Nothing moved within the darkened candleless room. Perhaps the guard had been mistaken?

"I'll simply wait for him here. There's no reason to run around the entirety of the palace for him." Fiona slid her hands over the stacks of paper on the desk. The pages were mostly blank except for a few beginning drawings that looked like a forest. Or at least the symbology of a forest.

She walked through the bookshelves and to the two arches. She hesitated on the threshold of the bedroom. What little she knew about Richard told her he would be upset if he caught her snooping within. She would hate it as well if it were her. As she reasoned with herself that she was simply looking for him, she hovered at the entrance and poked her head into the chamber. The understated bed was large, taking up most of the room. A fire crackled in the hearth, giving off light and warmth but no smoke. The whole fireplace construction was from Copper, no doubt. Expensive to be in the room of a historian. Only the Queen had one other Fiona had noticed.

It was a room with little in it. No personal objects at all really. No portraits or tapestries. Fiona ran her hand across the inside of the doorframe. It was quite dusty—he didn't let servants come in here either.

"What are you doing?" Richard said behind her.

Fiona was pleased with herself for not jumping and turned to face him. "I came looking for you and figured I'd wait here."

"In my bedchamber? Alone?" Richard said quietly. He raised an eyebrow, but there was a hint of a smile on his lips.

Fiona felt her face grow warm. She crossed her arms. "Of course not. In the archives. I was curious if you had a privy I could use so came toward your bedroom," she said, trying to put him ill at ease.

He tossed his head and laughed, golden curls shaking. "Likely story. Well, come back to the main room, Investigator, and try to keep your hands to yourself."

"I'm not going to throw myself at you." Fiona rolled her eyes.

"I meant my books." Richard smirked. He turned sharply away from her and strode back into the archives.

Fiona took off after him. "If you're done being rude, I was hoping to speak to you about our cases."

Richard nodded, all smirking aside. "Yes, how fared your simpering morning at the Hawkports?"

"It was not simpering," Fiona said. She turned away pointedly and ran her fingers across the spine of one of the books on the table. "It was quite lovely actually. The grounds are beautiful and the manor intriguing."

Richard snorted and sat in the wooden chair. "Probably more interesting than the big-nosed chap you were with."

Fiona pursed her lips. "John was lovely as well. Why are you so down on him?"

"I am not down on him," Richard said, rubbing his jaw. "I couldn't care less about the lawyer or the whole bloody family. Anyways, what did you find?"

"Quite a bit actually." She recounted Dodger's letter of evidence as well as what she had gleaned from her visit to the Hawkport facilities. "Without a doubt, someone well connected to the Hawkport facilities must be helping the Painted Edge. And it was apparently Lord Henry Hawkport who reported the airship stolen as a solid piece that the Painted Edge took."

"Blasted nobles," Richard said. "That's quite more than I've gotten. These erratic downpours are keeping even the most stalwart confidants inside or shoring up their homes from flooding. There are reports of officials being bribed in Woolring and the Rock however."

Two counties currently south of the Plateau. Though Woolring made sense—it was the site of their secret meeting with Henrietta—the Rock was nothing but broken mountains inhabited by those who truly didn't want to live anywhere else. Not very many people there. Odd. "Well, that would explain why the Woolring guards took so long to get together and storm the hideout." Fiona leaned in. "But the Rock...that's the Queen's land. What would they be bribing for there?"

"Yes, their entire goal remains unclear, but I've suggested to Queen Brilliance to have her guards and the armed forces on high alert around the Plateau. There's no telling what they are going to do with those crated supplies."

Fiona frowned. She had never mentioned the supplies in the crates. "Did you see what was in the crates? I thought you left before then."

He glanced away. "I may have come back to look. I had my own investigation, you know."

"I didn't tell you to go!"

"No, but you didn't exactly invite me to stay either." Richard rubbed his face and threw up his hands. "Look. A truce. We didn't exactly meet under the best of circumstances. Let's not get into it now. The Painted Edge must be planning something big, either to find the Guardians or with the Guardians, and that should be our focus."

Fiona raised an eyebrow at his vaulting mood but nodded. "Agreed. We should keep a persistent watch at the festival this evening. It would be the perfect time to make a move." Fiona thought back to the line in the message *Eyes naked*. If it meant being watched, that would be the place. "I just wish I knew what the move was. Either way I'll inform my people of what I've found." She sighed deeply. When could she slip a letter back to Dodger? She wouldn't have time to go herself unless she went first thing in the morning. They could get someone over to the manor and start asking questions of Lord Hawkport himself. She would be there, too, of course, to make sure all went well.

"In regards to the Guardians," she continued, "I gleaned nothing else really. Which is disheartening. If they are hiding beasts or taking care of one, then it is completely off the books. I will have to see if I can get more from Lord Hawkport today at the festival. Before I look into the other beast-named suspects,

I wondered if you could locate some family genealogy records for me. See how far back their families go so I don't waste what little time I have with them."

"Of course, of course," Richard murmured, staring off toward the arches. "Let me see what I can find in the archives. Griffintail, Bearspear, and Dragonkeep, yes?"

Fiona hid her surprise at his quick remembrance. "Griffintail has been discounted already. But add Lionheart."

Richard started but slowly rose from his chair. "Added a new one, did we?"

"John told me about them. Which was ever quite helpful," Fiona said, watching him carefully. Richard had reacted to the name, though he'd tried to hide it. Why?

He wrinkled his nose at the mention of John but said nothing else and disappeared into the end of the archive.

Fiona's eyes wandered over his desk. Quills, colored inks, and sheets of fine vellum and parchment were scattered about. There were several copies of the same leather-bound book stacked on each other. She flipped one open to see an accounting of some historical records, dates, and names. Curious, she flipped open others in the same stack. Each one was penned in different handwriting. These must have been the journals of the palace historians. She started off furtively, but as the minutes dragged on she got bolder reading through them openly. There were some accounts of Queen Pompania, the first to be leader right after the Inking. She always liked to read stories of Pompania, but these were simply dry accounts. The handwritings even started to blur together after a while, as if each historian was of the same mind, just different time periods. Maybe historians were all the same types of people—hotheaded and shockingly secretive.

Nearly half an hour later, Richard returned holding large scrolls. "My apologies for the wait, these charts date back extensively and took some time to find. I believe you'll find everything in order."

"Thank you, Richard. I'll return them shortly," said Fiona, taking the scrolls.

Richard tugged on his beard staring at her but then nodded abruptly. He began tidying up his desk as if dismissing her.

Fiona tried to tamp down her annoyance at being pushed away so easily and began to make her exit. If he had nothing else to say to her, then she might as well go. But perhaps he could provide insight on another matter? Being so close to the Queen, maybe he would understand her motives. She stopped. "Do you know why the Queen would reject anything Hawkport requests?"

He dropped his papers and moved closer, his brow furrowed. "If she had a mind to withhold or show control over them, she would reject a request outright. But only she can play that dangerous game. Why do you ask?"

Fiona thought about how much to tell him. If she was going to get him to trust her with his information, she should do the same. She relayed to him what happened at the manor in brief. "And then when I talked to John about buying an airship myself, he mentioned something about adding a new facility. For the manufacturing of it all. But then when I asked where, he said it was hush-hush until Queen Brilliance reversed the rejection. Something about the original land owner."

"I believe the owner is loath to give it up." Richard shrugged. "What the peerage does is sometimes far above my head. There could be any number of reasons that they are haggling over the land or whoever owns it."

Fiona nodded. "That's what I assumed. Well, thank you for the insight and the scrolls."

Richard blinked and scratched his cheek. "Er, you're welcome." He turned and began fiddling with papers on his desk. "Till the festival then."

Fiona smoothed down her bodice and left quickly, closing the door quietly. Her stomach twisted a little. Perhaps she needed a snack. She could certainly use another cup of coffee. She returned to her rooms to eat and pour over the charts with Henrietta. She was thankful for the suggestion.

The records indicated Bearspear had only been the same after the last forty years or so once they got a page turner in the family. Before then, they had simply been Pinewhirl. Perhaps they changed names to keep their lineage fashionable.

Hawkport's, Lionheart's, and Dragonkeep's lineages went back past the Inking. But it was clear that while Hawkport multiplied like rabbits, Lionheart did not. It seemed Baron Lionheart was the last of his long, illustrious line. Hawkport had over five children currently, not accounting for cousins and marriages.

"So it goes. I'll have to find Baron Lionheart and House Dragonkeep at the festival tonight. Luckily we'll already be with the Hawkports."

The festival was in full swing by the early evening. Revelers dressed in green and birch flower costumes danced around maypoles and perused market stalls. Minstrels played lively tunes, the trill of flutes swirling as one with the flittering banners in the cool incense-filled night air. On the right of the makeshift throne sat the family of the various earls in their costumes, crowded together with the immediate family in the higher tier and the lower family nearest to the ground. The same was done with the barons in many more sections than the earls. And then rounding out the rest of the right side was the lesser peerage. Commoners who could get into the festival, for it was very crowded, filled out the rest of the wooden seats to the Queen's left.

The cheering and excitement mostly came from that area and made even Fiona tingle with pleasure. It had been so many years, since she was a little girl, that she came to a costumed festival. She'd skipped as much as she could on her previous visits to see the sitting ruler. But she had to admit to herself that she was excited to see the acts with Henrietta in tow. The captain had dressed in part as her normal self: Saggy pear-green pants, boots made for stomping around a deck, and a blousy peach shirt gave the look of a pirate. A tall hat with big bright-pink feathers covered her graying strawberry curls—or tried to, as they seemed to have a mind of their own. She had a fake sword on one hip and a neatly trimmed mustache over her lip. She seemed so at ease in the clothing, though Henrietta couldn't stop tugging on the mustache and winking at people.

If only she could've brought her other friends too. What Fiona wouldn't give to see their costumes and reactions. Any other week they would've been welcomed, but people were surprisingly stiff about non-natives during the week of appreciation (to the Queen or to page turners, Fiona could never truly say). Even a human born on Spine was still Schiflan by law and allowed to come.

Lavinia entwined her green-velvet-costumed arm—she had come as a summer nymph—through Fiona's. "I hope you will do what you can with the Hawkports this evening after your ridiculousness this morning. But you should make sure to trade pleasantries with the other families as well."

"Why is that?" Fiona said, adjusting her enormous ballooned sleeves. She had decided it was best to blend in and so dressed as most nobles in an outfit befitting the Midsummer Festival, a mythical unicorn. A bright-blue brocaded bodice over a matching skirt. Feathers of orange stuck out from her hair, and one small wooden horn was centered in the crown of her brown curls. "I thought you would be happy about a close friendship with the Hawkports."

"I am, though I am still suspicious of how easily you are going along with it all. I assume it has something to do with the Queen," her mother whispered, casting her eyes about, "but I wouldn't want the fringe to think we are snubbing them over one house. In this case, quantity is better than quality, and the festival is a very public setting."

"That doesn't make a lot of sense to me. I'm only interested in talking to Lord Hawkport and Lord Lionheart truly."

Lavinia sighed. "Can you not see how being so particular to a few families makes our plans obvious?" She turned to Henrietta. "Oh, make her see reason, Captain. I am much too exhausted for her capriciousness this evening." Lavinia disengaged with Fiona and moved away, waving and smiling as if she hadn't just argued with her daughter.

Fiona drew in a deep breath to calm her nerves then released it slowly. "Why in Larrakane's name is she acting like this? She's been tightly bound since she arrived on my doorstep."

"It's not my place to say, mistress." Henrietta moved hair out of her eyes and tucked it into her hat. "But I think your mother there is having a hard time at court. I've even heard some whispers about her. Seems they've only increased since you started working for the Queen."

"Whispers? Please tell me." Fiona pulled Henrietta off between two stalls.

"Some have taken pains to snub your mother. It's in the small things, of course. Who's invited to a gathering. Who she's placed with at a table."

"Well, why should she care about things like that?"

"That is the world your mother lives in. She's not like you. Not as free. She's pressed by society life here. And as a widower dependent on her daughter..." Henrietta nodded pointedly in Fiona's direction. "She's not able to move as she pleases. Small changes like this have large ripples, lass."

Fiona had never thought of her mother as without control before. She commanded her to do a good many things throughout her lifetime. She was always direct about what she wanted and what she deemed was good enough. She certainly had no problems moving in charmed circles after Fiona was bound to Spine. Had she done something to earn the ire of the Queen? Or was the Queen just as impulsive as she seemed and her mother the latest target? Is this why she had come to Spine before the festivities started? "What does all this have to do with spending time with the Hawkports?"

Henrietta leaned in. "If you only talk to them, it will seem your mother is setting you, her well-known daughter and whispered Queen confidant, to catapult herself up. And unless you happen to go through with a marriage, which we both know you won't, it'll exile her from the royal court after this week. But if you talk to lots of families..." Henrietta waved her hand like a bird fluttering through the air.

Fiona worried her lip at the gesture. "If I engage with all the families, I'll just be the peculiar daughter who goes her own way. Not directed by my mother."

"Exactly. She wants you to have a good match, but she also knows you, Fiona."

"Does she truly?" Fiona scoffed.

Henrietta shrugged in her nonjudgmental way. "Well, she knows the royal court at least."

That she did. Fiona sighed and uncrossed her arms. "Well then, I suppose if I'm to be the peculiar one, I might as well make the most of it." She strode toward her mother and said hello to one of the people she was talking to. After a brief conversation she excused herself, moving on to talk with another and then another, following much the same family path of fringe that her mother had introduced her to before. She found it was much easier to get introduced to other people, like lightning splintering off the first strike. While she worked her way over to the Hawkports, she asked various benign questions but always slipped in one that could give her more information. It couldn't be a total waste of an hour and a half.

By the time she arrived at the lower edge of the Hawkport section, introduced John—dressed as a resplendent, green-velvet-hooded archer—to Henrietta, and reacquainted herself with him, her mind was churning. The only Hawkports who truly did anything with the airships was the lord, his eldest son, and their page turner cousin Bunny. It seemed most of the Hawkport children were either settled happily doing nothing or had left the page altogether for more provocative locations like Copper or Spine. Fiona wondered how a page turner like Bunny could be so involved in the day-to-day when she was bound to Spine. She was keen to meet this oft-discussed woman.

Dragonkeep had made up their name after the mythical creatures, something Fiona was finding more commonplace than she thought possible given everyone's reaction to her shortening her last name. But that made it less likely they were in any way connected to her fast-becoming-thin theory. Perhaps this wasn't exactly what the Elder had meant, but Richard had agreed it was clever, so there must be something there.

She tucked those thoughts to the side and turned to Henrietta, whispering, "Apparently there has been a tussle in the court between Earl Hawkport and Baron Lionheart. Most say the old man practically accused Hawkport of trying to steal his inheritance. So it reasons he's the owner of the mysterious land."

"If that's the case, then he doesn't own much at all," Henrietta replied. She leaned in closer. "He's baron over the Forlorn Tower." No one lived there. It was more like the floating earth isles that were imported to the page of air for skimmers to rest on than an actual fully populated county. But on it sat the crumbling ruins of a tower that had belonged to one of the erratic royals. Fiona couldn't remember which one. Odd that the lineage history Richard had given her hadn't pointed to any monarchs in Baron Lionheart's family line.

"I'll seek him out soon then," Fiona murmured.

"Fiona," Lavinia said, interrupting, "could you not talk business for one moment? Even the Queen can't expect you to keep on it forever."

Fiona opened her mouth for a quick retort but closed it. Her mother did seem more relaxed now. She would be in a fright if she knew what Henrietta had told her. Well, she'd have to keep that and the Queen's earlier threats under wraps. "Of course, Mama."

Lavinia smiled at her daughter, squeezing her hand. Fiona gave a tentative smile back. There wasn't much she could do, shackled into the stands with the Hawkports. She may as well enjoy the show. She could move more freely before supper.

John kept up a light chatter as the jousting and then the tournament continued on. He introduced her to more family than she could possibly remember but none with such a quirky nickname as his page turner cousin, who regrettably hadn't arrived yet.

After an hour of enjoying the jousting, small drops of rain begin to pour down. Fiona hoped that it would cease quickly. She didn't want to have to end what was her only relaxing moment this week so soon. Fireworks were set to shoot off for a dazzling display above the river. Plus, she had yet to see Richard at the festival. She had been keeping an eye out, but he must've changed his mind and stayed hidden in his archive.

As if pulled to her by thought alone, Richard appeared next to the stand like a bird out of thin air. He wore no costume but his attire was cleaned and pressed, showing he had changed since she last saw him. He bowed cordially to them all but asked to borrow a moment of Fiona's time to discuss some research. Without hesitation Fiona made her excuses and rose, to the questioning murmurs of John to her mother and

Lavinia's nervous laughter back. Fiona ignored it and stepped away from the platforms hurriedly.

Richard clasped his hands behind his back, gold eyes flashing as he smirked, "I find you hip to hip with the Hawkports then."

Fiona sighed loudly. "It's not hip to hip. We're simply sitting with them." She felt hot all of a sudden in her costume and said with light derision, "And you're one to talk. I'm gathering information. What have you been up to?"

He rocked on his heels. "Much the same. No one has spotted anything amiss during the festivities, but the guards are on high alert for anyone unrecognized."

Fiona felt slightly guilty for her admonishment. He *had* been keeping an eye out for the Edge. All guilt immediately vanished as he continued to open his mouth, however.

"You shouldn't sit with them forever if you're to talk to anyone else today," Richard said, shifting closer to her and crossing his arms.

"Need I remind you I don't work for you? We work together." She crossed her arms, staring into his golden eyes, baiting him to argue with her.

He grinned, unmoved. "That is why I thought I would lend you a hand. Divide and conquer, as it were."

"Now you're saying I can't handle it all on my own. Make up your mind, Sir Mourninghide, or I shall think you quite out of it."

Richard quirked an eyebrow but continued to smile. "I have actually. I know Dragonkeep well and can talk to him. I've met Baron Lionheart and know at least what he looks like. Out of this large crowd of people I can find them both and have a word." Drops of rain began to hit harder on and around them. He shook his head, reddish-gold hair moving restlessly. "Before we're all beset upon by the blasted storm that's brewing."

Fiona thought it sensible but was still reluctant to let him win. "I've already discovered all I need to know about Dragonkeep, but your plan isn't a terrible one. You can focus on Lionheart and I'll focus on Hawkport. We'll reconvene at supper."

"I look forward to it," he said in a warm, deep voice.

Fiona's face warmed at his tone, and she was glad she had the deep-brown complexion to not show it.

Richard bowed, seeming to know when to walk away with his victory, and started to stride off.

"Why don't you join us inside, Sir Mourninghide?" called out a voice above them.

Looking down at Richard, Lord Hawkport stood among the family. He held a silver tankard in one hand and beckoned to the historian. The others, who had begun to get up due to the rain, glanced at each other and then at him, but that was all they showed of their confusion.

Richard bowed. "You do me a great honor, my lord, but I must get back to my duties."

Fiona raised an eyebrow. She knew he was stuffy, but this was a bit much. This was a suspect begging to be investigated. She watched Richard's face as he carefully rained in frustration. What was he so upset about?

Lord Hawkport gestured with his tankard to Richard. "Why don't you come by Shade Manor tonight? You would be welcomed as anyone of the party."

"Alas, I have writings I must get ready for the Queen tomorrow." Richard nodded his head with a small measure of politeness.

"You do love your books. By Larrakane's light, I wouldn't have recognized you if the sun was out." There was a ripple of laughter around the earl.

Richard didn't respond but instead bowed again and stalked off. It seemed Fiona wasn't the only one who couldn't be bothered to be cordial on principle alone.

"Does your uncle know Sir Mourninghide well?" she said as she returned to her place.

"Better than I imagined apparently. I wonder what their discrepancy is," John said, glancing at his uncle.

Watching them, Lord Hawkport raised his tankard in a toast. He seemed in very good spirits, even as the rain continued to pour. It was clear that the family was waiting on him to go inside, but he was unmoved. Instead, he leaned back as if holding court, a gesture supported by his costume choice for the festivities: gold regalia befitting royalty but with the absurd blue hawk of the family insignia blazoned in the middle. Almost shockingly large, as if he were the King or a summer lord.

Fiona turned around, not liking the way he watched them. "Yes, it's very curious."

"Is that your investigator brain spinning along?" John said with a wide smile.

Fiona blushed. "I can't help but look at a question and see an opportunity."

"That's very admirable."

"You think so?"

"Oh yes. Life is somewhat predictable here. But you make it seem so much more...questionable."

Fiona tried not to react to the compliment. She hadn't realized she had been showing John that a predictable life wasn't what he wanted. Drat.

"Well, life can be predictable anywhere when you've lived in one place for so long." She turned to suggest to her mother they go inside before they catch a chill from the rain, but there was a jolt as the ground shook, knocking her into her mother.

"What in the dark edge is that?" Fiona said.

The remaining people around the platforms murmured as another rumble shook the seats beneath them.

Fiona felt nauseous as if the whole world was starting to spin. She grabbed on to the wood seating to steady herself.

"What is going on? Fiona?" Lavinia said, wrapping her arms around her daughter.

The night sky rippled in the distance as if someone was turning the page but to a heightened degree. Fiona had never seen anything like it in her life. The fold took up the horizon. The rainy gray edges of Rise pulled away, the darkened night sky and full moon of her page folded back. A similarly dark but eerily quiet sky revealed itself. And the world panicked.

PEOPLE ALREADY ON THEIR way inside from the rain ran for cover toward the interior of the palace and away from the platforms. Others who had been dawdling leapt out of the seats and dove for cover. Screams tore the night air, muffled by the pounding of the increased rain. A page had never opened so large before. Another jolt shook the earth beneath their feet.

Fiona jumped up, pulling her mother with her. The nausea was starting to dissipate thankfully. "Make way to the palace."

Henrietta held out her hand and Lavinia grabbed it, pulling herself over the short balcony and onto the ground. "Where are you going?" her mother asked.

"Higher up to see while it's still open," Fiona shouted, picking up her skirts completely. "Henrietta—"

"I will keep my finger to the wind, mistress. Don't worry."

Fiona nodded, thankful not to have to explain her concerns to her friend, and ran to the highest point she could, the Queen's balcony. She climbed the steps quickly until she could see farther in the distance. Cupping her hands to her face, she caught the sky rippling again, folding back slowly, and uncovering the gray mists of Rise. What she had thought to be darkened was faintly lit with a blue-green gradient, but she didn't recognize the page as its vignette grew ever smaller. The turn snapped shut and Rise was simply Rise again.

Seeing her, a guard called out, "What was that?"

"Someone turned the page. And the Plateau, it moved," Fiona yelled down.

"The Plateau isn't set to shift for another fortnight," the guard said, confused.

"And yet it just did." At least a little. Did the page turn spur the Plateau's seasonal spin? Fiona continued the last few steps up and pulled herself into the Queen's box to an unusual sight. The area had been emptied, the Queen likely taken to a safe space. But Richard held the throne's arm, clenching it with a drawn, pale face.

Fiona went to him, breath hitched, and laid a hand tentatively on his shoulder. "Sir Mourninghide, are you hurt?"

Richard grasped her fingers, his rough hand holding tight. His wide eyes took her in. "It was the Forlorn Tower. It's gone."

Fiona stopped, brows creased. "Gone? What do you mean, it's gone missing? It's an island." She glanced back into the night sky unable to see anything more than the sporting arena and the peaks of a temple in the distance. "How can you tell?"

"The direction...the size." He wiped his face with a handkerchief. "It must have been the blasted Painted Edge. What else would the equipment be for?"

That's what they had been gearing up for with the ropes and pulleys: an island theft! Transporting an entire island, even one as small as the Forlorn Tower, was somewhat imaginable if you threw limitations and expectations into the dark edge. It would take cunning and a great deal of power to turn the page with something that size.

"We must find it." Richard swallowed again and straightened up, tugging at his doublet. His face reddened but from boiling anger rather than embarrassment. "How dare they trifle with the page in this manner! They will regret it."

Seeing Richard changed back to his old self, she let go of his arm and took a step back. "We should act quickly in case there are any other surprises in store for tonight," Fiona said. Her mind was a whirr. Did the Travel Guild already know? Surely someone thought to alert them, but if not... She needed to get back to Spine at once.

Guards entered the room, their captain striding forth. Richard met him and began talking earnestly to him about the safety of the Queen.

Fiona was almost away unheeded when Richard called out to her, "Fiona, I will talk to the guards and my local contacts. You will talk to your page turners, yes? Outside the page?"

She frowned. "Of course. Are you questioning my ability to get answers?"

He tugged at his beard. "No, I want answers from cover to cover. Report to me at once with what you hear." He nodded tersely and strode away.

Fiona had half a mind to call after him about his brusque attitude but swallowed it. If she was honest, she was as disturbed as he seemed to be. It was clear he was struggling with what happened, but his coldness pinched her, and she didn't have time to mull on why.

She hurried on her way to her chambers for her ornithopter. She opened the door to find her mother pacing the floor and Henrietta nowhere to be seen.

"Larrakane bless, Fiona, you're soaked through," Lavinia exclaimed. She began unlooping her dress. "Get out of those wet clothes or you'll die of a cold." Without giving her time to respond, her mother shouted, "Have you heard? Someone has somehow hidden one of the isles. An *island*, dear. Can you believe it? How is that even possible?"

"That is just what I intend to find out," Fiona said, flinging off her loosened wet clothes as she hurried into her room. She quickly put on her wool stockings, doublet, and sturdy boots, glad that they were warmed by the fire.

"Where are you going?" Lavinia stood in the doorway mangling her handkerchief. "Wouldn't it be better to stay here at the palace? It can't be safe if someone attacked us and has the power to take a whole island. It must've been those painted ruffians."

Fiona was surprised her mother had heard about them. Perhaps she paid more attention to the *Card* than she pretended to. "I'm going to Spine, but I will be back. Where has Henrietta—"

There was a commotion in the corridor of loud voices and running feet. The woman in question bounded into the room with several boisterous people behind her. They were dressed finer than most of the people running up and down the halls of this side of the palace. For the page to be in a crisis, the group were more jovial than expected.

"One moment, gentlemen," Henrietta called out into the hallway. "I must exchange costume for real." She tugged the hilt of her costumed sword, removing it from her outfit. "Lavinia. Mistress. These rapscallions have offered to take us somewhere less chaotic on their airship. If we leave now with my hand on the wheel, we'll make it clear to the other side of the page in no time."

"Yes, yes," the thick baron intruded, "the Rock would see us comfortable, my dear. Feel free to bring your friends."

"Henrietta, I have to get back to Spine. There's so much happening."

The captain's brow furrowed, and she tugged on her doublet. "You can get back? They've closed off all the pagemarks to officials only."

Fiona jerked back. "They have? That was quicker than expected."

"Captain, we must be going. It's getting right poor in this part of the castle," the thick baron called out from the hall. His friends laughed along.

Fiona realized that they must've partaken in a large amount of wine and beer at the festival. Were they simply using Henrietta as a means to leave the Plateau? "Do be careful. I worry they aren't respecting you as they ought to be."

Henrietta cleared her throat and looked back at the group. "Those who bond fleeing a crisis bond for life, eh?" She strode across the room and picked up her bags and her true rapier. "If you hear of anything, I'd certainly like to know. Care of Baron Bearspear at the Rock should get a message to me quickly." She nodded to Fiona and said, "Lavinia, would you do me the honor of accompanying me?"

Lavinia stopped pretending to be ensconced in staring out the window of their chambers and glanced at Fiona, eyebrows drawing together, "Are you sure you have to go to Spine?"

"Without fail." Fiona said. Perhaps going to the baron's holding would be a safe place for her mother. She didn't quite trust that the palace wasn't crawling with Painted Edge spies still. "You should go with Henrietta."

Her mother gazed back out the window. "Of course. Henrietta, let me grab my things." She moved from the room quicker than Fiona had ever seen and without a backward glance at her daughter.

Hoping to alleviate the tension, Fiona said, "Would you please keep my mother safe? I wouldn't want anything to happen to her."

The captain nodded quickly. "Of course. And will you please tell my dears I...well, I quite miss them. I'll be home soon as they open up the 'marks."

"Certainly." Fiona squeezed her shoulder and trotted out the door, pushing past the barons, who called out to her in jests as she ran. If they were unconcerned, perhaps more people were as well. But no, the open courtyard and the carriage stands outside told a different story. All around her people were chattering as the information about the stolen island trickled about. People trundled into the palace looking for safety and reassurance or to their homes as quickly as they could, properly terrified. As well they should be. She agreed with her mother—something she didn't think would happen in her lifetime—that the island had to have been taken in a powerful way. What would have the power to do that, though, she was at a loss about. Could they have already secured the Guardians? But no, a Guardian couldn't leave their page. Not unless that page was already in turmoil, it seemed. Perhaps it was needed to wake the Guardian?

She tugged her scarf out of her sleeves and wrapped it around her waist under her doublet. She twisted it, frustrated. "If I had been paying more attention to the Edge—" She cursed. Where had they taken the blasted island to? It couldn't have been easy to orchestrate. There was more here than Fiona could think through by herself. She needed help. She would go to the one place where she would find that in spades.

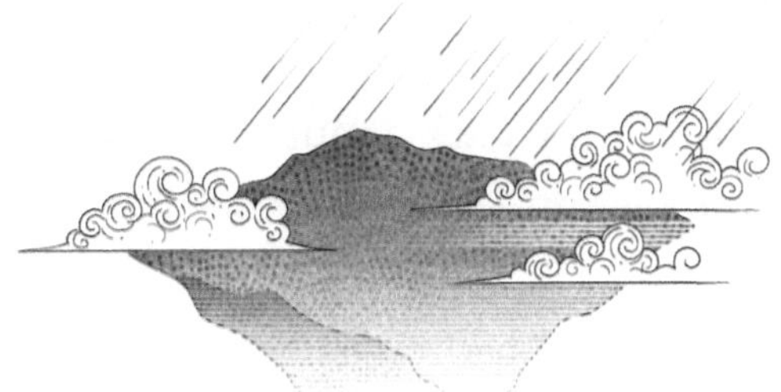

Henrietta's telling was true. The Travel Guild pagemarks had been immediately blocked from entries and exits within Rise. Well as fast as airship messengers could fly. She had to pretend once again to work for Dodger and was only a little surprised that it succeeded. Though it had taken a bit of finagling getting out of the page and back to Spine, she had made it to the Hinge, Guild HQ, in one piece. Dodger seemed to know why she was in his office before she could open her mouth, a fact she was quite thankful for. His jackets had scant reports, only that the Hawkport airship captains were poor witnesses due to the rain. No other reports had yet come in from field agents in other pages, but Dodger insisted he would let her know when they did. Giving her a Travel Guild–stamped decree put even more of his faith in her and showed that the threat of the stolen island was enough to wave quite a few lines of regulation.

The Queen immediately sent for a stronger jacket presence in Rise. It seemed nonhumans were invited to the festivities for once. Fiona didn't know if Dodger was using the word *invite* correctly but she felt comforted by the fact that there would be more eyes to watch for the Painted Edge. Marcia, his boss and shape shifting hag, would be leading them herself as well. According to Dodger, Marcia had been quick to suggest it when she heard how it had happened. Fiona thought there was something there, perhaps with Sadie, but Dodger was still in the dark about the sisters. It wasn't her place to illuminate him, so she lost the chance to ask Marcia outright.

Fiona left the Hinge as quickly as she could and was thankful to find her urgent summons, care of the Guild, saw Gaili and Matteo ready and waiting to be gotten up to speed. The fauns were already poring over maps and animatedly talking in the office when she arrived home. Two heads, one pink and one black, bent together made them look like bookends around the shared desk.

"Once again they've managed to scarper off with something of unimaginable size and no one has fiber to show for it," Fiona said, closing the office door behind her. She strode straight to the small stove for a cup of coffee, thankful to be free of the skirt and bodice she had worn at the festival. Her daily clothes were a comfort in this situation.

"Was the island important?" Gaili said, leaning back. A smudge of ink stained her cheek.

"I can't imagine why it would be, but someone must know," Fiona murmured. There were fifteen counties surrounding the Plateau. Most had too many people and the others too many animals or crops. The Forlorn Tower was singular. You could walk from one edge to the other in a matter of hours. "Perhaps Baron Lionheart, the owner, could tell me." Had Richard talked to him before the world changed? The conversation seemed so long ago already.

"A whole island? How is that possible?" Matteo ran his hand through his ebony locks and across his small black horns. "And where would they hide it?"

"That's what we need to determine. Well, us, a quarter of the Travel Guild, and Sir Mourninghide."

"That's Richard," Gaili whispered poorly to Matteo.

He shook his head minutely to her and asked loudly, "Who is Richard?

"Oh!" Fiona said, tugging at her scarf, cheeks warming. "Don't pretend Henrietta didn't write you both about everything going on this week. You three are as bad as turner gossips. He's thoroughly irritating, utterly ridiculous, but for the moment we are allies. That is all." She hoped he learned much while she was away. Then she could demand he report to her in the way he had done. "But that is in Rise. Out here I have you darlings. Speaking of Henrietta, she says to say she misses you both and she'll be back as soon as they open up the pagemarks." Fiona bit her lip to stop from saying more. She didn't want to worry them unnecessarily if her thoughts about the baron were wrong.

Gaili pressed her lips tight and Matteo nodded thoughtfully. There were twin looks of surprise on both their faces, but Matteo was the first to brush it off. "Well, we are ready when you are."

"Can you help me figure out where the pages connect if I show you a map? I know pagemark to pagemark, but random points are not my strong suit."

"But of course." Matteo clapped his hands, then rubbed them together. "I live for a good map."

"He keeps several on him so he can update them at any time," Gaili said, massaging his shoulder and smiling.

"Aye, if I was a page turner, I'd be a spotter no doubt," he said, unrolling a large rectangular cloth from one of his leather-wrapped cases. "But as it is, I have to rely on others for my turning, and that puts a crimp into it. Ah, here is my latest map of Rise."

Fiona stared down at the map of the fifteen counties with the Plateau in the middle. The edges of the fabric faded into inky black. The dark edge. This map showed Rise in the middle of winter, so the Plateau was east to west, as opposed to how it was now. "Do you have a summer view?"

"Ah, I can do you better." Matteo opened the stopper of a small vial, dipped his finger in, and then rubbed the cloth Plateau in a circle, spreading the substance outward. It slowly rotated. The River Tam grew bigger and the lower island lakes and waterfalls adjusted as they did during the summer season. "It is layered, you see. It reacts to the right pressure and the element spread across it."

Fiona grinned. "Clever. Can you show me where it aligns on the other maps?"

"Ah yes, the Book from Her Light is my favorite view." He pulled out similar rectangular cloth maps and aligned them precisely on the table. With a small bit of showmanship, he produced a beautifully etched glass case in the same size and fitted it snug over the maps. The case had a thin slit that curved from one side to the other, which he slid copper tongs through. And, after affixing a vial of what Fiona could swear was emptiness to a hole fit for it within the glass, the maps began to hover over each other with Blaze at the top. Each element of its heated landscape magnified in detail by the glass. Matteo stepped back, smiling wide, and bowed slightly. "It is how I imagine it."

Even as a cartographer, Matteo had the same knack as other faekin for producing exceptional inventions. Was it in their blood or residual faeness that produced this ingenuity? Fiona shook her head in amazement. "That is genius, Matteo. Truly wonderful. Oh, I could be distracted all day by how much you can see here." She bit her lip, focusing, and grabbed the copper tongs to turn the maps as if they were pages till she got to Rise. "Okay, so then, if the island is here, it couldn't be turned to Mistral." She flipped the map again, turning to the page of air. "They would be taking it smack into Empearal."

Matteo whistled. "Not enough paper in the Book to try and traverse that hurricane."

Fiona shook her head. "It was quite dark as well, and I've never known Mistral to be anything but bright. And the Depths is out too. It's directly over Whirlpool."

"That leaves Copper—" Gaili started.

"No, the sky wasn't golden either," Fiona murmured, thinking back to the darkened vignette. There had been light there and shapes, but where would that place it in the Book?

"Well then, Kerus," Gaili said. "But if it appeared in the sky above the desert, format will have it soon enough. Can't keep all turners silent."

"I suppose it being an island, it could become one with Cobbles maybe?" Matteo added in, eyebrow arched.

"Yes, but so would anyone traveling with it, and I doubt it was a sacrificial mission." Fiona rubbed her forehead. "Or at least, I think I doubt it. I need to understand why that island!"

"Well, there is one other option," Gaili said quietly. "They may have taken someplace we don't have contact with."

Fiona looked up quickly. "You think they know but we don't?"

"They've been ahead of everyone this whole time. It would make sense they know about unknown pages as well."

Fiona ran her finger down her scarf slowly. It would make sense if they could turn the page to a place where nothing could impact the island's journey or them. If they had scouted a new page, like the earthy-smelling one that Clara had opened up last month, then they could be there. With a small gasp, Fiona tugged off her scarf and pulled out the parchment papers from a golden pocket. "Part of their instructions were to *align the stone and Hazel's vine!* A pagemark. I didn't see any vines in the sky, but I was miles and miles away. Come on. I think it's time to get an expert on that particular point."

Gaili's expression turned blank, but she said nothing as she and Matteo gathered their things and followed Fiona out of the office, across the street, and straight to Mistress Didia Humbledraft's door.

Fiona quickly rapped on the door, then winced. "We should've brought cake."

Before she could scamper back and grab a visiting gift, a tall, slender tawny man opened the door, sage temple librarian robes swirling to a stop around him. "Fiona?"

She smiled up at her old friend. "Hanno. I didn't know you were back from Rise." Hanno had gone through Travel Guild turner training at the same time as her. While he was a few years older than her fourteen, they had connected over their curiosity of the Book and its hidden secrets. Though he had gone on to work for the temple and subsequently the library, they had both continued delving into mysteries of their own. "Are you working with Mistress Humbledraft? Is she in?"

"He's not working, he's gossiping," an older woman croaked from behind him. Mistress Humbledraft stood in the manor hall, interest plain on her dark golden-brown face. She was largest in the middle and wore the tucked and puffed-up gowns of their human page—an older style than what was currently in fashion but more in line than Fiona's own eggplant hose and black velvet doublet. Her wavy gray hair was loose from the remnants of a bun, and her round glasses were pressed tight against her face. "Get in and close the door before you let the cat out."

Fiona bundled in past Hanno, who stared after her as Gaili and Matteo slipped in. Ignoring his open mouth, Fiona addressed Humbledraft. "It is very rude of me to show up without an offering and with company, but needs must."

Mistress Humbledraft nodded. "Format has it they've gone and pinched an island. Glad I came home early. Hard bind for the Queen this week."

"Yes, and moreover there's no news of it being sighted yet. But that is where I bring you all together." Fiona bowed slightly. "Mistress Humbledraft, may I introduce you to Gaili and Matteo. Gaili is—"

"Oh, the alchemist! How lovely," Mistress Humbledraft said, cutting Fiona off. "And the consummate paramour. Cartographer, yes? I do hope you brought your goodies with you. Come in, come in." She waved them through to the parlor.

The room was better furnished than the last time Fiona had been in. A comfy settee sat right in front of the window looking out. The walls were still decorated with tapestries and trinkets from Didia's spotter days. A golden tapestry of a young Queen Pompania the Good being crowned caught her eye. The crowd of people around the Queen—all men, oddly—seemed more distinctive. Had she had the tapestry painted over?

"I must say, I love to see young love. Keeps me spirited. But where is your third?" Mistress Humbledraft said to the fauns.

Gaili blushed. "She's in Rise, pushing the breach, as she calls it, Mistress Humbledraft."

"Please, let's not stand on ceremony here. You may call me Didia, and I know you call her Fi."

Fiona, roused from her study of the familiar tapestry, grinned. "I see nothing truly gets past you."

"Only if it flies over me, dear, and even then, I've got the glasses." Dida pushed them up on her face. She called out, "Hanno, be a dear and make the coffee tray, please."

With a quickness that told of his familiarity with the home, Hanno did indeed make the coffee tray with complementary cake. As he did, Fiona went into better detail of what had transpired in Rise with the missing island and what little she and the others knew. Matteo brought out his maps, showcasing what they both thought about it being in one of the seven pages.

"I know you'll both be the soul of discretion when I say that this next part is a secret." Fiona stared at Hanno and then Didia. "So keep it in the flax."

"I have confidences older than you, so that shouldn't be an issue," Didia said and sipped her coffee. "But wise of you to say."

Fiona raised an eyebrow but nodded. "Recently Gaili and I discovered what may be a new page. It is there we think the Painted Edge could be hiding out."

"Well, they certainly aren't always in Spine," Didia said, "but a new page? How would they find it?"

"Someone had to be experimenting," Fiona said carefully. She wanted to talk around what her and Gaili had seen done with the Seasonal Crowns since they weren't widely known. "We've seen the page with our own eyes. It felt...original."

"Did you get a bookmark for later?" Hanno said excitedly. He set down his cup and pulled out a cylindrical leather case.

Fiona shook her head. "But if it exists, there must be a way there. If the Travel Guild turns up nothing in the other pages, it would be good to figure it out."

Hanno unrolled his map. Instead of being layered like Matteo's, it was wide and large with all seven pages laid out and Spine next to them. Fiona recognized it from the wall of his room. It was heavily annotated, even more so than before. Hanno had always been interested in "hidden page" theories. It's what made him a good researcher to work with the former spotter, Didia, though the employment had not been by chance. "There are several good working theories, but without a bookmark we're stuck with conjecture."

Fiona wished she had the nerve to keep the fourth crown she had confiscated at Clara's experiment, but she had left it with Mac, the rightful owner. Should she bring her in on this too? The poor Summer Monarch was still reeling from the last event.

"I did keep something from the experiment," Gaili said, blushing and looking at her feet. "While not a bookmark, perhaps we could use that to try."

Fiona's mouth fell open. "You did?"

"I thought I would need it to..." She waved her aged hand. "But I didn't. So I've been studying it thinking that I might best understand how the experiment was done." She gingerly pulled out the metal clock hand that had housed the fourth crown and set it on the table. Its blackened metal shone in the light of the lantern-lit parlor and all eyes riveted to it.

"This experiment, did it go well?" Hanno said.

"No," Fiona said, "so take precaution. I'll be back as soon as I can."

Gaili nodded and refilled Didia's coffee cup. Matteo began pulling out more of his maps, arranging them together to set up the View from Her Light.

"You're going to go back now?" Hanno said, tearing his gaze from the maps.

"I've gotten as much as I can from this side of the Book and I'm no help to you four." She smiled looking at the group. A cartographer, an inventor, a spotter, and a librarian. She had little doubt that with enough time they could deduce even Larrakane's whereabouts. "I'll be at Thorn Palace, or at least in Rise, should you need me. Send word as soon as you can by Travel Guild jacket, and I'll be back."

"Stay safe, Fi, there's no telling what they plan to do next."

"Yes, that's exactly the problem," Fiona said, pulling on her gloves. "I am determined to understand their motive for this. If that can be uncovered, we may be able to pull ourselves ahead of them for once and stop them for good." There was little doubt now that these rippers had a grander plan than all their sum parts. Smuggling creatures and stealing an airship was one thing. But an island? That was a bit out of her league. She would need powers to match. She would need a Guardian.

FIONA ENTERED THE HUSHED grand archive, footsteps thudding on the stone floors. Richard glanced up from his desk, worry easing from his tawny face. He gave her appearance a once-over as he rose. "Ah, Mistress Thornbeard, back so quickly. I hope with good news."

"I think I have a way to find the island." Fiona sat at the table and clasped her hands together. She recounted what she had learned from Dodger and where she thought the island may be hidden if not in Kerus. She assured him her side was working away and would alert her as soon as either had something. "The main thing, I think, is to understand why *that* island. Even if we find it, the Painted Edge will simply keep tearing the Book apart. We need to understand their larger motives."

Richard waved away the notion. "What do you mean? You don't need a motive. You know what they're doing."

"Yes, but while you can sell a gem the size of a serving platter or illegally created goods on the market for paper, you can't sell an island. Even stealing the airship meant quicker mobility. But the Forlorn Tower..." She pinched the bridge of her nose and sighed. "It throws their seemingly profit-focused crimes into a new light." She remembered what Soots had said about the Painted Edge possibly trying to get rid of them. Perhaps this too was in that vein? "Tell me everything you know about the island. It may have something to do with the Guardian."

Richard threw up his hands. "The Guardian. *The Guardian.* It's always about the bloody Guardian! We should be dealing with the rippers directly. We need to be doing something now."

"What do you think I'm doing? That we're all doing?" Fiona rose, closing the space between them. "Solutions cannot be granted in a moment."

"We should go directly to the Hawkports and demand they tell us everything."

"Demand with what?" She lowered her voice, aware of guards that trooped the hall. "They may have helped the Edge steal an airship, but we have no tangible proof. What little exists is locked away on their property. And if you recall, they sit higher in the royal court than we do at the moment. If we make demands of Lord Hawkport and nothing comes out of it, we won't be able to do it again without a literal display of clear evidence and a troop of jackets, neither of which I see us getting anytime soon."

Richard paced. "I can make them talk."

"But can you make them talk to the Queen? To the Binder?" Fiona sighed. "Look, we can go to the main airship facilities on Shade, we can search for evidence. There must be something there. Lord Hawkport clearly didn't want me nosing around. Either there's another connection to the Edge or something about their plan." Fiona reached out and placed her hand on Richard's arm, stopping him. She leaned in. "I know you want me to stop talking about it, but the Guardian may be able to help if we can find them. One has to exist."

"What do you even think this Guardian can bloody do? What makes you so sure they have the ability to stop this?"

Fiona bit her lip and looked away. Why wouldn't they have the ability to move literal mountains in Rise if they wanted to? Soots certainly could. "Because..." she started. Could she tell him her secrets? In all honesty, she wanted to trust Richard rather than keep a wall up with him. Larrakane be kind, she wanted to confide in the stubborn man. She took a breath and rubbed the edge of her scarf. "I know they exist for the elemental pages. Why not ours?"

Richard glanced at her, mouth open, but then shut it. "One didn't stop what happened in Copper, did it?"

She narrowed her eyes. He hadn't confirmed he knew about Soots, but that he definitely knew about the incident in Copper proved he was more knowledgeable than he had previously let on. Fiona had wondered why a Copper Guardian hadn't intervened but never mentioned her thoughts to anyone but Gaili. Fiona's trust was limited these days with Sadie's whereabouts and connections unknown. "How do you know one didn't intervene in Copper?"

"I get all the Queen's reports." Richard shuffled uncomfortably, avoiding her gaze. "Look, let's go to Shade. I concede. Larrakane help me when it comes to arguing with you. We'll find actual evidence or else."

"Or else what?"

"I'll make them talk."

Fiona studied Richard. He seemed barely able to keep his temper in check. While she didn't often love Rise, she could understand the frustration of having your home tampered with and wanting to do something about it. "Okay, either we find evidence, or we do it your way."

Richard took a deep breath and nodded. "Thank you."

Fiona penned a quick note for Henrietta telling her to keep her mother and herself safe, that the fauns were working on a solution, and in as vague words as possible where she was going and why. If anything should happen, she knew Henrietta would alert the Travel Guild. She directed the note with a flash of her Travel Guild decree via a clearly burdened messenger. Letters and notes must have been running clear across the page and back again from the palace as the island continued to be missing. She hoped her note wouldn't take too long and tucked a few extra papers in the messenger's hand as a tip.

Palace guards and Guild jackets decked every doorway like statues. Richard opened his mouth to speak but she quickly stepped in front of him and showed her Guild insignia decree. Fiona was thankful for Dodger after a few minutes of showing it repeatedly. She wondered if it would be faster to adhere it to her doublet.

"Friends in high places indeed," Richard said as they continued out of the palace grounds.

"But not enough to commandeer an airship." Fiona tucked the decree into her scarf quickly as they headed for the docks. "It will take longer to get to Shade without one, but I don't trust anything Hawkport right now. I can turn us to Mistral and fly us nearly there and above with ornithopters. Then we can turn back and make our way to the manor quietly."

Richard stumbled. "Turn us? You mean take us to another page and then back again?"

The wariness in his voice made Fiona pause. "Are you scared of turning the page?"

"It's not something I've, er, often done," he said, rubbing his brow. "I like my books and my archives. Things come to me…"

"Yes, well, we don't want them to know we're coming, do we? Two people on ornithopters will be spotted in the air long before we desire." Fiona turned to the guard station, forcing Richard to keep moving. He sounded just like her mama when it came to traveling the Book. Perhaps it was more questionable for the less adventurous. Didn't everyone want to see the Book from cover to cover?

After a quick glance at her writ, the guardhouse gave them an additional ornithopter. Fiona kept hers, as trusty as it had been all these years. It was like an old friend, and she wouldn't give it up now for a new model. She wished Gaili or Dodger were with her, but she knew they all had their parts to do here.

Richard shrugged on his ornithopter, its bulk sitting well on his tall frame. All worry was gone from his face once it was securely strapped on, replaced by a frown at Fiona.

"What are you staring at me for?" she asked as they continued away from the palace. She wanted to have as few eyes on their departure as she could manage.

"Is that going to hold up?" He nodded at her ornithopter.

"Don't talk about her like that. She'll be just fine. Never you mind." She spotted a shed that should do nicely and led them toward it. "Now we'll be miles and miles away from any sensible people when we get to Mistral. Finding a pagemark here that connects safely would take too long. It's imperative that you stay next to me since finding your way to a pagemark in Mistral from the middle of nowhere will be next to impossible."

"For me, you mean."

Fiona tilted her head and smiled weakly. She pulled the rip cord on her ornithopter and then on Richard's. "Luckily we're simply flying by time." Fiona held out her hand to Richard. He hesitated before grabbing it, his rough one pressing into hers. She felt his tremor and gave his hand a squeeze. "Don't worry. This is the part I'm best at. I won't let you fall."

She reached into her scarf and pulled out her favorite feather, bookmark to the page of air. Rubbing it between her fingers, she concentrated on the elemental chapter. Once she felt the correct spot, she bound herself to the page of Mistral and then to the area, an unknown pagemark, in that page. The world folded away and into blue skies. The sound of the wind pitched high. Richard clung to her hand and mumbled under his breath. While she couldn't understand the words, she agreed with the meaning. She took a step forward with him trailing behind into the unexpected gust.

The winds battered them as soon as they entered the airy page. She hadn't expected to encounter any adversity in this area of Mistral. The last time Fiona had been out this way was in search of a rumored onae colony, birdfolk of the page. It had been bright and clear, but that was many years ago. What in the dark edge had moved in?

Richard grabbed her forearm, feet dangling, a look of pure terror on his face. That look focused Fiona right up. She moved closer to him, their bodies barely inches apart, and yelled over the wind, "We'll be alright once we get out of the breeze."

"This isn't a breeze, woman, it's a maelstrom." His golden eyes were wide as he glanced around at the vast sky.

Fiona shook her head. "I promise, this is just a tickle." She put on a forced smile to ease his fright, ignoring the bits of a cloud's trail as it raced by. Taking a quick peek at her heavy pocket watch, she noted the time and then set off in the direction she clocked as the page turned. While there was no perfect way to tell distance or direction in the elemental pages, time often worked. If it took three hours or so to fly from the palace to Shade, then it would take the same amount of time in Mistral. But one place could have more air traffic than another, and that had to be accounted for. An experienced turner could do the process quickly and adjust as needed. An unread turner would likely be lost within a matter of minutes.

Gaili had mused on creating a compass for this sort of thing. Fiona would have to put in a commission for how often she was turning to Mistral to save her time or cover her tracks.

She held fast to Richard, thankful that his ornithopter was doing most of the work. For as much as they were moving in the right direction, they were continually battered by the cold, howling wind. Her curly coils tore out of her pinned style and whipped at her face. She hesitated before diving lower, trying to shake the current. If she went too low, she'd be too close to the ground when they turned the page back. But the wind was uncaring. It was as if the gusts were trying to block their way forward. Fiona stopped heading down, pulling Richard in front of her so he could hear and she could keep her direction. "Something's different about this area."

"You don't say?" The sleeves of his doublet threatened to loosen themselves as the wind continued.

Fiona pursed her lips but said nothing. He used ornithopters all the time in Rise. Why was he so tense?

He wiped his face roughly. "I'm sorry. I'm on edge but I shouldn't take it out on you."

"Well, this wind wall, if it is that, could last for hours or even days. We'll need to find a hole or turn back." Fiona looked around, trying to find a place she could push them through. If they got stuck in the middle, it could throw them completely off course. Then her only recourse would be to turn back to Spine, probably thick in the forest, and lose hours traveling to a safer pagemark. All the while they would be out of knowledge of what was happening in Rise or with the island.

Frustrated, Fiona flew closer to investigate it, letting go of Richard's hand.

"Why are you near my perfect gale?" came a windy voice above them in Aer.

"Apologies. What do you mean?" Fiona shouted back in the elemental language. She winced at her pronunciation, but she wet her lips and tried again. "Is this wind wall your doing?" Looking around, all she saw was sky. Larrakane help them if this creature was an empearalan. They had the temper of storms and the attitude of a walnut.

"My perfect gale. Don't break it, land dweller," the voice said much closer to them.

Fiona reached her hand out casually to Richard, who had turned from tremoring to glowering in the direction of the voice. He seemed to understand her meaning and interlaced his fingers with hers. His warm hand squeezed hers, drawing Fiona's attention with the familiar gesture. *Focus, you blotter.* She called out to the sky, "I wouldn't dream of it, I assure you. Will you do us the honor of letting us pass through it perhaps?"

A spiraling creature of mist and white cloud, like a whirlpool, came closer to the duo. It was barely perceptible to Fiona, but what was clear before her became hazy. She pulled Richard in tighter, wary of being separated. She hadn't encountered a creature like it before, but it was clearly a native to the page.

Well, when one encountered a stranger, it was always best to be respectful. Fiona cleared her throat. "We are happy to give you a gift if you can help us."

"What are you saying to it?" Richard whispered.

Oh, of course he wouldn't understand. Most humans didn't bother learning the languages of the Book. "I am asking for help in exchange for something."

"Gift?" the creature said, watching their interaction.

Perhaps that didn't translate so easily in Aer. "An object you might like." She shivered as its form pressed close to hers. It seemed to have absolutely no issues with personal space.

"I will intervene, if you want," Richard said, voice hesitant.

Fiona glanced at him. His face was pinched but he seemed resolute. It was the first time he hadn't assumed he should jump in and protect her. It touched her. She shook her head. "I've gotten it in hand. I asked if it wanted a gift. An object."

The creature whirled around him and beside Fiona. "Don't interfere, land dweller." A blast of cold air hit Richard, pushing him toward the wind wall.

"No, stop. He wasn't going to do anything," Fiona yelled in Aer. She thrust her hand into a thick silk pocket on her scarf, thinking of her feather plume fan, and brought it out. She unfolded it and held it out. "Here, take it."

The creature looked to Fiona and then to Richard, swirls of cloud shaking back and forth, then took the fan, its cold and transparent self covering it and lifting it away from her. The fan danced in the breeze of the creature, feathers separating and gently moving apart. It settled and the creature withdrew away, taking the cold air with it.

"I hope you like it. Now help us pass the wind please," Fiona said slowly, trying not to butcher the elemental tongue.

"I'll help you pass, land dweller."

Thank Larrakane. Fiona gripped Richard's hand, pulling him back toward her. "Hold on to me."

With a restrained nod, he squeezed her hand tight and wrapped his other around her waist.

A strong blast of wind came from behind them, and Fiona gasped. The force of it directly into her back could've been painful, but a cold bubble of air encased them. They were pushed rapidly by the gale into the wind wall. The sky blurred past in strips of azure.

Fiona panicked and pulled her rip cord, then Richard's quickly In a gale like this the ornithopters would be ripped to pieces if they were still going. She wanted to shut her eyes but didn't dare for worry of losing her sense of direction. The heavy blast pushed them past the wind wall and hurtled them through the sky. After a few minutes it abruptly stopped. She quickly pulled her rip cord again as her stomach dropped. Richard clung to her waist.

"Pull your cord," she said frantically.

His weight leveled out as the ornithopter pulled him back up. "I'd really enjoy land again," he muttered. He rubbed his face with his free hand. "But if I'm going to be wind tossed, at least, well, you're quite the adventurer aren't you?"

Fiona sighed and pulled out her pocket watch. It had been an hour since they started, but she frankly had no idea where they were. In the right direction, sure, but the blast may have pushed them past Shade for all she knew. It felt as if they had been thrown from a moving carriage. "There's no help for it. We're going to have to turn back and see where we are."

"Even if we're not in the right place, forget about coming back here."

Fiona winced. "Usually this is my favorite place to take people."

Richard looked at her wide eyes and then chuckled with a snort. "If this is your favorite page, I'd hate to go where you loathe."

Despite her frustration with the situation, Fiona laughed. "Come on then." She held tight to her ornithopter and Richard's hand, using it to turn the page to Rise. After a few moments of concentration, the vignette of Mistral folded away from them to reveal Rise's deep-black night sky.

"Well, the good news is we haven't blown past Shade from what I can tell." Richard said confidently. He started to fly closer to the land mass beneath them.

Fiona raised an eyebrow. He was extremely good at telling from this height. She followed him down. "What's the bad news then?"

"Bad news? Why does there have to be bad news?" he said as they landed on a bridge. He shrugged off the ornithopter and folded it up, stashing it in his satchel.

Fiona looked at the easy fold with envy as she shifted her ornithopter's weight on her back. "People don't normally start good news without bad news following it."

"Ah. Well, the bad news is now we must get to the facilities, investigate, find heavy evidence, and not be discovered."

"We already knew that," Fiona said. They moved away from the bridge and hurried toward the side of the road where the trees could give them cover. Their feet stuck in the mud as they trudged through the thicket.

"Yes, but you wanted the whole tin, so I gave it to you."

"Has anyone ever told you how odd you are?" Fiona said gruffly. Now that they were in the trees she relaxed a little.

The Hawkports would still be at the palace or at their manor, the airship workers in their homes. Simply the mass of guards like the other facility to watch out for then.

"Has anyone ever told you you're nosy?" Richard answered back. He glanced at her and smirked. "Nosier than a turnip, as my mother used to say."

"And the oddness roars back to the front again." Fiona dusted her hands off and began stalking through the trees. Of course she was nosy. What proper investigator wasn't? And usually people who didn't have secrets were amiable to small, peppered questions. With the right meal of course. She turned to him to say just as much, but he was nowhere to be seen.

"Richard," she whispered. "Where are you?" In the darkness all there was were trees and the shifting of the forest. She took steps back toward the road. "Richard," she hissed.

"Calm down or the whole world will know we're here," Richard said from near her feet.

What Fiona had simply taken as another pile of leaves was moved back to reveal a cellar-like door at the base of a tree. It wasn't made of wood, cut, and dyed, but more as if the tree itself had decided to build a hidey-hole. It was cleverly hidden. Richard was standing within, looking up at her with a wide grin.

"What are you doing?" Fiona said, taken aback.

"Finding a tunnel entrance. There are miles of tunnels within these islands." He tilted his head. His face creased as he paused and he tugged at his beard. "But don't go telling the whole Book about it."

"I'm nosy, not a gossip," Fiona said as she started down the dark stairs. It was a tight fit as she brushed past him on the way in. He felt warm and solid to her, and she hurried past, pushing herself up against the wall. Roots poked from the packed earth and snagged her clothes as she got to a small landing. The tunnel carried on, wider than she expected. A wheeled cart stood in an antechamber but otherwise there was no sign of previous use, dirty as it was.

Richard closed the door, the only sound the creaking of the steps as he came down them.

"How'd you know there were tunnels in the island?" Fiona said. She motioned for him to get ahead of her.

"Well, it pays to have friends in low places too." Richard took the lead, pulling out a candle to light. "Not every island has deep tunnels, mind you, but this one, the Plateau, Forlorn, and of course Middle Market has them."

"What do you mean of course Middle Market?"

"You can't have a proper market without tunnels." Richard waved his hand. "I thought your pirate friend would've taught you that."

"Henrietta is not just a pirate. She's quite the captain and experienced skimmer," Fiona said hotly. "And how do you even know she's a pirate?"

Richard sighed and turned around. "It's not hard to pick up the pieces if you know where to listen."

"You have spied on me!" Fiona poked his arm.

"As you have done me. No doubt checking my background. Find anything interesting?" Richard asked, staring into the dimly lit passage, his voice a touch frustrated.

Fiona paused before saying, "Only that you've had your fair share of loss. I'm sorry."

Richard fumbled for a moment but began walking again. "It was a long time ago. Do not worry on my account."

Fiona was silent. She didn't know Richard well, but it was clear he was more than the sum of his parts. A widowed spy. A historian. A gruff and terse man. But so young. So golden eyed. What had happened to make him hot and cold? She found herself speaking up in the quiet. "I lost my father when I was thirteen years old. Before I was inked. It's been quite hard for my mother and I to reconcile our differences without our playful arbitrator."

"Your mother seems like a formidable woman."

Fiona snorted. "That she is. She always wants what's best for me, but best in her eyes is simply unreachable."

"Perhaps she wants what's best because she didn't get the opportunity to have the best."

"She had me and my father. That should've been enough." She was surprised she had actually said what she felt out loud to him.

"Maybe she misses him so much she can't stand to see you not have the same too."

Fiona bit her lip. "Perhaps." Her mother wasn't warm in the way mothers should be. In the way Mac was when she grew up on Spine. She was pushy, and that pushiness was always directed at Fiona. "I always thought if I had a sibling we all would've fared better. We could've split the duties and feelings of Mama equally. And if I was still inked and they were not, then my sibling could've stayed home while I went off. Maybe Mother would be too busy getting them married off instead of me."

"Not all siblings work as well as that," Richard said, his voice gruff. He sped up a little.

Curiosity pricked by his reaction, Fiona said, "Have you any siblings?"

There was a pause before Richard said, "I did."

"Oh? Did you two get along?"

"No."

Fiona felt she had done something to regain his terseness but beyond her normal inquisitiveness. She decided to move to a safer topic. "So exactly where does this lead out then?"

"Do you mean to say you've been following me but without any idea of where?" Richard said, his voice tinged with humor.

She rolled her eyes. "If you're leading me into some sort of trap, that would be a grave mistake on your part, for I do not disappear lightly." She wiped dirt off her face and said quietly, "But I trust that you know what you're doing."

Richard grunted. "Instead of stomping down the long roads or through the forest, this tunnel will take us to the other side of their facilitates. Well, one of the openings will. Closer to the docks."

"And from there light steps and darkness should cover us." Fiona nodded.

"Yes." He trudged on in the dim light.

Fiona lapsed into silence, a rarity for her. She didn't know why, but pushing Richard until he broke his terseness felt wrong right now. They traveled on in the underground tunnel as it began to narrow. They walked close past spidery runoff passageways until Richard took a turn. There were steps leading up to a dark door.

Richard blew out the candle and stuffed it in his bag. Climbing the stairs, he pushed on the door hard but fell through when it gave way easily. He cursed under his breath, the same unknowing language he seemed to use when frustrated.

Up through the cellar doors, lantern light flooded the room and into the passageway. It wasn't quite the cover of darkness they were hoping for.

RICHARD QUICKLY SCRAMBLED BACK into the cellar and pushed Fiona farther down the tunnel away from the light. "Someone's up there working."

"At this time of morning?" Fiona pinched the bridge of her nose. "Are you sure it's not a guard?"

"No. I can hear the bang of a hammer." He turned to look at her, golden eyes flashing in the bright light. "Guards are easy to deal with. They look for trouble. It's the workers who'll get all spooked and make a mess of things."

Fiona moved toward the lit open doorway, skirting around Richard. "Perhaps they won't notice us if it's simply a few. We can be quick."

"Not notice us?" Richard stepped into her way, hands moving to grasp her shoulders. He stilled and dropped them. "We're not exactly easy to ignore. You with your wool stockings all the way up to your—" He motioned to her waist and doublet.

"All the way to my what, Richard?" Fiona tilted her head.

"Ornithopter," he ground out. "That's quite obvious we're not workers."

"Alright, alright. I grant you that." She shrugged off the contraption and set it against the wall. "Look, I was in the other facilities only yesterday. There's a room for workers' uniforms and the like. If we can make it there we can dress appropriately."

Richard tugged on his beard. "It's not a terrible plan. But if they notice us, let me talk to them first."

"Why, because you're more charming than me?" Fiona smiled wide, happy he was back to normal—grumpy and demanding.

Richard grunted and waved his hand for her to follow.

Fiona made a deliberate sigh but walked quietly beside him. There was a faraway sound of wood hitting metal from somewhere within the workshop. Peeking out her head, she saw that they had come around to a sign-in bay, usually where captains let off passengers and someone signed them in and escorted them to awaiting carriages. There was a worker—early to rise, apparently—repairing one of the dock stations. Near them was the exit out into the wider facilities.

"Distraction A," Fiona whispered as she reached into her scarf and pulled out her new slingshot. She clumsily searched for a rock around her as she watched the worker. "I need something to throw."

"What?" Richard said, glowering into the distance.

"Oh, never mind," Fiona said, exasperated. She didn't want to part with anything on her person, but she reasoned that it needed to be something innocuous in case anyone found it. Taking off her heavy pocket watch, she secured it in the sling. "Move to the side."

Richard quickly did as suggested. Fiona pulled back and shot the watch past the worker.

It landed with a loud clatter on the ship the worker was nearest. His head immediately went up, like a gopher from its hole, and he scurried to see what the commotion was about.

"Well done that," Richard said.

"Let's hope no one finds it."

They ran from the stairs and across the bay to the only door in sight. Fiona grabbed the handle, but it was locked. She cursed under her breath and quickly pulled out her lock-picking tools, bending to get to work.

Richard was only a step behind her but abruptly moved back.

"What are you doing?" Fiona said.

"He's coming back already. I'll cover for you. Apparently next time you'll have to sling several watches."

She worked quickly to get the tools into the lock, taking a shallow breath to calm her nerves. She cringed at the thought of Richard knocking the poor man out and hoped he would be gentle about it.

The worker plodded back to his area and stopped. "Ho, who are you?" he called out toward them.

"I lost my pocket watch and came to check my ship. No worries, though, I've found it now and will be on my way. No *need* to worry about it," Richard said confidently.

Fiona almost dropped her tools at the absurd story. She almost dropped them again when the worker said, "Right. Glad you could find it then." His booted feet tapped on the wooden boards as he walked away.

The door clicked and she quickly crawled through. Richard followed and closed the door, locking it behind them.

"What was that story?" Fiona said as she rose from the ground. "I could've worked up a better one half asleep."

"It was a simple lie told to someone who wanted to believe they wouldn't have to worry about something bad happening. Luckily your slightness made it easy to hide you." He motioned to her form.

Fiona frowned, noticing his eyes wouldn't meet hers. Had he known the man? Is that why it was so easy? As a spy he would have all sorts of codes with people. Perhaps that was one of them. She wanted to ask more questions but not when they were skulking around. "Fine. For now. This way." She waved at a darkened hallway. The wood floors creaked lightly beneath their steps as they carried on into the facilities and away from the dock.

The moon cast dim light through the warehouse's high windows. They kept to the shadows, ears strained for any sign of the guards. Though Fiona swore anyone with the slightest hearing would hear their loud breathing, no one came running to apprehend them. There were the faint sounds of rhythmical footsteps, someone pacing perhaps. At the end of a long passageway, a hallway branched off, lined with closed doors. Fiona gestured to Richard, and they crept toward it, pausing at each intersection to check for guards. A certain mixture of trembling anxiety and excitement bubbled in Fiona. Richard had been keeping up with her step by step. She didn't need to worry about him talking too loudly or fidgeting. Was this what working with someone else in your field was like?

Halfway down the hall, echoing footsteps approached. Fiona pulled Richard into a dark alcove, and they pressed against the wall, scarcely breathing as the footsteps drew nearer. Richard's golden eyes focused on her. Her breath hitched, stilling. The warmth between them grew immeasurably. Her heart beat loudly to her senses. The guard passed, lantern light in hand, and continued on, seemingly unaware of the two hidden in the darkness. The warmth vanished, Richard quickly moving out into the hallway as the guards' footsteps faded. He glanced back at Fiona and then away again.

Fiona took a small breath and stepped into the hallway, following after him. *What was that?* For a moment everything seemed to settle into place. Like turning the page back to Spine after a long day away. She shook her head. She was imagining things. Perhaps without others to watch over, she was becoming the fanciful distracted one.

They continued down the hall, stopping at each door to peer through cracks and keyholes. The next door revealed neat rows of wooden cubbies. After checking for occupants, Fiona and Richard slipped inside. They moved quickly to the wardrobe, finding simple uniformed trousers, shirts, and overalls.

"These will do nicely," Fiona whispered. She pulled a set of overalls from the cubby, unwilling to think about changing in front of Richard. She found herself staring at his broad back as he slipped off his doublet and into a pair of overalls himself. *Focus, Fiona.*

Richard kept watch as she finished pulling on the uniform. With more confidence than before, they slipped out of the room and softly closed it.. Fiona led, her memory of the other facility and the signage pointing them to the owner's office. It was a much larger warehouse than the one on Smallcrest with higher windows, wider passages, and more closed rooms. Perhaps much of the family worked out of this office. She found what she was looking for, the Hawkport private offices. Fiona made quick work of the lock while Richard kept eyes to the hallway corner, obscuring her from view. They slipped inside and closed the door. Fiona relaxed against it for a moment and sighed.

The office was large with several desks held within. It was clear that one was for an assistant, tidier and small, while the other two were large and covered in papers, books, an inkpot, and more. Richard wasted no time waving her toward the center desk. He settled in to look out, ear pressed to the door.

Fiona took her cue and began systematically scanning through the desk files. Quickly she realized this was Lord Hawkport's desk. There were quite a few shipment orders with his name scrawled on them in a stack to one side. Unreviewed ones stacked in another. Beyond the orders for minor parts, route schedules for the various airships were splayed out on the desk. He must've been viewing them very recently. They covered many of the ships leading to and from the Plateau. The airships given to the Queen for use. A priority for him to have his eye on, no doubt.

A large desk calendar lay underneath the piles. Fiona flipped through the calendar, looking for anything amiss on the dates or names that drew her attention, but found none. At the back of the calendar, however, she found airship route schedules pressed in between months long past. Next to certain ship captains' names were the initials *PT*.

"Look at this," she whispered, holding up a route schedule. "It's a duplicate route to the ones posted up in the docks and on the desk. Who has those initials?" She ran through the list of nobles in her head but came up with nothing.

"Perhaps it's not a person but persons. Page turner?" Richard raised an eyebrow.

"It's all for the same airships too." Though the captains seemed to cycle through different airships, whenever they were combined with one of the PT ships, it denoted it. "Strange. Why would they mark that page turners were on board?"

Richard frowned. "Let's get to those ships and find out."

They hurried from the office back to the docks, encountering no guards or interference on the way. Fiona thought it odd, but perhaps there was a shift change about to take place. The first few airships they came across were not marked *PT* on the route schedule. They hurried on farther away from the dock and public area where they finally found one of the marked airships.

Richard stared up at the bottom of the ship, squinting, and then bounded toward it.

Without waiting, Fiona followed after him. What had he seen?

He crept quickly up the gangplank, wood creaking beneath his feet. Fiona followed, marveling at how eerie it looked, empty of all people and in the twilight hours of morning.

Richard moved expertly around the deck of the ship, seeming to know his way quite clearly. He opened a hatch and descended.

Fiona thrust her frustration at Richard's lack of communication to the side for a moment and descended as well into the empty ship's belly. They reached the bottom compartment, the room stretching out from them into small passageways and other passenger rooms. This was a cargo ship, smaller than the type that ferried skimmers back and forth from the pagemarks. It was silent as Fiona looked in the small rooms, making sure they were alone. Crates stacked on crates and boxes filled the storage hold. "What did you see, when we were down below?"

Richard paced. "There were holes at the bottom. They shouldn't be there."

"You seem to know a lot about airships," Fiona said.

Richard tugged on his beard. "Yes, well, I used to be a mechanic for them."

"And you're just now bringing this up?" She couldn't quell the suspicion inside that Richard wasn't being entirely honest with her. He had no cause to bring it up before, but he was able to deduce an issue with the ship just by a glance! As if he had known it would be there.

"It was a long time ago and it doesn't matter one hair." He paced the center passageway but stopped and frowned at her. "Does it?"

"It doesn't," Fiona said, tossing the matter aside. It came back to her just as quickly. "I simply like to know if a person is lying to me or not. I thought we were working well together but—"

Richard strode over to Fiona, but he stopped, seemingly reluctant to tower over her at this moment. He shook his head. "We are working well together. I used to work on airships. I used to do a lot of things before I became a historian. Some of it matters but a lot of it doesn't." He stopped and gestured as if he didn't seem to know how to go on.

Fiona's agitation subsided, and she sighed realizing she was being so unlike herself. What had gotten in to her to distract her so? She looked around the space. "Where exactly are these holes?"

Richard strode to the middle of the storage hold. "Here. But there's nothing to indicate what they would be."

She looked around the cabins and noticed that a thin rail ran around the hold but not within the cabins. It was much like the rail on Captain Henrietta's ship. Pushing a crate to the side, Fiona ran her hands under the railing until she found what she was looking for: a latch. She flicked it open. "This is one thing my captain friend taught me. When hauling goods, it's best to have another hold."

A door opened from one of the crates. Inside, a rope ladder was tied to the top. They unfurled it and climbed down into the secret compartment. It was large and empty with an unpleasant odor in the room that Fiona couldn't place.

Richard inspected the space, running his hands along the inner wooden wall that met with the floor toward the front of the airship.

Fiona walked around the room, its sticky slick floor puzzling her. There was thick rubber on the portholes as well as the seams of the ship. She had seen these many times before on the large ships used for skimmers to tour underwater in the Depths. Those were seals.

"This isn't right. The hull's been reinforced here." He knelt and pushed on the floor, revealing two large openings and what appeared to be metal tubes with many holes. "What in the—what are these?"

She bent next to him and rubbed her hands lightly over the surface, drops of water clinging to her dry gloves. The holes weren't perfectly circular but large enough. They reminded her of her childhood and the trickle irrigation on the farms. "These can release water into the chamber."

"Why would you want to fill the chamber of a ship with water? It would make it heavy." Richard frowned, rubbing his own hand over it.

Fiona ran a finger across the floor, feeling the liquid here, too, was warm water, though with a slight texture to it. She channeled her inner Gaili and licked her finger timidly. Salty. Not from the rivers of Rise then. That could only mean one thing. "A page turner could turn the page to the Shimmering Depths and fill this room. With the seals, it would stay full." It was a little-known fact that the lake in Spine operated under the same principle. Even she'd had to work her way into that information.

"Until they opened the irrigation compartments..." Richard continued.

"...flooding the land as the ship passes by. Endless covering rain." Fiona met Richard's gaze. "They've been using this to hide the Painted Edge's activities."

Richard nodded. "This, this is proof that even that slimy Hawkport can't refute. The damage reports, the floods. It's been him. All along." He stopped and clutched his chest. His eyes widened and he jumped up from the floor running to the hatch.

Fiona shouted, "Richard what's wrong?" and followed quickly after him.

They raced back to the top. The twilight sky had lightened up considerably since they had gone below. Richard halted on the deck, staring into the sky. "Oh, oh no."

Fiona gasped. A massive isle of earth towered over the island. Where once Shade was level with the Plateau, it was now far below it. "What happened?"

"The islands. They're sinking."

RICHARD UNFOLDED HIS ORNITHOPTER from his bag quickly. "We have to stop them. Now."

"How can the islands be sinking?" Fiona took his arm. Sinking! If they continued on, they'd move past the cloud lines in less than a day. And then what? Fall into the endless ocean never to be seen again. Various legends, teachings, and fables from ancient civilizations had warned of the ocean below the clouds being worthless and monstrous. Those who'd scoffed and flown down never returned. "It must be because of the missing island. The Guardian must've been taken with it. It's the only reason the page would fall apart." Like when the Blackstone was taken from Blaze.

Richard pulled the rip cord on his ornithopter. "Let's have the questions on the way to the palace shall we?"

Far off, a door banged open, making Fiona seize up. Hawkport guards rushed through and spread out around the dock like tiny ants searching. They had to have been alerted to them being here. There were so many, more than she suspected had been in the building.

Fiona reached to pull her rip cord but realized she had left her ornithopter in the tunnel. "I have to find another one." Surely there were some on board in case of emergency.

"There's no time," Richard whispered as he pulled her down and crouched below the deck wall.

Fiona staggered to the floor and shook her head. "You run to the Queen. Tell her what we found and have Hawkport seized at once."

Richard rubbed his face. "No, I won't leave you to be taken by his guards."

She thrust the airship schedules into his hands and squeezed them. "You most certainly will. One of us has to get away. And you know the Queen personally." Fiona pushed his shoulder, ignoring the drop in the pit of her stomach. "Go, you stubborn man."

He glanced toward the side of the ship at the searching guards and frowned. "I'll at least try to distract them while you hide. Please, run away to Spine as soon as you can." He sprang up, ran to the bow of the ship, and took off into the air.

There were shouts but Fiona wasted no time in watching him leave. She crawled to the corners of the deck, looking for another ornithopter or a way to hide herself. Finding nothing, she wedged herself into a slim space between crate and hull as the stomping of feet came nearer on the gangplank.

"He took off from this ship. Tell the others to get in the air and after him. I'll search for the investigator."

How had they known she specifically was there? Richard had hidden her from the dock worker, and they hadn't encountered the guards while searching around. The only person she had told, written to more like, about going to Hawkport's was Henrietta, and even that had been in the vaguest terms. Fiona cursed internally. Of course, why wouldn't Hawkport have spies at the palace? They clearly had them as couriers and messengers. Hawkport knew her moves as soon as she sent them back and forth. Foolish of her not to have delivered the note through trusted means. He had probably been following her all along, but why?

The footsteps drew nearer. Fiona pressed herself as small as she could and said a silent wish to Larrakane to simply let her have this hidden moment.

Alas, Larrakane seemed bound to ignore her. A guard jerked her up, his hand roughly grabbing the neck of her doublet, ripping it as he pulled her out of the corner. "How could I miss someone as lovely as you in a corner?"

Fiona knew her strength was inadequate to fight the guard, but she wasn't going to be so easy to take. She mustered up every visage of her mother and shouted, "Let me go, you blotter, or you'll be hearing about this from the Queen directly."

The guard's eyebrows furrowed and he hesitated.

"Release the lady. *She* isn't important," Richard's voice boomed behind her.

The guard immediately released her and took a step back. Richard swooped in, grabbing her by the waist. Fiona held on to him tight as he took off down the side of the ship. He navigated up through the small gap between the isles. As they moved past the rocky surroundings, it was clear that more than just Shade had been sinking. Smallcrest was almost parallel to the other isle.

"This is madness. An ornithopter can't bear both our weights," Fiona said, holding on tightly.

"No madder than me leaving you there to find yourself in Hawkport's hands," Richard said quietly.

"You hadn't needed to rescue me," Fiona said. Though she wasn't too put out he had come back for her, she did have a plan.

"I wasn't rescuing you." Richard sighed. With some reluctance he said, "I was rescuing me."

Clinging to him, Fiona's hand spanned Richard's back as his firm grip held on to her. His heart was pounding quickly. Fiona's face warmed as she couldn't do anything more than press herself to him, her face nestled on his shoulder. "That doesn't even make sense."

"Aye. Nothing does with you, blasted woman," he muttered.

"Richard—"

The whooshing of a gaining airship stopped her words. Hawkport-emblazoned and slimmer than a passenger ship, it was speeding right toward them.

Richard grunted. "That'll be the reinforcements."

Was Lord Hawkport with them? Fiona didn't dare move to look at the ship closely. "We can't lose them at this rate. Ornithopters can't win a race against an airship."

"Listen to me, Fiona," Richard said as he maneuvered them closer to the Plateau, presumably to make it harder for their chasers. "Do not try to reason with them."

"Why would I reason with them?" Of all the times to be giving her orders, he was picking now. Ridiculous.

"I simply mean, don't try and talk your way out of this. Once we're on the ship, just keep your head down. I'll find a way to get you time till you can go back to Spine."

"I can't—"

"That's our only chance. You turn to Spine and you go straight to the Binder."

Fiona worried her lip. She wouldn't be able to turn the page on a moving airship. He didn't understand. The ship rose beneath them rapidly, swallowing them like a fish caught by a giant whale. Guards grabbed them, jerking off Richard's 'thopter and tossing it overboard.

The guards bundled them down into the hold, stuffing them into a small room. They bound Fiona's hands with turn stoppers. The metal warmed instantly on her wrist, like a kettle just heated. Nausea swamped her, and she rested with her head against the hull of the airship. She needed to focus on something, anything to push away the sickness she felt as the manacles severed her senses from the wider Book.

"So," she began lightly trying to compose herself, "what is the plan then?"

"We'll we're confronting Hawkport, for one thing. I knew he was a rat, but this is worse than that. Endangering our people," Richard said, jaw clenching.

He was much too focused on Hawkport. Her mind tried to understand why, but it was hard. "And then? How do we escape?" Fiona shook her head but stopped. The nausea was too much. She closed her eyes and breathed deeply.

His rough hand grabbed hers. "You look sweaty. What is it?"

She raised her manacled hands weakly. "Turn stoppers. Cutting off my senses from the Book."

Richard hooked his fingers underneath the manacles and tried to pull them away, but they were fastened tight.

Fiona shook her head. "It'll lighten soon, or so I'm told. Focus. If we can't get to the Queen, we have to get them to take us to the island. It must be the key to what's happening.

If we can get to the island, all hope isn't lost. Returning the Blackstone fixed Blaze."

Richard said nothing but reluctantly let go of her hand. He swallowed, tense.

Fiona bit her lip but couldn't help saying, "Richard. You know more than you're telling me. What is it? What are you so afraid of?"

"I don't keep quiet because I want to. I have duties… I have to answer to her."

Fiona sighed. "The Queen is ridiculous but powerful. I know. I want you to trust me, but I understand how hard it is to trust after working alone for so long. Doing your own thing your own way. It takes time. But if there's anything I can do so we can solve this together, I'm willing to do it. I care about the Book, and that includes Rise. It includes the home where I grew up and the people who are still here. I may be a page turner, but I'm also human."

It was quiet, no sound but the whooshing of wind as the airship flew rapidly, disregarding all proper flight requirements. Fiona's chest tightened and her body felt heavier and heavier as the seconds passed by. She had been as stubborn as he was not too long ago. But with patience and care from others she had learned that trust was a many-faceted thing. Would Richard be able to trust her enough to let her help? How could she continue to show him she could? Though she wanted to know more, she wouldn't press. In her own way, it was all she could do. She did, however, make a plan. "Once we get to Hawkport, we must be convincing. We must get him alone so we can determine his motive. Understand what we can offer him that the Painted Edge hasn't." Fiona opened her eyes and leaned into Richard. "We need to divide and conquer them."

Richard nodded but said nothing else, a pensive look on his face. The ship shuddered to a stop, landing. Guards came for them and pulled them outside onto the ship deck and down the docks. They were back at the Hawkport facilities. Why come back here? Instead of going through the facility entrance, they dragged them around the side to a smaller, nondescript door. Fiona couldn't believe it had been less than a couple of hours since they had broken into Hawkport facilities in the first place.

The room was barren of furniture, but the tracks through the dust from door to door told a story of a heavily used area. A window looked out to a private dock area where an airship was landing. The Hawkport insignia was painted delicately on the hull, but beneath it was a second insignia, that of the Queen. This had to be the family ship.

Fiona tried to open the window, but it didn't budge. The guards had stepped back and created a perimeter from the airship dock and the doorway. From the gangplank of the airship strode Lord Henry Hawkport still wearing his golden king costume. He shouted something back toward the airship before being directed toward Fiona and Richard.

The door swung open, and Lord Hawkport began clapping as he entered. "Excellent work, all. Truly." He closed the door and bowed to Richard and Fiona. "We meet again, Sir Mourninghide. Mistress Thornbeard."

"Hawkport," Richard ground out. "Can't you see what you've done?"

"What I've done?" Hawkport pointed at himself, laughing. "Isn't that the kettle? You and the Queen have done more than enough. You and all the monarchy."

"You want power," Fiona said, ready to enact her plan. "So you work with the Painted Edge to get it. What did they promise you?"

"Fiona," Richard hissed under his breath, "stop."

"No, no, Richard, let the woman speak. It sounds like she has quite the view of things." Hawkport waved his hand as if giving her permission. "Go ahead, dear."

Fiona licked her lips and stood up taller. "Whatever the Painted Edge has promised you, they won't go through with it. They let their own go to prison once. Why wouldn't they do it again?"

"Ah." Hawkport nodded. "Yes, the smugglers you captured, correct? Well, I certainly think they are a little lower in the food chain than someone like myself. But I am open to hear what you're offering." He looked her up and down. "Yes, I can see why John likes you. You are more than a distraction, aren't you?"

"Stop ogling the woman, farm boy, and let us go. You *needn't* worry about us."

Hawkport smiled at Richard. "Fascinating. She said a promise was powerful, but she didn't say how effective it would be." He strode to Richard and grabbed his face, bringing him closer. "I have my price, and all I had to do was nothing more than I already do."

"The islands are sinking!" Fiona moved toward Henry, but Richard reached out, interceding between them. "If they continue, everyone will be lost below the clouds."

"Well,"—Hawkport tilted his head—"not everyone. The Plateau stays, you see. I've already started offering travel from all the counties to the Plateau on my ships. For free, of course."

"The Rise will be decimated. People's lives destroyed. What would be the point?"

"Oh dear, I thought you would understand." Hawkport leaned toward her but kept his hand on Richard's face. "The Rise won't be decimated. It will be saved! And in the new world, I will be one of the greats. King Henry Hawkport, the man who made everyone fly."

"Surely even the airships need more than your thoughts to fly. Fuel? Parts? All that will be sunk as well." Millions of people couldn't cram onto the Plateau. They would be displaced throughout the Book. "We have to get people out of Rise."

"Oh no, no. We can't have humans scampering off. No one is leaving the page." Hawkport waved to the surrounding area with a flourish. "So enjoy being back home."

"It's happening all over again," Richard muttered to himself. "It can't. It can't right?" He turned to Hawkport. *"You need to release us at once and take us to the tower."*

There was a buzz of energy in the air, crackling like lightning. Fiona grasped her head and ducked, unsure of where the energy was coming from, but it never hit her. She looked up to see Richard staring open-mouthed at Hawkport.

Hawkport, for his part, laughed, a wide grin on his face. "Oh, you should see your face, old man. It is good to see you taken aback."

"How are you like each other?" Richard said, staring at Fiona. "Why doesn't it work?"

"Why doesn't *what* work?" Fiona yelled, then took a deep breath, the nausea threatening to overwhelm her. Quieter, she said, "Richard, please enlighten me as to what in the name of Larrakane is going on." Fiona placed her manacled hands on his shoulder. "You can count on me."

But he said nothing, a pained expression etched on his face.

"This old codger won't explain. He's a liar through and through." Lord Hawkport shook his head and leaned against the door, smug.

"Hold your tongue," Richard said sharply.

Fiona gritted her teeth and willed herself to stop focusing on the nausea. In the back of her mind, she let herself connect the dots she had been keeping apart. He always knew when there was trouble with the islands. It seemed to pain him each time as if he was feeling it keenly, not simply because he felt it was his duty to care. And there was no reason a historian was so close to the Queen. A spy, yes, but he hadn't wanted to report what he knew to her, he wanted to go directly after Lord Hawkport and to the island. Even though he had no power over Hawkport. But he was confident he could make him talk. Why wouldn't he be? She had seen him do it several times already. Only someone of immense power could make people do what they want. And for once in her life, she let her affinity for someone cloud what was clearly in front of her. She turned to Richard, still wanting him to confess it himself. "Are you—"

"Don't say it," Richard ground out. He grabbed hold of her hands. "If you say it, you'll be in too deep, and I don't want you to be a part of this. For Heaven's sake stop trying to figure it out, you blasted woman."

Fiona's thoughts froze at the unfamiliar word, *Heaven*, and his hold of her hands. She took a deep breath to focus. "Why won't you simply admit that you're the Guardian?"

Hawkport raised his eyebrows in a cringy smirk. "Yes, Richard, tell her why."

"Because it's my curse to bear. And no one else's," he said. He rubbed his thumb over Fiona's hand. "Can't you understand I—"

"Oh posh," Hawkport cut him off. He pushed hard against Richard's chest, breaking them apart. "How noble of you. I suppose that's why you call yourself Mourninghide, Lionheart, Brightblade. Oh *yes*, I've figured out all your aliases, you blotter." He grabbed Richard by the shoulders. "Thousands and thousands of people have to deal with the mistakes you made, but absolutely, make it all about yourself. I've had enough of this."

"Don't say another thing," Richard said.

Hawkport leaned forward, his face inches from Richard. "You may have given us wings, but you are not my keeper. I am a Hawkport. I fly where I want." Hawkport called to Fiona, eyes still trained on Richard, "This righteous old bastard called my family to his service. Can you believe that? Larrakane gave him the tools to make ships fly around this page, and instead of doing the work he was tasked with, he elevated my family and pressed us into duty."

"Richard and Larrakane gave you the power to make airships?" Why was that part of being a Guardian? The islands had always been separate and floating. Why did Larrakane only grant flying ships when the Inking occurred?

"Yes, the way to make them has been in the family for two centuries now. Funny thing is we can't remember how fast enough to bloody well write it down. My eldest, me, my father, his mother—we all have to put the finishing touches on *every single airship*. It's most peculiar. Alone, we are powerful. Watched, we are nothing. Do you know how frustrating it is to not be able to capitalize on your good fortune? Hmm? To have to increasingly satisfy such an aggravating monarch like the Queen? To be stuck under the servitude of someone who wants to hide away in his little hole reading books and pretending he doesn't exist?"

Richard scoffed. "Servitude? As if you aren't just under the servitude of someone else now."

"At least this warden gives me control."

Fiona leaned against the wall, too weak to remain standing on her own. She let her mounting frustration clear her head. She had to keep asking questions, keep this going till she could come up with a plan to get them out of this. "Why, Richard? Why are you still lying about being the Guardian? Why are you hiding it at all!?"

Richard closed his eyes. "I don't have any fight left in me."

"First truthful thing I've heard you say." Hawkport sighed, contented. He glanced out the window and nodded. "Ah, looks like cousin Bunny is ready for us. You to her and me to the palace!"

Fiona glanced out the window to Hawkport's nod but uttered a curse shocked. Waiting on the gangplank was none other than Sadie Stoneguard. Fiona took a step from the window's view. Was that really her?

"How do you know Sadie?"

Hawkport raised an eyebrow, "Sedhare, you mean? Cousin Bunny was inked a little over a year ago. She's more homesick than most of you lot. Brighter too." Hawkport tugged Richard's manacles and pulled him out of the room with a force that surprised her.

"Don't come after me," Richard called back to Fiona, voice trembling.

She had to warn him about Sadie. "Richard, listen to me, I—"

Hawkport cut her off. "Don't worry, she won't be able to come after you for some while, old man." He nodded to a guard, who entered the small room and pulled Fiona away from the window to the other exit. Fiona jerked away, fighting to go after Richard, who cowed as Sadie pulled him into the airship.

THE GUARD DRAGGED FIONA through the other doorway and down a flight of steps to a cellar. She fought him every step of the way, demanding he let her go. He seemed cold to her appeals, and not for the first time Fiona wondered how many people were normal Schiflan citizens and how many were Painted Edge members around her. He swapped her turn stoppers for ones with thick chains and thicker manacles. The nausea and fogginess effect that had lightened considerably came back with full force. It felt as if she had run into a stone wall. Were these more potent than the Travel Guild ones? How dangerous would they be if left on her for a long time? Surely Hawkport wouldn't keep her here forever.

The cellar door closed, leaving Fiona alone in the dark. Her mind wandered. She hoped her mother was okay. She would be worried sick, as it had been hours since Fiona had sent word. Hopefully Henrietta took the temperature wherever they were and would get them both out of Rise if the danger increased.

The palace wasn't safe with everything going on, and Lord Hawkport would surely be after the Queen in no time. With a sinking in her stomach, Fiona realized that if he'd intercepted her note, there was no way Henrietta or her mother even knew she had taken off with Richard. They might assume her to still be in Spine.

What had Richard meant about her being like Hawkport? Why would he think something so idiotic? Well, the power he had, or whatever he was wielding, didn't seem to work on her. Not that his other charms did either. He was insufferable. And stubborn. She was worried most about him. What did Sadie need him for? Why was Sadie here and not on the run? Sadie and the Painted Edge, together. Fiona needed to tell Marcia, tell the Travel Guild, tell someone.

Fiona realized with a jerk that she was falling asleep. The manacles were doing more than they should. Definitely not Travel Guild–issued equipment. She needed to get them off. But how?

She drifted in and out of the haze of sleep. Her mind foggy, she forced herself to continue her questions. There was something she was forgetting, something she could do. The guards had put her in here alone. They had carried her, bunching up her doublet, looking for weapons. As she faded in and out, a memory came back to her: she'd been so excited to change clothes out of her dress and into her normal wool stockings, her scarf tied about her waist under her doublet. Her scarf wasn't a weapon, but it did hold her lock-picking tools.

Fighting the overwhelming urge to nod off, Fiona painfully maneuvered her hands down to the scarf. With great effort, she retrieved the tools and set to work picking the lock on her right cuff. It sprang open. The turn stoppers' effect lessened considerably. She shook her head and focused on the task at hand, muttering to herself about the type of coffee she was going to try and the number of baths she would allow herself when this was all over. The thick-chained turn stoppers dropped to the floor, clattering.

When no one came running, she felt along the grimy stone wall to the cellar door. What she wouldn't give for faekin eyes right now in this darkness. She bent down, rubbing her fingers against the lock, but was knocked off balance by the shuddering ground. That was new, wasn't it?

She got back up off the cold ground and carefully worked to pick the cellar door lock. Her hands shook, but she took a deep breath. As long as the rumbling was far apart, she could do this. Slowly she continued on until, with a satisfying click, she was free. She swapped her beloved tools for her new sling, then stored her scarf tighter and higher up on her body. *Let them figure out how she had escaped and scratch their heads for a while.* She opened the creaking door and began to creep upstairs, wary of any remaining guards. First one flight of stone steps and then another. The ground around her rumbled again and she grabbed onto the stone walls trying to balance. No one was running for her. Something was extremely wrong.

She pushed open the wooden door at the top of the stairs, the creaking of it loud to her ears. But there was no one around. The hallway was quiet as she made her way back to the small room. It had all been abandoned. Not a guard remained. How long had she been falling in and out of sleep? And why would they leave their posts with her captive like that? Fiona hurried to the window, watching for anyone who could stop her, and gasped at the sight: Shade had sunk farther below the Plateau. They had gone miles down at this point. No wonder it was empty.

Fiona swung between competing urges. She wanted to get back to Spine, but where would she end up at this point in the landscape? And her mother and Henrietta might still be in Rise. Were they safe? Hawkport had spoken plainly about his feelings for the Queen. Whatever he had planned on the Plateau could end badly for everyone. No, she was the only one who knew he was a danger. She had to get to the palace to warn them and then her family. With the island sinking, she required a fast way off it. Hopefully there was an airship left to see her safely. Fiona strode out the unguarded door and ran toward the docks.

She wasn't a pilot. There were the basics she learned watching others as a young girl interested in flying and what little Henrietta had taught her and Gaili over the last couple of months. It would have to do. She reached the large docks that should've been packed with people. Fiona's heart sank. Row after row of the landings were empty. The only airship left had clearly seen better days. She rubbed her temples and moved quickly to it. "It can't be as bad as it looks." She hurried to the gangplank, leaping up it as fast as she could. The wooden deck had many holes that she could slip right through if she wasn't careful. Boards peeled up as if they were old paint. The hull seemed to be scraped repeatedly by some heavy cargo, leaving it thinner than it should be. The faint smell of sheep and dung still lingered as she moved carefully about it. Clearly not a premier-class ship. Whatever it had been used for before, it had to be her friend now. She patted the ship as she had seen Henrietta do a hundred times. "I'll call you *Second Betty*."

Fiona unleashed the ropes as another rumble tore through the sinking island. It was clear that whatever was causing the islands to sink wasn't letting them fall in any sort of natural, graceful way. The sooner she got off the island, the better. She checked the gauges as the captain had taught her and moved to the steering wheel. There was not enough power for a full flight. But perhaps enough to get her in the air and seen by another ship?

She flicked and pressed and flicked and pressed, but nothing happened. "Come on, *Second Betty*. We can do this." But the ship refused to budge. Frustrated, she hit the steering wheel with her fist and kicked the pedal. The airship seemed to roar with life, the noise of it filling Fiona's ears. She glanced at the gauges, but nothing had changed. Everything was still at zero. What then was that noise?

An elegant airship crested over the side of the building and beelined toward Fiona. Its bronze and mahogany hull shone in the sun as it approached the ship, lining up side by side. A small window opened in the top cabin and Henrietta's voice rang out, "Need a lift?"

"Yes, Captain!" Fiona grinned, rushing to the side of the ship. Deckhands tossed her a rope ladder and she grabbed on, pulling herself up the rungs as best as she could. As soon as she got to the gleaming wooden deck, the ship lifted off and away from the island.

Fiona quickly made her way to the captain's cabin, where Henrietta commanded the wheel, calling out orders to prepare for a wind-throttling affair.

"How did you know I was here?" Fiona asked after hugging the captain.

Henrietta chuckled, peach cheeks reddened once again from the whipping wind of sailing. "I know how to read between the lines of your notes by now, mistress. Thought it was a bit odd that the ink was smudged and note was already opened though. I was sure you hadn't sent it like that."

Fiona sighed and paced the small cabin. "Indeed, I had not. Lord Henry Hawkport instigated this entire affair. I should've known that someone might be reading my correspondence, but I didn't think it would be him."

"That explains why those lazy barons knew they would be safe on the Rock. A Hawkport captain showed up to see them off the island, but I made sure we didn't go with them. I took your mother back to the palace and placed her in care of the Travel Guild." She squared her shoulders, standing taller.

There was a story there, for sure. "Lazy barons?"

Henrietta's nostrils flared and she shook a fist to the air as if they were right in front of her. "The most they accomplished this week was getting too sotted to properly save themselves. I'm all for a good drink but they aren't worth flying into the wind if you get my meaning. To the dark edge with them." Henrietta tugged on the brim of her small cap. "If retiring into court means I have to sit around and wait on the charity of those not fit to lead, then I was better off before. I get more done for people flying the good flag than they ever will." She moved a graying strawberry curl out of her face and grinned at Fiona. "Besides the crew on this ship deserves a good steward. They agreed to host my talents quickly enough. Isn't that right, crew?" Henrietta shouted out.

"Aye aye, Captain," said sailors just outside the doorway.

Fiona laughed and surged forward. She gave her friend's shoulder a quick squeeze. How Henrietta had gotten an entire crew of people to follow her in less than a week she could absolutely fathom. "Well, seems with a lick of paint you've got a foot into Rise and outside of it now."

Henrietta winked. "Hold on there, lass. She turns tight like you wouldn't believe."

Fiona sat in the only available seat in the cabin and allowed herself a brief moment of relief before turning her focus to her next task.

Henrietta pushed the airship for all it was worth. It should've taken half an hour at full speed to get to the palace, but with the island so far sunk it was half an hour just to get halfway up the Plateau. It seemed the island was farther west than before as well. Were they not only sinking but spreading farther from the Plateau? Why? Henrietta didn't bother trying to hide from other airships. Speed was her objective, and as they got toward the top of the Plateau, she truly shined.

With more momentum than Fiona thought any airship was capable of, they darted toward the palace grounds. Henrietta weaved in and out of the buildings, and just as it seemed they were about to crash into the air docks, she maneuvered the ship swiftly into place. "Throw out a rope, crew, and guard the *Nimble Faun* as best you can. Captain Henrietta needs a place to stash her for a bit. When it's all said and done, you'll be treated handsomely."

The crew nodded to the captain, clearly already smitten with her, and she saluted back as her and Fiona turned away from the docks and toward the palace proper.

The courtyard was choked with frightened people clutching their belongings, displaced from their swiftly sinking homes. Fiona pushed through the crowds, flashing her decree at a Travel Guild jacket.

"Find Gilded Marcia and bring her to the Low Gallery at once!" she ordered.

Fiona raced into the chaotic palace, frantically searching for her mother. She found her with Henrietta in their quarters, her mother anxiously pacing as the captain tried to calm her.

"Fiona!" her mother cried, pulling her into a fierce embrace. "My dear girl, I was sick with worry."

Fiona squeezed her mother tight. "We must go back to Spine at once, we're not safe here."

Her mother opened her mouth to argue, but the captain cut in, "The lass always speaks true. We best be on our way."

Lavinia nodded slowly, shock threatening to overcome her. She looked around the room, grabbed her gloves and squared her shoulders. "I'll follow."

With no further protest, Fiona led them swiftly to the Low Gallery. What was usually an empty thoroughfare where statues and tapestries outnumbered the guests was packed with nobles going to and from their rooms. Several were arguing with palace guards about getting their belongings to a safe location away from the displaced commoners outside the palace. Travel Guild jackets watched on from the fringes, only intervening when a situation was escalating.

Gilded Marcia arrived, pale human face tight as her short black hair was pulled into a severe—even for her—bun at the top of her head. Her back was straight as a board and her mouth set in a thin line. Among the many humans, she stood out, even if Fiona didn't know she was secretly a faekin hag in disguise. Luckily no one looked twice at her, perhaps too afraid to. Though she didn't reach the height of most jackets around her, it was clear by her very demeanor that she commanded them. "Investigator Thorne," she said curtly.

"Gilded Marcia." Fiona stepped closer to her and whispered, "Jackets are needed to guard the Queen and find Lord Henry Hawkport. He's working with the Painted Edge, and I believe he's going to do away with the Queen in the midst of the chaos."

Lavinia gasped, hand clapping to her mouth. "Fiona!"

Marcia nodded, ignoring the interruption. "At once. Anything else?"

"I've seen Sadie," Fiona said, leaning in and dropping her voice even lower, "and more importantly, I think I know where she is. I believe if we can retrieve the island and the person she took, then we can save Rise. We need to get back to Spine first."

"Then I'm coming with you," Marcia stated and raised her chin, watching her.

Fiona didn't argue. She would be glad to have Marcia's talents in search of Sadie and Richard. They needed all the help they could get. She nodded. "Glad to have you, Gilded."

Marcia wasted no time in leading them all toward the banquet chamber. It had been taken over by the Travel Guild as soon as necessary apparently. Jackets flanked every entry and exit. Rows of Travel Guild ornithopters lined tables, while other equipment spread out from wall to wall. In a matter of moments, she had given orders to many jackets, sent a coded message back to Guild headquarters, and instructed ornithopters to be given to the assembled group.

It was a strong command center run by a strong woman. Fiona was a bit relieved she wasn't fighting against Marcia and her force. Fiona put on her new ornithopter, briefly saddened about her long-standing one now living in the tunnels of Shade, and then helped her mother with hers. She muttered, "May the forests of Spine forgive us for our abrupt entry."

Marcia grinned, a wide, elusive thing. "I think we can do one better than that." She cocked her head to the Privy Garden, the largest green area on the palace grounds. It had been cordoned off and jackets stood guard blocking the entry. "We don't have time to get to an official pagemark," she said and grabbed a satchel off the table, "so we've had to make our own."

The Privy Garden was big enough to turn the page, but where would they end up? Fiona grabbed her mother's trembling hand and squeezed it reassuringly. Henrietta whispered to them both, "What a way to start another adventure."

Lavinia nodded and smiled, her shoulders relaxing a little. "I suppose it's good to be careful what you ask for, isn't it, Captain?"

Fiona frowned at the odd statement, but before she could ask any questions, Marcia grabbed her hand and Henrietta's. With no more than one breath in and one breath out, Marcia turned the page to Spine amid the manicured lawns and pink roses of the garden.

THE WORLD GAVE WAY before them to a forest below and bright blue sky around. Marcia pulled her rip cord and took a step, tugging the rest of them with her. They all followed suit and soon hovered above the army of perpetual fall trees in the unending forest.

Fiona tried to determine where exactly they were, but everywhere she turned was the same. They were truly in the thick of it. Before she could look toward the sun and figure out their position, a page turner secondhand reflex, Marcia whistled loudly, gaining their attention.

"We'll land over here," she said, pointing to a thicket of trees, "and then you can tell me where we're headed."

Fiona opened her mouth to argue, but Henrietta and Lavinia did as commanded immediately. Sighing, Fiona followed suit. "We need to go back to my home. I left Gaili and Matteo working on a way to get to Sadie." Though she hadn't known it at the time, of course. If she had, she would've focused on finding the troublemaker from the beginning with Richard someplace safe.

"Which page is it?" Marcia said. She began to rub her hands in circular motions over the bark of one trunk before moving to another and doing the same. What in the world was she doing?

"I think the time for working with the Guild has come, mistress. For better or worse." Henrietta whispered to Fiona, then helped Lavinia down through the trees.

She hadn't realized how much she had been hesitating to answer until then. Fiona nodded, unaccustomed to being so transparent with the Travel Guild. But where would secrecy get her? It didn't help Richard or Rise. "Gaili and I discovered a new page, or at least what we assume is a new page, a few months ago during the incident on Copper." She quickly went into the details of what she saw when Clara tore Copper, adding that it was her idea to keep it a secret and not Gaili's, lest the withholding of information be in some way unlawful.

Marcia squinted, her eyes turning to slits in a very unhuman manner, and she shook her head at Fiona. "You should not have kept that information from the Guild. We've had an incredibly hard time tracking them down, and it would have been better to know they may be somewhere even our spotters haven't found." Marcia leaned against the tree, her frustration with Fiona clear and making her human visage a touch more frightful than she could possibly know.

"I know you believe me selfish, but there's more than just my needs entwined with that reveal." Fiona stopped, not wanting to get further into it. They should be moving to get to the city as quickly as possible. What was Marcia waiting on? Did Fiona dare risk her temper again by asking?

In fact, what was Marcia's compulsion? Did it compare to her sister's alliteration in obfuscating her name and her penchant for riddles, or Mac's creations and her preference for never leaving the Thread?

The trees rustled as if agitated themselves at her thoughts. She shifted away from them, shaking her head. The forest didn't move. Well, it didn't stir as if it were upset, at any rate. What was going on?

From the trees strode the Elder druid, their pine-green hair windswept. Their chest rose rapidly, seemingly out of breath. How had they found them?

Marcia moved from the tree she had been leaning on and bowed to the druid. "Elder. We need to be in the turner district. At once."

The Elder turned to them, blinking with almost reptilian eyes. Or so it seemed. In a moment the odd look was gone. Fiona wondered if she had really seen anything at all.

The druid frowned, assessing the group. "So many?"

"Time is of the essence, Elder," Fiona said, shaking off her amazement and taking a step forward. "A Guardian's life is at stake. If you can get us there quickly, we can answer your questions afterward."

The Elder sprang back. "Yes, of course. We'll need a larger tree." They strode away at once.

The group followed quickly after. Fiona glanced at her mother, whose mouth had been resolutely shut the entire time, but her wild eyes told her that she was overwhelmed. She had never been in the position of comforting her mother more than she had this last week. What could she possibly say? Her work wasn't for the unread. Deep inside she knew her mother thought what she did was unusual and perhaps frivolous. To see one's home cataclysmically change, to see what people once thought impenetrable crumble around, could upset an entire worldview. What must her mother be thinking?

The Elder stopped ahead of a large spruce tree, its trunk the width of a Guild-run carriage. They placed their hands on the rough bark and spoke in a low voice. Fiona strained to hear but didn't understand the almost throat-ripping words. Before she could remark on it, the tree opened its trunk, bark peeling away like double doors, and a welcoming air of scented needles wafted toward them.

"Follow me." The Elder stepped into the tree.

Marcia waved her hand. "It's safe. Just follow."

"That's safe?" her mother said incredulously.

"As much as walking down a lane." Marcia nodded with a measure of softness to her face.

"More so, I suspect. No rippers in here, Lavinia," Henrietta said, entering first and disappearing.

Fiona was practically overflowing with questions, but she grabbed her mother's hand and pulled them both in.

Warm.

Dark.

Sleep.

They stepped out onto the edge of trees and a familiar path Fiona knew to be a short distance from her home and the edge of the turner district. The Elder was already on the path standing next to Henrietta, rocking back and forth on the balls of their feet. "Come, come. Don't stay too long."

Lavinia yawned. "My, I could use a nap."

"Yes." Fiona nodded, feeling oddly drowsy herself. "But that will have to wait."

Marcia exited and the tree closed with a resounding snap. "Joining us?" She said it with more familiarity with the druid than Fiona could quite believe. Marcia was not of the same rank as the Elder. But perhaps she had been in Rise too long. Rank wasn't everything.

"Needs must keep me away, I'm afraid. Does the Binder know?" The Elder tilted their head.

"I sent jackets to report as soon as I arrived in Rise. But the Guardian...that is new information. Will you?" Without waiting for the Elder druid to answer, she barked out, "Fiona? Where to?"

"Right," Fiona said, snapping out of watching them. She trotted toward the path. "This way."

The Elder bounced back away from the rest of the group. "Fiona, a quick word if I may," they said in a cracking voice.

She hesitated. What could they possibly have to say to her besides admonishment for going and getting the Guardian captured? Perhaps it's what she deserved. She turned to Henrietta. "Will you show them to Mistress Humbledraft, please?"

Henrietta patted her on the shoulder and led the way out of the forest, tugging Lavinia with her.

"I am sorry, for what I said a few days ago." They rubbed the edge of their ear, looking away.

The unsureness of the druid took Fiona by surprise. The gesture made them look a touch younger than she had ever noticed before. Fiona squared her shoulders and stepped closer. "You were right, however. I let the Guardian of Rise get taken. He practically walked himself out, no less. But he's been fighting so hard for me to not know. Almost as hard as you did."

The druid smiled tightly. "It's not shocking that those who meet you care about you, Fiona. I know it's caused more headaches than help. But it was foolish to not share everything with you. After all you did for Blaze, for Copper…" The druid took a deep breath. "If I had been more transparent, regardless of the long-term cost to you, you may have known what to do. You could have made your own choice. When you return, please come to me at once and I'll explain all. May you and Larrakane forgive an old druid."

Fiona looked up into the druid's grass-green eyes, trying to understand their thoughts. She had expected admonishment, not an apology from someone as powerful as this. The familiar kinship she usually felt when talking to the druid surfaced, her chest loosened, and she grabbed their shoulder lightly. "Of course. You did what you thought was best, Elder." Though she had questions, desires, oh so many things she wanted to ask, she simply squeezed them reassuringly.

"Nicolosia," the druid said with a quick nod. "Elder is so stuffy between friends."

Heart warmed by the sign of trust, Fiona grinned. "You can bet on seeing me as soon as I've retrieved the stubborn man and taken him home."

The druid raised an eyebrow but only inclined their head in acknowledgment, words seemingly spent. With little movement, they sprang back into the thicket of trees and disappeared from sight.

Fiona ran up the path and toward Didia's home. The door was open as if waiting for her, and she strode in directly to the parlor, where much loud conversation echoed.

Gaili and Matteo were crushed between Henrietta's arms as she profusely hugged and kissed them both on the cheeks. Fiona's eyes met hers, and though the captain winced, she tightened her arms around the fauns and winked at Fiona.

Fiona was glad Henrietta had sorted herself out before seeing them again. She hated to see the tension on all their faces.

Didia rose from the settee, adjusting her glasses as she took in Fiona's appearance. "You took your sweet time getting back. Your mother is having a lie down in one of the guest rooms."

Thank Larrakane for small favors. She appreciated Didia seeing to her mother's comfort. "I was somewhat apprehended," Fiona said, taking the proffered cup from Hanno. She drank the delicious coffee in two gulps. "Have we found our way in?"

"Oh yes," Gaili said breathlessly. She looked up, but her face scrunched at seeing Fiona. "Has it gotten worse?"

"Much worse. Everything but the Plateau is sinking. The page of Rise is dying."

Gaili shook her head sadly but then got on with it. "We've used the clock hand to determine a way in. Well, what Clara had done really. It's quite clever if you think about it. You see, we can use the hand like a dowsing rod. Like the fae..." She trailed off as if editing herself. "Well, fae used to do it before we made better methods for finding ore. It'll help us find the page, somewhat like a bookmark but not in the exact same way. And because we're page turners, it'll use our power instead of, say—" She glanced around at the company of people. "—the *items* Clara used."

Fiona frowned, confused. "How is that possible? Is it made of something special?"

"Quite special in fact," Didia interjected. "I've only heard of this material from mentions in other spotters' journals. Mythical really. It's rumored the only sample even around is under lock and key with the Binder."

"Yes, Clara must've done considerable work to find enough of it to make two rods. She must've scoured the pages." That faun had been working on what seemed a far-reaching plan. What else did she discover?

"Well, that's quite an achievement. Let's go forth then," Fiona said, setting her coffee cup down.

"It's not as simple as that." Didia raised her hand, stopping her. "It's dangerous and almost impossible to turn the page without a bookmark. At least most page turners have been to the elemental chapter or somewhere in the mortal one. Accidents happen, more so when traversing a new area in a known page."

"Didia was one of the Guild's best spotters," Marcia said, smiling down at the older human woman. "She's trained quite a few too."

It was as gentle as Fiona had ever seen her. She raised a deliberate eyebrow. "What aren't you saying?"

Didia clasped her hands together. "I'm saying, beyond messing up and landing somewhere you didn't want to be, you could be tossed into the dark edge. This rod will only tell us which direction the page is in. What if there's something else in between?"

"And what if the place we saw is somewhat deadly?" Gaili said. "Or unbreathable? There's no way to be sure we're fully prepared."

Marcia started to speak up, but Fiona placed a hand on her arm. "They are right. It's a risky mission. And not all of us are trained jackets. But there need be only one person to go and come back with a bookmark. I can always find my way home to Spine."

"Oh, Fi, I knew you would say that," Gaili said, waving her hand, "but it'll take all of us looking out for each other to survive this."

"And how can we pass up the chance to chart a map in an unknown land?" Matteo said.

"Or see my studies prove actually useful for once?" Hanno said.

"I'm no turner, but I'm not too old for another adventure today," Henrietta interjected.

"You can't stop me from going." Marcia crossed her arms. "I'm what gives this mission legitimacy."

Fiona pressed her lips together to stop from mentioning Dodger's writ. She sighed, all the faces of her friends looking to her as if she gave the orders around here. When had she gotten so elevated? "Well then, we need to prepare as best we can and quickly."

"We were hoping we'd convince you not to try and go it alone." Gaili smiled. "But that was quicker than even I counted on. Matteo's determined we should turn from Spine since there's no telling how the divining rod will interact with Rise."

"It's clear that Spine has some special affinity with the pages," Matteo said. He grasped Hanno's arm. "This one has been studying the layout of Spine for some time. A rival for my genius, he is."

Hanno blushed. "N-never. But Spine should connect with all pages, even if we don't know about them. The same way the dark edge endcaps all pages, except Spine. It was decreed by Larrakane when the Inking occurred."

"And I've collected as much as I could from the shop. Considering no liquid came through the gap Clara made, I have a variety of jelly breaths to try when we get there, dark goggles, and plenty of vials for the ornithopters should we be gone awhile." Gaili pulled a large satchel from behind the settee and patted it. "Foodstuffs too, though I hope we don't have to dig into them."

Didia pressed a thin notebook into Fiona's hand. "This is a quick check for scouting a new spot. No one's ever discovered a new page, so you'll have to wing it a bit, but good reading for the carriage ride over to New Rise." Her warm, scratchy hand encompassed Fiona's and she patted it. "It's got Hanno's notes from the books you retrieved for me earlier this year. I think they might help, overall, that is."

Equal parts warmed and intrigued by the notebook, Fiona curled it inward and slipped it into her many pocketed scarf. She sighed. "Please tell my mother I'll be back as soon as I can. But she needn't know everything else."

"I don't, do I?" Lavinia said from the archway, face stern. She clasped the front of her bodice, straightening it, and stood her full height. "Fiona Isabella Thornbeard, were you going to run off on some dangerous mission without saying goodbye? I think not."

The room went silent. Fiona stepped around her friends and face to face with her mother. She heard them shuffling away but kept her gaze locked on her mother. "I wasn't going to run off. You'll be quite safe on Spine with Mistress Humbledraft. I have to leave."

"No, no, you don't have to do anything." Lavinia swept around Fiona, blocking her path. "There are Guild jackets and Rise guards. Other people who can take on danger. Even Henrietta has a sword. Why does it have to be you who goes?" Her voice cracked, but she cleared her throat and stood up taller again. "No."

"Mother—"

"No. I am your parent and for Larrakane's sake, Fiona you will listen to me for once." She huffed, her voice thick. Lavinia took a deep breath. "I can't lose you too. I barely get you around enough as it is."

Fiona's throat tightened as her mother's eyes welled up. She swallowed and laid a hand on her mother's shoulder. She had never seen her this upset, not in years. Not since her father died. Was that simply because her mother didn't let her see it?

As if reading her thoughts, Lavinia sniffled but turned her face away, hiding her tears. Fiona pulled her into a hug, pushing past Lavinia's weak muffled protest about emotional propriety.

"I will come back, Mama."

"I know," Lavinia said pulling out her handkerchief and dabbing at her eyes. "I can see that you're much better at this than I thought. You're so in control, Fiona. Larrakane only knows how you got that way. Must've been your father."

Fiona tilted her head. "There might be a smidge of you in my manner."

Lavinia scoffed. "Someone save us all then. There doesn't need to be two of us."

"Oh, I think that's what makes the Book all the better." Fiona took a step back, giving her mother some space.

Lavinia wadded up the handkerchief. "I've always wanted to go on an adventure, but I think I've had enough excitement for a lifetime today. Do be careful."

Fiona smiled warmly. Of all the miracles in the Book, her mother coming to terms somewhat with her job was the most unexpected but fulfilling one. "Yes, Mama." She pressed a kiss to her mother's forehead and then strode toward the front entryway, where quite a few people milled about pretending to be admiring the architecture.

"Well, let's get to it then," Fiona said brightly as if her tone would mask the myriad of emotions plaguing her. In other times this would be the happiest of expeditions. She was glad not to be going alone. On her own was always more trouble than it was worth.

They hastened from Didia's, leaving her and Hanno watching from the porch. Didia called out, "Don't forget your bookmark!" Fiona patted her scarf and waved it.

Gaili, Matteo, Henrietta, Marcia, and Fiona squeezed into a waiting carriage with their various satchels. It seemed fortuitous until Marcia nodded toward the distant wood line. Though Fiona didn't have faekin eyes, she suspected the Elder nodded back.

Inside the carriage a silence permeated the air after Matteo gave the driver directions. Even Gaili's natural chatter ceased during the cobblestone-pounding ride through the backstreets of the city. Fiona cracked open the journal Didia and Hanno had given her, eager to be as prepared as possible for turning to a new page. Would it be elemental? Mortal? Or something new?

They arrived after the longest and somehow quickest hour in her life at the edge of New Rise. They pivoted, driving toward the forest line until they were a sound distance from the human district. The Kerusian driver, a black panther with jacket insignia, nodded toward Marcia as they exited and hurriedly drove away.

Fiona glanced around. "This is as safe a point as we'll get, I do believe. If anyone wishes to turn back now?"

All shook their head no. Marcia held out her hand for the rod.

"I've held them before," Gaili said quietly. "I know what it's like to share the connection. I may be able to pick it up once more."

Fiona winced but didn't argue. If they were going to be successful, they needed to recreate the experiment as closely as possible. She grasped Marcia's hand, and then Matteo and Henrietta grabbed on to Gaili's other hand, and together they circled quietly.

"Wait," Fiona said before Gaili began. "There's another thing we had that might matter. I was…bonded at the time. The tears into another page took that from me."

Gaili frowned. "I didn't think—I was hoping that with enough page turners we wouldn't need that sort of fae power."

Marcia quickly hid a look of surprise but shrugged. "I have my own bond. It'll have to do."

Fiona slid a glance toward Gaili. *Which Seasonal Monarch was Marcia bonded to?*

"Let's start," Marcia ordered, drawing their attention back to the group.

Gaili gripped the clock hand and closed her eyes. Fiona focused on the sky, its bright light mimicking a sun and how it all worked in order not to affect the turn. But nothing happened.

Gaili sighed, frustrated.

Fiona placed her hand on the rod. "Let's try together."

"That could screw everything up. Turners shouldn't interfere with each other," Marcia said.

"This is no normal turn. Come now."

Marcia also placed her hand on the rod, gripping away from the two.

"Let's all focus on Gaili's words. Go ahead, tell us what you saw," Fiona said.

"A dark place, an earthy smell, looming thick cap-like shapes with fluttering blue light in the distance."

Fiona focused on the picture Gaili made, willing a connection through herself and to the page they sought. The rod jerked and Fiona held on tight. She imagined stepping into that unknown world. Her body flushed from head to toe, first warm and sticky, then cool. Drops of dew formed on her brow as if a light rain shower had burst into being above them.

With the ripping of paper, the sky darkened as the world around them shifted. Blaze. Depths. Mistral. Cobbles. Rise. Kerus. Copper. Darkness. Roaring. Bright. Echoes. Tick. Blaze. Depths. Mistral. Cobbles. Rise. Kerus. Copper. Darkness. Roaring. Bright. Echoes. Tock. Blaze… Instead of a page opening to reveal the next, glimpses of the pages flashed by their eyes, unstopping. They started to grow, encompassing the area.

"Well, I hope it wasn't supposed to do that," Henrietta said, holding tight on Gaili's hand.

Fiona's heartbeat raced as her chest tightened. She took a deep breath and shouted, "We have to stop it in the right page."

"We need a way to focus it. Without a bookmark I don't know how," Marcia said, gritting her teeth.

"Maybe we can do it with ourselves," Gaili shouted over the din of clashing sounds coming from the pages. "Clara opened the Shimmering Depths when the clock hands were nine and three. She moved them closer together when she tore the other page." Gaili turned the rod farther away from herself. It felt to Fiona like her body was being turned as well. The flipping slowed but continued through some of the same pages. Rise. Kerus. Copper. Darkness. Roaring. Rise. Kerus. Copper. Darkness. Roaring. Rise. Kerus…

"You said it was dark and quiet right? I'm going to jump for it after Copper," Marcia said. "Follow my lead. If something goes wrong, I order you two to stay here."

"Marcia—" Fiona reached out toward her, but Marcia jumped into the shuffling pages.

There was a thud, but the sound was soon overtaken by the most terrifying roars from one of the growing pages. "She forgets that I'm independent," Fiona shouted and tugged on Henrietta's hand.

Gaili nodded and closed the loop by pulling Matteo's hand. "When we see Copper, we go."

Fiona and Gaili focused on the shuffling of pages. The bright blue Spine sky turned to copper hues, and they all ran toward the horizon together.

FIONA FLOATED FOR A moment among the bright, beautiful, and cold stars. She looked for her hands, but then, what were hands? She couldn't feel anything.

"You've run a bit too fast, my dear," her father said.

"Papa?" Fiona said. She looked for him. He was here, wasn't he? Wherever here was.

"Not your time in the dark yet." There was a gentle push that quickly turned violent.

She stumbled in the air, too shocked to not be floating along calmly anymore, and landed on the top of a thick, soft, foamy mushroom. That it was a mushroom was quite clear by the earthy smell and familiar, but loathed, texture.

"Oof, that's one crash landing I weren't expecting. Glad not to be on ship," Henrietta said, muffled far off.

Moments later, Matteo and Gaili came flying out of the sky, their landing shaking the mushroom vigorously. A rectangle of light flashed in the sky, the sound of roaring was cut off, and the page from Spine closed.

"Well, we've made it...somewhere." Matteo sat up.

"Not immediately dying of breath, that's good," Gaili said. She rolled off her satchel and patted it with a smile.

Henrietta took a deep breath and let it out loudly. "Breathing better than I have in years, quite frankly."

"Did you...were you cold and dark during the page turn?" Fiona asked them all.

They looked at each other but everyone shook their heads.

Fiona tucked the experience away to be examined when she was sure she wasn't in immediate danger. "Let's find Marcia and be on our way."

"She came through before us," Gaili said. "If she experienced the same thing, she should be somewhere around here."

"Should we call out for her?" Matteo said.

"No. Didia's notes are very clear about how to proceed. Touch nothing, endanger nothing, and be quiet. Find the most unobtrusive bookmark you can." Fiona bit her lip. Taking a chunk of this massive fungus would be out of the question until they somewhat understood the impact of their choices.

As if reading her mind Gaili said, "Well, I think the 'touch nothing' part is somewhat gone." She motioned to their landing space. "We should get on from here. We'll go much faster flying overhead."

"Stay low," Fiona warned. "We can use the caps of these mushrooms as cover." Fiona shielded her eyes and peered into the dim distance, seeking a path forward. It was hard to see anything but mushrooms, the outlined thick stalks almost as big as the underground tunnels on Rise and the caps that were like house roofs to whatever lay below in the darkness. The eerie blue and green luminescence seemed to reside within each of the enormous fungi, pulsating slowly, as if it was a heart, but as they began to fly over the area, Gaili pointed out how the light wove into the fungi like veins, and indeed it did. She grew silent but Fiona could tell she was happily contemplating what marvels they were surrounded by. She couldn't help but think to herself of all they had to learn about this new page and wished for the first time in her life to not be so rooted to Spine.

As they flew on, the lights began to fade and sunlight, a proper sun, met them. The page was utterly transformed. Mushrooms that seemed intimidating took on a dewy, almost playful appearance like giant towers. Verdant vines mixed with pops of starburst and other odd-shaped plants created a kaleidoscope of colors that cascaded down toward the ground, disappearing into a thin green fog. The fog rose up, cooling their skin and carrying the scent of moist earth and a lush, almost exotic garden fragrance.

"This is breathtaking," Matteo said, sketching along with charcoal and parchment as he flew.

Fiona scanned the horizon for any signs of the island or anything that looked out of place in this world of teeming plant life. Did creatures live here, or was it all plant and fungi? Were they humanoid or more fluid like the elementals? So many questions! So little time for answers.

"There's movement surrounding something large in that quarter over there. That might be it," Gaili said, squinting.

If she had to squint, it truly was far. "A sign at least of some life. Let's head toward it but be careful," Fiona said.

Through the thin green haze of fog, they flew on. A half-crumbled tower began to take shape in the far distance. Blessed Larrakane, they were heading in the right direction.

"We'll need to get something as a bookmark, then turn back and get the jackets," Gaili said, angling her ornithopter to stop.

"I have a good approximation of how long and how far we've come," Matteo said holding up his map book. "We can lead them right here."

"I do believe we may have a hint of a problem before that," Henrietta said, peering into the fog and drawing out her sword.

Bursting from the green haze with an ear-splitting screech, a swarm of plantlike creatures flew toward them. They resembled birds with leafy wings and long vining tails. Razor-sharp beaks snapped at the group as the creatures dove in to attack.

Henrietta swerved sharply, barely avoiding the jaws of one leafy bird. "I've never known a plant to be a meat eater!" She swung her sword in a wide arc, slicing the creature.

"So much for not endangering anything." Fiona veered wildly, trying to evade the apparently hungry birds. Thorns and vines shot out from their tails, trying to entangle the group, but clearly they were not used to prey who could properly evade them in the sky. The fauns spread out, making it hard to target them together. Fiona dodged out of the way of a quick vine while Henrietta flew in front, slicing at the vines with no small amount of gusto. She seemed quite in her element.

For a brief moment Fiona wondered just what happened in Mistral where Henrietta flew.

Fiona pulled out her slingshot, aiming for a hawkish one with the small supply of rocks Gaili had given her. It was hard enough to get a good shot with the thing while standing still, but this was almost impossible.

"We have to get away from here. Maybe double back?" Gaili said, being chased as she flew farther down and away.

"No, we have to keep going," Fiona shouted over the shrill cries of the creatures. "We'll try to hold them off. Gaili and Matteo, turn the page to Spine. Get the jackets."

Henrietta swung her sword, taking out more of the creatures, trying to evade their attacks. Fiona flew toward her. "If we go higher, that may drive them away from the others so they have time to turn."

"Won't we be seen from this distance?" Henrietta cried, slicing a vine with her blade.

"Perhaps. But it's a chance we'll have to take." Fiona flew up and away from the rest of the group. Henrietta wasn't too far behind her after shouting a quick farewell to the fauns.

They were besieged from all sides by the furious swarm as they flew higher. Vines clutched and clawed from every direction as the plants sated whatever malicious desire they had.

There was a flash of light in the distance and Fiona risked a glance to see Gaili and Matteo turning through to Spine. Thankful there were at least some graces still left in her life, she shouted to Henrietta, "Let's find cover."

Through the gaps between mushroom caps and tangled vines they flew, ornithopter blades chopping at plants, until they were on the ground. The beasts did not follow.

"Well, that's an ill omen when creatures such as them do not brave the forest floor," Henrietta said.

"I think because this is no ordinary forest," Fiona said, lowering her slingshot. The mushroom trees swayed and wiggled of their own accord, making Fiona take a step back. She dragged her loose curls away from her sticky face, the humidity already making her sweat in clothes better suited for the breezy sky. Mushroom caps created shadowed spots on the thick and woven terrain of roots and mycelia. It was intricate and yet springy to Fiona's feet. If she wanted to get out of here without a sprained ankle, they would have to walk carefully and watch their steps as much as they watched their surroundings. Tramping across the ground wasn't her favorite idea, but what else could they do?

"I already miss our mapmaker," Fiona said glancing around at the thick vines surrounding them. They had come down facing the island. Where was a brightly lit path when you needed one? "This direction, I do believe."

Henrietta licked her finger and stuck it in the air. "Aye, that's the way. Wind was blowing from our back the way over here."

Fiona raised an eyebrow. "Do all captains know how to tell the direction of the wind so clearly?"

"Only the surviving ones." Henrietta sighed as she stowed her sword and began tromping muffled steps across the tough vines. "I wish I had *Big Betty*. Make this trip in half the time."

"Reinforcements should arrive soon enough. I hope." If they had jackets on their side to deal with the Painted Edge, then there would be one quarter taken care of, but if they didn't...well, perhaps they could still release Richard and he could get the island back to Rise. She didn't know how his Guardian abilities compared to Soots's.

They plunged their way through the packed earth in the direction of the isle. They would need to take flight again to make it to the top of the island, but Fiona wanted them to be a surprise to the Painted Edge as long as they could. Once again her thoughts flew to Marcia. Where did she go? Why didn't she wait for them? Impatient to deal with her sister, sure, but this was a new world. It was a blotter move to wander off alone.

"Fi!" Henrietta's quick shout broke through her pondering. She was fast sinking into the ground as if being engulfed by it.

Fiona dove forward over the stubby roots and threw out her hand. "Grab on and pull yourself out."

Henrietta grabbed with one hand, her sword raised in the air with the other. She pulled, but the ground rumbled and sucked her farther in. "Not happening."

It wasn't exactly like quicksand, legendary dangers of the Kerus jungles. It was as if the ground itself was trying to swallow Henrietta. Root her down.

The captain struggled against it but slid farther in. She stabbed the woven mesh of root and mycelia with her sword, but it could barely pierce through.

Fiona stretched herself along the ground, trying not to fall in, muscles burning as she extended her body to its limit. "Grab my hand."

Fingertips brushed against each other but to no avail. Henrietta was pulled in to her head and then out of sight.

"No!" Fiona searched frantically for a way in after her that would allow her out again. The sides of the hole were much smoother than above. She couldn't even climb down. The vines that hung from beneath the mushroom's caps might do for rappelling, but when she grabbed on to one, a thin thorn pierced her skin and she pulled back quickly. Was there nothing here that would bear her weight and leave her unharmed? She couldn't leave Henrietta behind to find help. There was no telling what was happening to her below the ground. Getting captured by the Painted Edge had more possibilities for escape than this.

"Henrietta! Can you hear me?" Her voice rang out in the still silence of the jungle. The fluttering of wings above the caps told her the beasts from earlier heard her. But nothing else answered.

Fiona took a deep breath. She would have to follow. There was nothing else to it. She took off her ornithopter and folded it into her bag, wishing the hole was big enough to use it. With a wince and a small prayer to Larrakane, she jumped into the hole.

Vines wrapped around her torso, jerking her in midair. Fiona gasped and spun around, trying to see what had captured her.

Over a dozen creatures surrounded her, the likes of which she had never seen. Several were a mixture of thin vines that seemed to be wrapped into a tight, almost humanoid shape. Others were grassy, green and orange with something akin to legs that hovered off the ground. They had no visible mouths nor ears, but wide unblinking eyes watched her. One, their vine appendages spread farther than most, had unraveled half of their body and wrapped it around Fiona. They pulled her back from the hole, dangling her above them. Many had long spears with large bronze tips drawn and pointed in her direction.

She struggled against the vines. "I have to save her. Please help me."

Another set of vines rappelled into the hole from a different creature. In a still moment it pulled back Henrietta's sword, covered in mud. They presented it to Fiona. There were quick looks among the crowd. The largest of them stamped their feet, raising their spears and swords in a manner Fiona did not appreciate.

Understanding how things possibly looked to clearly territorial beings, she stopped struggling against the vines.

"Please, we didn't come here to fight you. My friend is in the hole. She's like me." She pointed toward herself. Oh, what sort of language to speak? She wasn't even good at the ones she knew. She pantomimed as best as she could Henrietta and the hole, pointing. Frustration and fear welled up inside her chest, making it burn.

One of the plant people, shorter than the others with a more bulbous head, seemed to puff up. Golden green spores swarmed from the creature's body and enveloped Fiona's head. Many thoughts combined into one. It was a soft rustle of sound, like wind passing gently through the branches, that shifted into a high rustling. Curiosity, confusion, and distrust were intermingled in Fiona's mind. Fiona's fear and distress poured from her as she coughed and said once again, "Help."

The plant people rushed to the hole. Masses of tendrils shot down, and seconds later up came an unconscious Henrietta, mud and roots slopping off her. Fiona hurried toward her, kneeling and pushing mud away from her face. She breathed into her mouth, pushing on her chest the way she learned during turner training. There was a gasp of air and then a loud curse in Henrietta's thick accent.

Fiona wrapped her arms around her, uncaring about the mud, and gave her a tight hug. "Are you okay? Does anything hurt?"

"Oof, nothing now, but I'm sure to be right sore later." The captain rubbed her back. "I wasn't cut out to be on the ground. I knew it then and I know it now," Henrietta said with shaky laughter. "Who are all these then?"

"They saved us," Fiona said. She thought to the people, *Thank you.*

Green spores floated toward Henrietta as she began to stand. She shook her head for a moment, confused, but then her eyes widened. "*Well, that deserves my hearty thanks,*" Henrietta's voice sounded in her head. Henrietta got up slowly, pulling Fiona with her. She bowed to the assembled plant people. "*Thank you for saving my wingless life.*"

"*We help you, but we detain you.*"

Fiona wasn't sure who put that thought in her mind or if it was a single one of them. She stood up on shaky feet. "*Why is that?*"

"*Your kind took our space. Blocked our light.*"

"*Not our kind,*" Fiona thought. "*They are dangerous, and we've come after them. To stop them and take the light blocker back.*"

The plant people looked at one another. "*Perhaps you speak the truth. Come.*"

Fiona patted Henrietta's shoulder, bewildered at the turn of events. "Well, it seems breaking the 'be quiet' rule wasn't too bad." They followed the plant people on farther into the dense jungle. "Larrakane help us as the welcoming party for the rest of the Book," she whispered to Henrietta. If they didn't cause an incident with these new people before the end of the day, she would think them most lucky.

THE CREATURES SURROUNDED THEM, marching toward some unseen point. To Fiona's relief they were heading closer to the island, its cold shadow ever present as it loomed in the sky. Fiona shivered. The Forlorn Tower was one of the smaller and lowest islands in Rise. But here it seemed massive. As if it had tripled in size. Or perhaps this world of plant life was simply smaller than the page of humans.

They continued in the island's shadow, deeper into the jungle. The plant people marched on, though some of them raised their spears toward the island menacingly. Fiona didn't think she would have to do much to prod them into a fight with the Painted Edge. They seemed quite ready already. How long had the island been here for them? Did time here work the same as it did in the other pages?

Fiona tentatively pushed her question out through the connection.

One stopped, making wide-eyed contact with her.

"Two light cycles."

Taking that to mean two days, it wasn't too bad. A little faster than the other pages, but nothing a Travel Guild timetable couldn't solve. Oh, how to explain things to these people about the Book. About the Guild. Fiona thought back to Didia's guide, chewing her lips as they marched on: *Don't treat the creatures you encounter any dumber than you would treat yourself. A surefire way to underestimate the unknown and get yourself hurt.*

"How long do you think it will take Gaili and Matteo to get to Dodger?" Henrietta asked.

"Only a couple of hours, hopefully." She rubbed her arms, prickled with goosebumps as a cold wind swept through. The smell of salty sea hit Fiona's nostrils. Were they nearing the coast? So it wasn't all land then. Oh, what a delight it would be to study this page from above.

They entered the vined walls of a sturdy rectangular building, almost invisible within the jungle had it not been for the guards posted at its entrance. Once inside, there was less jungle and more brick than she had yet to see in the page. Thick slabs of sun-dried stones were stacked to make the building's wall. There was little to the interior but wooden benches along the walls, a weapons rack holding more spears, shields, and bronze swords and a small wooden bowl with what looked like burning incense, and a rough statue of a thick humanoid on a chariot with a spiked crown. Pillows, the softest thing in the room, sat in front of this small corner. She supposed it to be an altar to their deity.

The room quickly crowded as larger plant people entered to see the unfamiliar. They were quite striking towering over her and Henrietta with long vines less tightly wrapped than their compatriots and colorful beads encircling various parts of their body. They made appendages as needed, grabbing weapons as they strode in, the beads of blue, yellow, and green shifting to wrap around. Though there were differences between most of them, the combination of being made of vines and using telepathic communication was the same. They no more talked to each other out loud than they did with Fiona. And while there was no background chatter as in most cities, there were still sounds of a large, active population floating through the guard station door.

One of the taller plant people with more beads than the others stepped forward, staring unblinkingly at Fiona and Henrietta. *"Who are you?"*

Though she would be hard pressed to pass an exam, she thought there was a slight change of speed depending on who was communicating. *"I am Fiona,"* she thought back. *"I've come from far away."*

"Myceliumeans?" the creature said gruffly, their tenor deepening.

"Farther," she said simply. She was glad not to have to lie about whomever that was.

Many looked at each other and then her. Where anywhere else there would be murmuring, it was silent except for the rustle of fabric, clanking of spears, and tiny clicks of beads. They were speaking to each other, but it was wholly within their heads.

Fiona pressed on, lest they make decisions without her. *"I am here to help resolve the problem of the sun-blocking island up above."*

"Your people." It was not a question but more of a frustrated statement.

"My kind but not *my people,"* Fiona said.

They nodded again. *"We have the same. Our kind, plantian, has been working with your kind for many light cycles now. They've betrayed our home and our counsel. Taken our people hostage when they would not go freely. Turned their back on us and blocked the Life Giver, Helios.*"

"I don't think they've gotten wind of Larrakane yet," Henrietta muttered out the side of her mouth. She looked still like a statue to Fiona's eyes, but she had spoken.

Well, this would be sticky. Perhaps she needn't explain about Larrakane. Let the deity do her own dirty work. "*We have more coming to get rid of the people and island above. You can tell them by the clothes they wear.*" She tugged on her own doublet, realizing that the creatures weren't actually wearing any cloth. "*And by this symbol on them.*" She held up her writ from Dodger and pointed to the Travel Guild symbol of the open book and various creature footprints above it. It was official: she was going to have to get this piece of paper framed for how handy it had become. She tucked it back into her scarf.

"*We will not endanger our captured people with an army,*" the creature said. "*You must call me Caliope. Tell me everything you know about the ones above, and in exchange you come with me to scout.* Caliope motioned to the others. "*Prepare as we planned. When the others of her kind come as she said, leave them unharmed. Do not fail to strike out at our foes as our Lady of War has commanded us.*" She banged her spear against her shield and raised them high.

Her fighters rallied behind her. One gave Henrietta back her sword reluctantly. They all had bronze swords or spears compared to Henrietta's light rapier. Fiona wondered what they made of the weapon but quickly turned her attention to following Caliope out of the guard station. Though she was reluctant to follow the commands of someone so militaristically set in mind, she thought back to another of

Didia's suggestions: sometimes you must go along to get along when encountering something new.

She was all for scouting ahead while Caliope's team worked in the shadows, but how would they get to the island without being noticed? *"Henrietta and I have a way to fly, but how will you get there?"*

Caliope stared at her then, shot her vined arm to the highest point they could see, like an arrow from a bow. The thin green vines wrapped around other trailing plants and she darted away, pulling herself up.

"Well, I suppose that's—" A vine shot down encasing itself around Fiona while another tugged on Henrietta. They whistled through the air up to the top of the tree as Caliope settled them next to her.

"They come to our nation. Why?" Caliope thought to Fiona.

Fiona brushed her velvet jacket down, trying to calm her nerves from the sudden flight. The plantian might not care about falling, but Fiona sure did. They didn't need to know how out of sorts it had made her though. *"I believe they've come to hide here rather than for your nation specifically."* Or at least, that's what she assumed. While it was clear Caliope's people were intimidating, she wasn't sure what would make the Painted Edge seek them out. Or why any of the plantians would help the rippers.

"They block the Life Giver from entering our city, depriving us of his rays. We cannot be weakened by such a paltry attempt."

"I am on your side." Fiona crossed her arms. *"If we can get to their leader, we can capture the island. They have one of our people as well. If we can free him, we can remove the island altogether."* Though she had little idea of what Richard could do he had seemed confident that him getting to the island would fix

everything. She trusted that he knew his Guardian abilities. She had to. It was the only reason she could think of for why he would so willingly go with Hawkport and Sadie.

Henrietta grabbed a grapevine, steadying herself as she leaned in. "There's some sort of watch happening. Look, around the side."

Indeed, several humanoid forms flew off from the side, traveling around the edge of the island.

"We need to get to the top of the isle without being seen. They'll raise an alarm if we're spotted," Henrietta said.

If only they could make the attempt invisible. Perhaps through the island instead of on it. "Maybe we can get inside," Fiona said. "Richard said there were tunnels that ran through the island."

"Smuggler road? Fancy that." Henrietta grinned. "I thought that was just Middle Market."

Fiona raised an eyebrow, noting her friend never mentioned it before. "Apparently not."

"Probably ends at the tower then," Henrietta said. "I'd heard there was something below the tower, but lots of rippers have tried to find it over the years only to come up empty handed."

"*What are you saying?*" Caliope demanded, pressing her shield between them.

Fiona took a breath to calm herself and quickly translated their conversation and her plan. Rather than get to the top and be out in the open, as Forlorn Tower had nothing to hide among and no trees to call its own, they could use the tunnels within it to make their way in. Caliope quickly agreed. Together, Caliope—ivy-like arms swinging from vine to vine—and the humans flying as close to the tops of mushrooms and thick jungle trees as they could, made their way to the bottom of the flying island.

Thick old roots from long-dead trees pointed out of the sides. Caliope flung out a vine, clinging to the root, but pulled back immediately. Fiona and Henrietta flew to her and stopped, holding on to the massive shaggy-leafed tree.

"What's wrong?" Fiona said.

"That sapling is dead and won't bear my weight." Caliope's voice softened in reverence.

"One of us may have to carry you then," Fiona said. If she could last a few heart-pounding minutes clinging to Richard, surely she could carry this creature.

Caliope seemed to eye Fiona warily. *"How does it work?"*

"I don't really believe we have time for an alchemy lesson." Perhaps it wasn't the best way to address a new leader of what seemed a strong society. She took a deep breath and rubbed her temple. *"Sorry, I simply mean that it's safe and my people use them daily. We have yet to plummet to the ground."*

"Yet." Caliope wrapped her vines around Fiona. *"I will allow this."*

Without any more hesitation, Fiona jerked her head to Henrietta. "We need to find the entrance, quickly."

"If it's made for the same reason as Middle Market's, I know the place." Henrietta nodded and flew up. Fiona followed.

Henrietta flew along the tip, close to the island, avoiding roots and long-forgotten fencing that had tumbled its way down and gotten stuck. Fiona kept an eye out for any signs of Edge scouts while Caliope sent her pressing questions about the island: Where had it come from? Why was it in the air?

Fiona answered as best as she could, skirting the edges of the truth. She wasn't the most diplomatic of people, even when she wasn't pressed for time. Sure, she knew how to push people to get answers out of them, but her focus was divided. She felt the weight of Caliope, the edges of her vines scratching Fiona's jacket and wool stockings. She tried to focus on not dropping her and giving as much direction to the ornithopter controls as she could to stay out of sight and near the isle. After the third question she wondered if Caliope was trying to distract herself from the situation.

"I suppose this is new for you," Fiona said hesitantly.

Caliope's body twitched. *"It is. No unfamiliar creatures in hundreds of years. Wondered what was over the ocean but never thought it would be creatures like you."*

Fiona understood the feeling. She wanted to revel in the newfound place, ask questions herself, travel, and more. Perhaps in curiosity they were more alike than she had previously thought. She hoped that they would take to the Book once they learned of it. And not in the conquering-other-pages sort of way that the cats of Kerus had.

Henrietta waved her over toward a tight opening halfway up the small island, and Fiona flew to it. She landed on the lip, where Caliope immediately removed herself. The plant person quickly ruffled all of her leaves, fanning them out the way Fiona had seen the birdfolk of Mistral do. She turned away to give the leader a moment to compose herself.

"Smugglers road." Henrietta folded her ornithopter and shoved it in her bag. "Though it's a bit danker than I would've expected. Can't see that it's been used lately." She pushed back a strawberry and gray curl from her forehead and then pulled out a small lantern. "Gaili said it's smokeless."

Fiona rubbed her aching neck. "Bless her thoughtfulness."

Henrietta shook a vial from her pack and placed it into the lantern. A soft glow sparked and then grew brighter, casting shadows on the dim interior. It was rocky but soon gave way as they walked to smooth, worn stone. The pathway indeed went up, decorated in corners with ancient cobwebs and giving off a dusty smell that made Fiona sneeze.

"Nothing has been alive here for quite a while," Caliope said keeping her vines close to her body. It was as if she didn't want to brush against anything within the tunnel if she could help it. *"When did it die?"*

"When did what die?" Fiona frowned at the word.

"Your land. There isn't a drop of life in this earth."

Fiona narrowed her eyes, peering into the dark. That was unlikely. There was certainly grass along the top the last time she had been to the island, many years ago. *"It may be recent. Since it was taken and moved here perhaps."*

Caliope was silent. Henrietta's booted footfalls echoed on the stone as they continued through the tunnel. It grew narrow and wide in some places, but there were no runoff passageways lining the tunnel of Shade island. Fiona listened intently for the sounds of voices or even the wind, but there was nothing. Dusty, cold stone filled their senses as the silence became oppressive. They hurried their steps, and after some time hit upon a door built into the gray stone wall. Henrietta pulled out a small mug and pressed it against the door. After a moment she motioned for Fiona to have a go.

Voices whispered on the other side. It was hard to make out what they were saying, muffled as they were. But why whisper unless you didn't want to be heard? And who wouldn't want to be heard? Gossiping turners or prisoners.

"Can you open the door?" Fiona whispered to Henrietta.

"There's not usually doors in smugglers road." Henrietta ran her hand along the seam of the door. "If this was hiding anything good, they wouldn't bother securing it from this side."

Vine shoots shot around the door, edging it in spindly green leaves as if the carpenter added a decorative border. Caliope's chest puffed out for a brief moment and then the door was pulled off its hinges in one fell silent swoop.

Fiona didn't know who was more shocked about the sudden disappearance: herself, Henrietta, or Richard, who stared at her with widened golden eyes. He was bound to a large four-poster bed with heavy ropes on each post. Beside him lay Marcia, still in her human form, with turn stoppers around her wrists and ankles. She looked unusually pale and sweaty, her eyelids heavy and unmoving.

"You stubborn woman," Richard said when he regained his composure.

Fiona smiled, glad to see he wasn't completely worse for wear. "Hello to you too, Sir Mourninghide." She hurried over to him. The cavern room was small but well furnished like a king's bedchamber. A large dresser stood in a corner, and carpets laid out on the floor haphazardly covered every inch of stone. Piles of books sat in corners and precariously on tables. While the large bed the prisoners were on took center of the room, wooden stairs leading up and out of sight edged the opposite wall.

Henrietta rushed to Marcia and sawed through the ropes with a quickly appearing dagger.

"Get the manacles off her quick," Fiona said as she worked to untie Richard.

"You must go and get the Guild. At once," Richard ground out quietly. "There are too many of them for us to take them all."

"*Who are these people? You're releasing them?*" Caliope thought to Fiona.

"*They are our friends. Our allies. I told you one was captured.*" Though she had thought Marcia lost to another page and not bound here. It must've been the work of her sister, Sadie.

"*Who is the other? You did not mention two.*" Caliope's voice rose within Fiona's head.

"*We both want to get rid of this island from your city and stop the people doing it. That's our focus. I didn't lie to you,*" Fiona thought back in earnest. She didn't have time for details. They needed to move quickly. "*Can you deal with that for now, or not?*"

"*Obstruct us from punishing these captors and vengeance will be swift.*"

Fiona sighed and nodded. Vengeance always seemed to be swift with some people.

Richard watched the two wide eyed and said, "We must get the island back to Rise. There's only so much longer before all the islands sink and are irretrievable."

Henrietta stood from unclasping Marcia's manacles. "I don't suppose this thing can fly like an airship."

"Unfortunately, no. But the one they took seemed to be modified to tug this island along with the page turn." Marcia grimaced and rubbed her wrists. "Sadie loves to gloat."

"This entire island?" Fiona said. She kept a careful eye on the door, lest anyone come through. "Why didn't you wait for us?"

Marcia frowned. "I did for almost half an hour, but no one came. I thought you listened to my order or something went wrong."

Time was running much faster indeed on this page. Fiona rubbed her neck and sighed. "We have to get to the airship, then do what we saw in the previous ships. Open the page to Rise and tug it back." Fiona repeated the plan, with some general modifications, to Caliope, who seemed to accept that the island would soon be leaving.

Marcia stretched, her human form seeming to accommodate for her natural hag size. The dazed expression on her face began wearing off. She swallowed, looking at the vine creature before her, and then stood taller. "You three go to the ship. I'll stay here to subdue anyone who may come for us and wait for, I assume, notified reinforcements?"

"Gaili and Matteo left for the Guild as soon as we found the island. And Caliope's people, plantians, are infiltrating quietly."

"Good." Marcia tilted her head, assessing Caliope. Caliope in return didn't move an inch, locking eyes with the Gilded leader. Marcia held out her hand, and before Fiona could intervene Caliope stabbed it with the tip of her vine. Marcia pulled away rubbing her hand, though she continued staring at the creature.

"She is an appropriate leader," Caliope thought to Fiona.

Fiona rolled her eyes internally but thought back, *"The group that is coming take orders from her. Together, you may secure these people and find your missing plantians. We remove the island from your territory."*

"I see I'll have some Guild cleanup to do on our introduction to this new place," Marcia said glaring at Fiona as if she had bungled up new relations on purpose. "What in Larrakane's name are you waiting for? Go to the ship. That was an order."

"I certainly don't work for you," muttered Richard as he stepped toward the door.

Fiona smiled at his shared irritation. "Marcia, what form did you see Sadie in? Blonde-haired, blue-eyed human? I worry when she's not in sight."

"A good feeling to keep," Marcia said. She leaned in and whispered to Fiona, "She oscillated between that blonde noble version and a slim brown-haired woman. I don't think the Painted Edge knows of her as Sadie. Or at least not only her. If you find her before me say her name—her real name three times. I'll be there as quick as I can. I trust you remember it, but only use it when necessary."

There was something in her voice that made Fiona feel uneasy. Was her name more powerful for her or her sister? It called to mind what the Elder druid had said a few days ago about names. She nodded and then turned to Richard. "Is there another way out that won't run us smack into a dozen Painted Edge members?"

He waved her out the removed doorframe. "Come with me."

Fiona followed, taking one last look at Marcia and Caliope, who were staring at each other, still as towers. She smiled. Together those two could probably stave off an army of rippers. She picked up her pace and followed Richard and Henrietta out into the cold passageway. Larrakane help her if she had to do it instead.

"AT THE RATE THE islands were sinking when I left, they'll be past the clouds soon. We must hurry." Richard grabbed Fiona's hand, tugging her down the tunnel.

"How do you know that? Is it truly ocean past the clouds?" Fiona hurried after him and Henrietta back the way they came.

"So many questions you have. You're always going on with them," Richard said with a small smile.

Fiona detected a hint of relief in his voice. Well, if he was happy to find her the same, she supposed he could handle her displeasure. "And you're always obscuring information. I suppose you getting kidnapped didn't change that part of your personality."

Richard huffed. "If that's all it took, I'd be wishy-washy long ago." He stopped in the middle of the tunnel and pressed hard against a stone wall. It swung open, revealing a corridor. Henrietta's lantern light cascaded inside, showing winding rough stone stairs that climbed up and into the darkness. They were broken. Uneven. But a worn rug covered the center like a well-trodden path. It was no smugglers road, that was for sure.

"You lived here," Fiona said breathlessly. The air from the passageway was stale and cold, as if unopened for a time.

Richard glanced at her, his face tight, nostrils flaring. A weary look crossed over him and he sighed as if finally resting at the end of a long night into a surprisingly soft bed. "I did, for a time." He started up the stairs. "For a hundred years, give or take a few."

A hundred years! That was long after the Inking. Fiona dragged her hand against the cracked cold wall, its surface thick with dust. He had been released for a hundred years now too. What did he do to be imprisoned within an island tower? Fiona bit her lip, but Henrietta saved her from the trouble of suppressing her curiosity.

"Who did you rile up?" Her light bobbed as she pointed it toward Richard. "Someone powerful must've imprisoned you here."

Richard jerked away from the light and went quicker up the stairs. "No one imprisoned me. I sequestered myself. I denied her request. Well, *deny* might be the wrong impression. I told Larrakane to shove her Guardianship—" He stopped and glanced back, brows furrowed. His look lingered on Fiona, and he cleared his throat. "You understand, I know... But she didn't take no for an answer. It angered her that I crowned someone else in charge when the Inking occurred."

Fiona nodded, a touch surprised at how much he was telling her. Letting her in. She stopped on the stairs, taking the moment to catch her breath. "Wait, the crowning of someone. You were there when they crowned Queen Pompania." Didia's tapestry of the event *was* an uncanny resemblance because it was Richard. "You crowned her yourself?"

"Yes." He started up the stairs again.

Fiona followed, squeezing past Henrietta. She lowered her voice. "You said before you had no right to be Guardian. Why did you refuse if Larrakane thought you could succeed?"

"I couldn't do it again. In here, I wasn't a threat to anyone, you see." Richard continued climbing but added quietly, "But she demanded that I be involved in the world. And what Larrakane wants she gets, whether or not it's right." His voice trailed off, seemingly exhausted, and he took two steps at a time, widening the space between him and Fiona.

Fiona ran a finger along her scarf's rough edges, letting the space remain between them as she chewed on this new information. She shook her head at the coded parchment they had sweated over, what seemed like ages ago. It had all been about Richard and this island. Was he the red claw or perhaps simply needed to be encouraged to get into action as Guardian? She would've thought it was a warning about his wrath but he seemed to have a hard time staying angry. It wasn't until the island disappeared that he rallied. But that he considered himself a threat, and one that needed isolating, confused her. What had isolating himself done except let people like Henry Hawkport amass power?

Her shoulder brushed against thick, dusty, tattered tapestries depicting outlines of three faded gold lions on a worn red background. Glimpses of the tower's former history, no doubt. Fiona ran a hand across one of the faint lions. There had been three golden beasts in the druid's poem. There were three on the banners. Was that all it meant? *Symbols of a royal line.* If Richard was from a royal line, that indicated there were others in his family. Did three lions mean three people? But he said he had no family. The heraldry was so different than

Rise's current house insignias, it was hard to understand its meaning.

Fiona ducked her head under a low arch as they finally reached a landing. Parts of the stone ceiling and walls were carved with ornate moldings and trim, now blanketed under thick cobwebs. An old wooden door, barely hanging on rusted iron hinges, led to a large empty kitchen. Nothing remained but pots hung to dry and an abandoned hearth fire.

After what felt like hours, but Fiona confirmed with her pocket watch was much less than one, fresh air brushed past the silent trio. Henrietta snuffed her lantern light as the stairs opened into a cavernous cellar room resplendent with broken furniture. Sunlight streamed through wide cracks in the wooden-beamed ceiling. Creaks echoed as people restlessly walked back and forth above them. A ladder leading to an uncovered hatch leaned against one end of the room. Fiona squinted at the ceiling, trying to make out if the small glints in the light were weapons or something else.

"I can talk to the guards," Richard began, "unless they too are shielded against me like you and Hawkport."

Fiona narrowed her eyes. "I don't even know what that means. I am not shielded against you."

Richard snorted softly. "Maybe not on purpose but you most certainly are."

She leaned in, arms crossed. "Well, that's not my fault. Maybe *you* don't even know what you're talking about."

Before Richard could retort, Henrietta broke in, "Look here, I'll distract them down this tunnel while you both make your way up the ladder behind 'em. I'm fair good at it, and that way you have time to get to the ship."

As much as Fiona wanted to push back, Henrietta was more adept at direct confrontation than she was. But still she hesitated, her chest anxious with worry.

Henrietta clapped her on the back. "We'll all get to Rise at the same time. I'll either be in manacles—temporarily mind you—or fighting mad as we arrive. You two go."

Fiona nodded reluctantly. "Stay as safe as you can though."

"As a bean sprout." Henrietta winked, crinkles at the corners of her eyes lifting up as she smiled.

Fiona and Richard crept toward the other end of the cellar and ducked to the side of benches and stacked chairs. Fiona had her slingshot in hand in case it was necessary. She hoped to Larrakane it wasn't.

Henrietta called up and out, "You two. There's some trouble with the prisoners. Need a little help down here." Her voice echoed through the cavernous cellar.

The rippers in their scruffy outfits stared at Henrietta through the cracks. One, beard desperately in need of a trim, tilted his head looking her over. "We know you…"

The other did the same but frowned. "Yeah you were at the meeting. Thought Sal told you to get lost."

Without missing a beat Henrietta said, "In front of you all, yes. Just gave me a different job outside the door. Listen, are you going to help a lass or not? The page turner's waking up and I'm not handling her by myself."

The men descended the ladder rungs, grumbling between them. They both had short bows but hip daggers as well. As soon as their backs were turned, Henrietta nodded but kept her eyes on them. Fiona glanced at Richard and waited.

"We've never seen this passageway the whole time we've been here," the bearded one said, poking his head into the open door where Henrietta stood.

"Yeah, why didn't Lionheart tell us about this one?"

Henrietta puffed out her chest and said with a cocky grin, "You just have to know how to get it out of them." The two exchanged a glance. Henrietta strode confidently back down the steps, not waiting for them to make up their minds, her voice fading away. "Come on now, I don't want to have to report they've turned the page while we're dawdling."

They quickly followed after that, seemingly fallen for her ruse.

Sparing a moment of appreciation for Henrietta's efforts. Fiona darted toward the ladder as quietly as she could and began climbing. Richard was on her heels. He stumbled, stubbing his foot. He cursed in his odd language but caught himself.

Henrietta's voice drifted up. "What was that? Damned page turner better not let him loose. Let's hurry, boys."

Fiona sighed with relief at Henrietta's skill and hurried to the top of the ladder. She climbed out onto the patchy wooden floor as Richard made his way up and through the hatch. Fiona grasped his hand, helping him. He gave her a quick squeeze of thanks and they moved hurriedly toward the windowed wall of this main room.

"Your pirate friend, Henrietta, I was wrong about her. She's impressive," Richard said.

"That she is. All the more reason we have to succeed. She put herself in danger for us to get to the airship. Is there a dock landing on this island?"

"No, but I know where I'd put an airship down all the same." Richard moved to a window and pointed. "North side of the tower, under the overhang."

There were people everywhere. This clearly was where most of them were hiding out at the moment. While there were a handful of plantians—squat, short mushroomed people and a couple that looked more like Caliope with tight vines—it was humans who were the most plentiful. Humans wielding swords and bows flanked the area. Strange that it was humans as far as the eye could see. There had to be more than that in the Painted Edge considering Sadie was faekin and Petronia had been smilodon. Were their forces split by page? Is that what they meant by Dots? They were almost as organized as the Travel Guild.

"We'll have to circle wide across the open ground to the side of the airship," Fiona said. "They may see us coming unless you think your Guardian powers can have an effect on them." Despite her occasional irritation with him, she felt no desire to upset him, but they didn't have the time to squabble about what he was if he had the power to help them get the island back home.

Richard nodded shakily. "I will, but it should be used limitedly." He hesitated, then rushed on, "Controlling memories in a rush can have unforeseen consequences."

Fiona nearly burst with thoughts and questions.

It must've been clear in her face, for Richard held up his hand and said with a soft smile, "Later. Trust."

Warmth spread through her. "You lead the way then. If they are shielded, as you say, then better one of us makes it unnoticed to get the island back."

Richard took no time in bursting out of the tower doorway and starting to circle wide. Fiona gave him a breath and then took off after him. With his long strides she wouldn't gain on him until he stopped. They raced across the flat rocky terrain, their steps pounding loudly in her ears. A crossbow bolt whizzed toward Richard, but he ducked with the instincts of a natural fighter and tumbled in toward the person who'd spotted him.

Fiona ducked lower as Richard's voice rose: *"Your watch is uneventful, and you have no reason to worry."*

There was a small rumble beneath Fiona's swiftly moving feet that subsided just as quickly as it came. She wanted to look back, to see if Richard's words had taken effect, but she continued on until she was pulled from the ground by a human woman who didn't appear quite friendly. She struggled with her, but the woman was more fit than Fiona. She clasped a hand over Fiona's mouth before she could say anything and began to pull her back toward the tower. Fiona tried to slip out of her grasp, but the woman just gripped tighter.

Panic rose in Fiona's chest as she glanced frantically around for signs of Richard. He was fighting his own battle, running from group to group and shouting at them. At least what he did seemed to be working. Fiona thought frantically of a plan, but ideas fled her. Luckily, her friends had not.

The air rippled above the island, pulling back the page to reveal the blue sky of Spine. A heavy scent of pine rushed through the opening as a large force of Travel Guild jackets in their black coats and bright insignias flew through the page turn. Wave after wave of jackets landed on the island as the sky turned back to the original page. The Travel Guild would have a whale of a time explaining that one to the new plant people.

The woman dropped Fiona as soon as a jacket landed beside her. Fiona wasted no time in running toward the airship and throwing herself up the temporary steps. She took in the empty deck and sighed with relief that she wouldn't have to battle once again on her own. Without more than a brief pause to breathe, she threw open the hatch and launched herself deeper into the airship.

"Come on," Fiona muttered in a hint of a prayer. "If you have any desire for us to save Rise at all, you'll make sure he makes it here in one piece."

Fiona ran her hands under the railing of the ship until she found the familiar latch she was looking for. This time a door opened from the lone crate in the room. She hurried down the rope ladder and into the secret compartment as before. It was as large as the ship at the Hawkport dock, but there was no unpleasant odor here. Instead, the heavy scent of fresh flowers permeated the air.

In the middle of the room was a device unlike anything she had seen before. Dark metal poles were anchored from floor to ceiling and from them hung straps of brown leather. Two at the bottom, like stirrups, and two toward the middle as pulls. A small wooden belt was mounted in the center so that the wearer floated in the middle of the straps. There seemed to be a wrapping of some sort, gauzy cream fabric better suited for a sun veil, encircling the top of the contraption that floated on its own, billowing out. Within was a darkened shape. Cautiously Fiona stepped toward the contraption, trying to look for signs of traps or triggers. Would the Painted Edge leave this room so unattended?

"What the devil is this?" Richard grumbled, dropping down the ladder. He closed the hatch after them.

Relief flooded through Fiona at seeing him, but she swallowed the feeling and turned back to the device. "It must be the modification Marcia mentioned." Fiona ran her fingers over the cool dark metal. It was the same material as the dowsing rod! For a near-mythical metal, there seemed to be plenty going around. Before she could focus too much on what it meant that the device was made of it, she pulled back the gossamer netting to reveal a thin band of bronze suspended over the chair. Its familiar branching vines and lush green leaves of verdant feathers made her drop the gauzy fabric and take a step back.

"It's one of the crowns," Fiona said. Her head churned with questions. Sadie had brought this here. Had made it part of the device. How did it work? Could she even use it, or did it have to be a faekin?

"A crown?" Richard stomped over and thrust the gauze to the side. "Well, it's not one I've ever seen before. What does it do?"

"I...I don't know," Fiona stammered, bewildered. Thoughts cascaded, making it hard to focus. What would it take from her? Everything the least bit advanced from Copper had taken something from her. If she couldn't wield it, could any human? What did that mean? Sadie wasn't a page turner. But could she use this to turn the page? It didn't make sense. But time for making sense was past. Someone would discover them soon, and while she could hope for it to be a friend, she had no chances to take. She pushed away the gossamer veil and climbed into the wooden belt. It fit snug against her thin frame.

"What will happen when you open up to Rise and we fly through?" Richard held the netting and straps out of the way for her.

"With any turn there's an element of focus. As long as no one else tries to take over, we'll be fine. And any page turner with training and sense wouldn't risk their lives trying to escape mid-turn." There were many insensible things people did, but page turners—experienced ones—didn't waffle with a turn. Unless... "Did your power work?"

"Yes. I had to repeat myself, but it seems to have done the trick for now." He looked uneasy. "Is that going to hurt you?"

Fiona slid her slippered feet into the stirrups. "There's only one way to find out. We don't have all day. I'm still concerned we haven't seen Sadie."

"As you should be," Sadie's voice rang as she dropped into the chamber from above.

She was the picture-perfect image of the leader Fiona had seen at the barn hideout over a week ago. Dark-brown hair, human, and scruffy looking. She should've guessed that the hag had more than one form around humans. It gave her flexibility to skulk that Fiona almost envied. Knowing that she wouldn't be able to safely turn the page or have Richard fly the ship with Sadie among them, Fiona needed to play for time and call on her sister. Would her real name rankle her? "Well, this is quite a new look. Not my favorite, Stella."

Stella blinked and glanced away, seemingly nonchalant. "Now, now, has my dear sister been telling you my secrets?"

Richard tried to rush the hag, but Stella dexterously twisted and sidestepped out of the way. She jutted out her leg, making Richard pitch forward.

"Act like the silly old historian you're supposed to be and stay weak, or I'll make sure you die early."

"I'd like to see you try." Richard grabbed on to her, grappling her from behind.

There was a bright glow from their forms as they fought each other.

"Stella," Fiona said, trying to draw her attention away. She just needed to buy time until Marcia could get there. "Stella! Why do you need him? Why do you need any of this at all?"

But it was to no avail. The glow disappeared and two Richards grappled with each other in the ship hold. They kicked and punched, both a match for themselves. Fiona couldn't tell them apart.

"I need a little help here," one of the Richard's shouted.

"Don't come closer. She's trying to trick you," the other one said.

"Of course, she's trying to trick me," Fiona shouted back. "That's what she does."

"Just put on the crown and turn us back to Rise," one of the Richards shouted.

"Yes, hurry up, we need to get back," the other one said.

Fiona started to reach for the crown, then stopped. Why were both of them trying to get back to Rise? One should've stated the opposite surely. "Stella, what's your game?"

One Richard had the other in a headlock. "Why are you standing about like a fish with your mouth open? Just get us home."

"She's just trying to lure you in. Don't ask anything else," Richard choked out.

Of course. She wanted to confuse her, make her waste time wondering. Well, she wouldn't fall for it again. Fiona reached for the crown, pulling it down and settling it on her head. The perfume of lush green trees and sweet florals surrounded her. The bronze band was slightly warm to the touch but began to cool on her head. But beyond that she felt little connection with it. Not the thrum that she felt when holding a bookmark and searching for the page she wanted to turn to. But the barest hint of something. The intoxicating scents began to fade. If Fiona didn't know any better, she would think the crown was confused by her.

The Richard with his arms around the other watched with amusement. "Oh, poor investigator. I was hoping the crown would overwhelm you! Oh well." Richard flexed out a hand and shifted it into a spotted smilodon claw, making it easier to tell them apart. She pressed the claw to the real Richard's neck. "Can't you see it's pointless? My group is more than a match for jackets. No one is coming to help you. And we've gotten what we needed." She caressed Richard's face with the clawed hand. "Come, Fiona. Don't you want to know what I mean? Three questions for three questions."

"Not on your life." Fiona swallowed and concentrated on Stella. Although she was toying with Richard, she wouldn't hurt him. Fiona didn't believe she had everything in hand. Her eyes flashed when she said it. And the sound of fighting outside still cascaded into the hold

Stella cocked her head and smirked with Richard's face. "Suit yourself, but I *like* you, Fiona. Aren't you sick of all the powers who play games like your Queen? Larrakane? They orchestrate everything to their pleasure. Aren't you against that sort of misuse of power? We are too. We just want to be free to live our lives. Isn't that what you want for people?"

"Once we take you back, *Stella*, the Painted Edge will tear apart without leadership," Fiona said.

Stella sighed heavily, face pinched. It was unbecoming in Richard's form. "I thought you were cleverer than this. You're far behind, investigator. Think, think, think."

Curiosity waved over Fiona at Stella's words. She shook her head, trying to ignore the distraction, but snippets pushed through regardless. The Edge members at the hideout did say their boss had put the brown-haired woman, a disguised Stella, in charge of them. While Stella had many forms to be sure, it didn't make sense that she'd play the boss and the lieutenant beneath. And Stella wasn't a page turner. A niggling fact that had bothered Fiona. Though she could understand page turners taking orders from someone like Stella, she had wondered how Stella, reliant on a page turner to move about the Book, could amass an organization like this so quickly.

"You're not the Painted Edge's leader," Fiona said, wide eyed.

Stella seemed pleased. "Simply the Book's best and brightest. We think you are too. Why don't you join us?"

"Ignore her." Richard broke from the choke hold. He pushed Stella against the floor. Stella swept her leg bringing them both down to the ground, where they rolled straight into the poles of the device.

Fiona saw an opening but couldn't block them out, not the way they were hitting the thing. She repeated Stella's name again, hoping that her blasted sister would get there.

As if a gift from Larrakane, Marcia dropped down from the hatch and sprung on top of the wrestling forms. She wasted no time grabbing one of the Richards. "Sister."

Stella's form rippled. The real Richard jerked away from her. Fiona closed her eyes, taking this brief moment of confusion as a win, and concentrated on turning the page. Her stomach dropped. She wasn't holding a bookmark.

"I need you," she said to Richard and held out her hand.

Without a thought he grabbed it in his rough one. Fiona focused, clasping his warm hand in hers and gripping tight to the leather pulls. She connected to the mortal chapter, then to Rise. The connection to their page was swift and unnerving. She felt its immediate presence and knew Rise was falling apart. She could sense so much panic. She pushed to block it all out and then tried to turn the page.

The world around them ripped open with such force that Fiona almost tumbled out of the stirrups, the pull from within her strong enough to tug her forward. Richard grasped her hand and the leather pull tightly and circled his other around her waist, holding her steady. "I've got you." He gave her a smile of encouragement.

Fiona nodded and took a trembling step forward. Where normally she physically walked from one page to the next, here inside the airship she felt as if she was pushing against an unyielding, frozen barrier. Focusing on her destination alone as she was taught, she peered out into the dim moonlit sky of Rise, concentrating on the place the island used to float. The titanic feeling of all the people and land that she was bringing along weighed on her. She took a deep breath.

A cold hand yanked her other arm. Her eyes flew to it, confused, and there Stella was with a smirk.

Unblinking indigo eyes swirled as she dug her fingers into Fiona. "People, like you page turners, want to go back to where they belong. You page turners are not the only ones cursed from that bloody *Inking*," she said with derision. She jerked Fiona's hand from the leather pull. "I'd rather face the dark edge than be imprisoned in Spine."

Fiona glanced frantically around for Marcia. She was curled up on the floor, unmoving. As Fiona's focus shifted, both pages around them blurred. The dim sky and moon began to merge with a deep, inky, star-filled one. Its cold and vast emptiness threatened to overwhelm her senses. This was familiar and yet ancient. This was the dark edge. Millions of lights burst into brightness. What was empty was now brimming with existence. "No, no, no."

Distant voices shouted her name. She couldn't drown them out. She had to focus. Had to take a step to the right place. But the coldness dripped into her. The dark edge was the place no page turner should go. But its familiarity surprised her. Quickly she tried to determine when she had touched it before.

"You've run a bit too fast, my dear," her father's voice cut through the noise.

Yes. Yes, it was between the Spine and the plant page when she jumped through. But how? With something akin to clarity, Fiona gasped. It was always there, the dark edge, surrounding them. It wasn't simply a boundary to the pages. A nothingness to fear. It was more than that clearly. A place of its own *between* each page. Possibly even one they could traverse through. She gripped Richard's hands, focusing hard on the calluses, the warmth and feel of him. The vignettes shook but did not separate. She needed a more powerful connection to Rise. A bookmark that could anchor them there. Richard. With a small tremble, she tugged him toward her, and before he could blink, she kissed him.

Everything snapped in place. She slammed against him, glad for Richard's strong arms to be wrapped around her. The airship shot forward into Rise, getting lift off some unseen current. The deep connection Fiona felt to the page flowed through her, and she sensed a history of words and people unknown to her. She jerked back from Richard and the connection broke off.

"Quite a way to get from one place to another," Richard said after a pause. The corner of his mouth quirked up and his golden eyes flashed. "Still better than the trip to Mistral, however."

THE PAGE CLOSED BEHIND them, its massive size taking a bit longer than a normal turn.

Marcia groaned as she leaned up off the floor. "What in the dark edge happened?" She glanced around and then jumped up, her energy seeming to come back rapidly. "Where is Stella?"

Fiona too looked around the large hold, but Stella was nowhere to be seen. There were only three of them there. She winced. "She tried to interrupt the turn and pull us into the dark edge. She almost succeeded in us all being stuck there, but I guess…" She stared at her hands. However dangerous, Stella being lost in the dark edge was a terrible punishment. "I'm sorry, Marcia."

Rubbing her arms, Marcia said, "And you think that means she's gone forever?" She shook her head, her confident voice not quite matching with her eyes. "We'll see." Marcia pinched the bridge of her nose, and her form shimmered for a moment. When the brightness dulled away, she looked put together, formidable, with not a hair out of place. How often did she shift to give the appearance of perfection when she was otherwise?

"What will you do now?" Fiona asked.

Marcia raised an eyebrow. "My job." She climbed up the stairs without a backward glance and left.

Fiona leaned, weak, against the contraption, still holding Richard's hand. "Is Rise fixed?"

Richard breathed a deep sigh of relief. "Yes. I didn't think—I was worried it wouldn't work. I should've known you'd be too stubborn to let it fail." His wide eyes searched her face. "They're almost past the horizon now. Soon they'll start to rise back up. I've got to get things into place. I've..." He squeezed her hand tightly. "Could you, for one moment, just do as I say? And not follow me?" He shook his head and strode without looking back toward the hatch. He pulled himself up the ladder and out of sight swiftly.

"Richard?" Fiona called out to him, whipping off the crown She struggled, pulling herself out of the pieces of the contraption. Why was he saying goodbye to her? He was being ridiculous. What did he mean? She had to follow him, if she could get out of this darned device. "How dare he talk to me as if those are his final words. Not if I have anything to say about it." She pulled herself out, thankful to be freed with only scratches to show for its use. Fiona balled up her fist and ran after him.

Up through the hatch and the second-floor deck stairs she ran. *Blasted man.* Thought he could say cryptic words and then run off in smoke. She would absolutely give him a piece or two of her mind.

The night sky was clearer than it had been in months. The moon was wedged so sharply in the horizon it seemed as if it was placed there. No one was on deck. Richard moved faster than one expected of a two-hundred-year-old person. She glanced over the railing of the ship at pockets of people—jackets, Painted Edge, and plant people. Some still tussled while others sat, turn stoppers on their wrists and ankles, devoid of weapons. What would the plantians think of this new realm? How would the Travel Guild handle it all? And where in all of this was Richard?

Fiona rushed to the bow of the ship and peered over the edge, past the coast of the isle. The Forlorn Tower, once the lowest isle around the Plateau, was now above so many. Were they rising up? He had said it so confidently it was clear his connection to the page was constant. Perhaps what he had to get in place was for the island's benefit.

She climbed down the rope ladder and dropped to the dusty dirt ground. The airship was askew, the page turn unsettling it somewhat. The thick metal chains that linked to iron hooks were being taken up by Guild jackets. Thick grooves where they had been dug were all that was left of evidence an airship had pulled the island once.

"There you are," a nasal voice said. The Queen's principal secretary, his wide ruff slightly askew, flanked by two royal guards, approached her from within a group of Travel Guild jackets.

Fiona swallowed and looked for a way to slip past the man, but the guards bookended her. She sighed. "How nice of you to find me before I came to talk to the Queen."

The secretary narrowed his eyes and his tawny face flushed. "With the events of this week, the Queen is under strong protection. That, however, doesn't get you out of the mess you've made here."

"The mess I've made!" Fiona took a step forward, but a guard blocked her. She ignored them. "I would have you know that if it weren't for me, there wouldn't be a Queen to protect or an island back in its place."

"Perhaps. But you still haven't completed the actual work the Queen gave you."

"She's still worried about finding the Guardian?" Fiona let out an exasperated breath. In all the powers of the Book, she had to be bound to one of the most short-sighted rulers. But short sighted and benevolent didn't go hand in hand. She needed to put an end to this line of inquiry for good. "There is no Guardian of the Rise." Fiona swung her arms wide. "Gaze about, Secretary. If there was a Guardian bound to protect our page, would any of this have happened? Wouldn't they have intervened in some way?"

He glanced around, eyes furtively taking in the scene. "Mayhaps the Guardian is simply locked up. It was your job to investigate—"

"And I did investigate." Fiona tugged on her scarf and composed herself. "And what I found was a plot to harm the Queen and throw Rise into chaos. The guardian of Rise, dear Secretary, is us. We humans are all we have here. Perhaps we should be kinder to each other so that the strength of us as one allows us to prevail when we need to most. Or other factions like the Painted Edge will continue to splinter away those who are unhappy with the powers at play."

One of the guards began nodding, seemingly rallied by Fiona's words. The secretary cut him with a glance, and he stopped.

"Please tell the Queen my findings and that I expect she'll be happy to see the page saved and the treasonous plot ruined. I ask for no payment in return, of course. But I do hope the next time she's throwing a court fest she remembers to invite my mother."

Fiona inclined her head politely and dismissed herself, walking away from the principal secretary. While she may have had no influence with her own leaders, she knew she had considerable weight with others. There was no way the Queen would know of Richard's existence without his saying so. He wasn't anyone's to own.

She strode over rocks and tufts of dirt, the island having seen more tramping of feet than in a very long time. The broken tower shadowed the moon from her for a moment, and she shivered, feeling a touch alone. Where had that blasted man scampered off to?

A familiar voice called her name, breaking Fiona's thoughts. Henrietta strode toward her, cap lost and curls flying wild at her speed. She was grinning and, although running with a slight limp, looked none too worse for their time apart. Relief filled Fiona. Her smile turned into a wide grin as Gaili and Matteo flew up behind Henrietta and joined her.

"This is a welcome sight," Fiona said, throwing her arms somewhat uncharacteristically around her friends. "I'm so glad you're all safe."

Matteo licked his lips, eyes dancing over her. "Was it you who turned the page? It was incredible. So beautiful and full of stars." He kissed his fingers and tossed his hands to the sky.

"Full of stars?" Fiona said. "I suppose they could've been stars. Only Copper and Kerus have any stars on record. They seemed..." She tried to find the right words. How to explain the perception of something so dangerous and yet so alluring?

"How did you turn with the whole island?" Gaili asked breathlessly.

Fiona's hand flew to her mouth. "Oh, Gaili! The Spring Crown. It's in there, in a device. We should get it at once before…"

Gaili nodded. "I'll retrieve it now. No worry, Fi." She squeezed Fiona's shoulder and walked quickly to the airship.

If anyone could handle the seasonal artifacts, it would be her. Fiona let out a sigh. "Did you see Richard come through here?"

"Aye. Headed for the tower." Henrietta raised an eyebrow and jerked her head toward the ruined structure. "He seemed bent on something, like lightning looking to scorch."

Matteo fanned himself with a light smile. "Yes, I'd be careful with that one." He tucked his arm through Henrietta's and leaned into her.

"He'd better be careful of me." Fiona headed for the tower. "I'll see you back at home," she called over her shoulder. Winding her way past the clumps of people, she entered the crumbling tower ruins. Where would that stubborn man be?

She picked her way down the stairs and back to the sitting chamber. No Richard in sight. But the smell of fresh ink lingered in the air. Where had she smelled that before? In Richard's office back in the library and in the hideout where they first met. He had been here recently then. She went to the corner where books were piled and picked up the open one, freshly written in. The words were in a language she couldn't understand. "Oh, Larrakane bless! Why does he have to make everything so difficult?" She ran her fingers over the dried and powdered words, hoping for them to be a code she could break. Instead, the words shifted on the paper into Schiflan. Wait, had they been Schiflan all along? It was hard to say.

And then Richard Lionheart said farewell to the feisty investigator, climbed out of the airship, and into his old tower. The fireplace still linked to his fireplace at the palace. A quick step and he would be there.

Fiona closed the book. The inks looked like the ones on the desk at his office. Why would he take the time to write what he had been doing? It seemed impractical. She picked her way over to the fireplace, looking for fae circles or something at least remotely familiar. There was nothing but dust, footprints, and the scent of him. She had never been one to ignore strange things if it could be helped. She took a small breath and stepped into the large hearth. A feeling, not unlike turning the page, thrummed around her. She clutched the book to herself, adrenaline from the past day still rushing through her and quickening her breath. She wasn't in control of this. Would it take her where the book said? Or somewhere else. She took another step, relying on the fact that she was an experienced page turner. Spine was her salvation, and she could always get back home. Repeating that thought, she took another step and found herself walking out of the fireplace into Richard's bedroom at the palace.

The sound of metal slamming against metal rang loudly throughout the archive. What was that noise? She peeked around the corner of the arched doorway and saw Richard bent over a printing press. She had never seen one up close before, but it matched the illustrations from her studies on the Binder. He was printing out reams and reams of paper. The smell of the same ink as the book she held permeated the air. Her wonder prevailed for a moment as she watched him, but confusion soon took over. This was what the long goodbye was for? To hurry up and come back to his books?

She pulled her scarf tighter around her neck and marched into the room. "What, by the good grace of my patience, are you doing?"

Richard stiffened, but upon looking at her face he relaxed for a moment. It didn't last long. He shook his head, moving stacks of parchment to a counter quickly and setting them aside. "Couldn't let me swan off into the sunset without pain could you?"

"There is no *swanning* off when half of Rise is still moving, there are dozens of captured Painted Edge to process, and you owe me answers." Fiona strode to the desk and placed her hand on the stacked papers he had. "Why are you trying to say goodbye to me?"

"I know I owe you answers. I understand." Richard sighed and gently moved the papers away from her. He continued with his work, taking more stacks and pulling them together. "But I have to attend my duties, now more than ever."

His hands were shaking. He was being honest. No terse, flippant answers. She stood watching him as he quickly laid thick covers on stacks of papers, lining them up. There were so many, but he seemed to be working as if he was more than one man. More than twenty. Was this his Guardian power manifesting in front of her eyes? Was there anything she could do to make this easier for him? "Can I at least help?"

He stopped and turned to her. He wet his lips and said in a quiet voice, "Fiona, I…" He cupped her face with his rough hands. "Look, I've no right to tell you these things, but I do care about you. Without a doubt you're one of the most stubborn and cleverest people I have ever met in my regrettably long lifetime."

Excitement at his words of affection tingled through Fiona. She pressed his hand to her face. "Quit saying goodbye then, you ridiculous man, and tell me how I can help with what's going on."

Richard moved closer to her, removing all space between them. He kissed her softly.

Fiona leaned in, her heart beating quickly. She hadn't been this vulnerable with someone in a very long time. She quite liked it. Perhaps she could hold off on getting her other answers a bit longer.

But all too soon Richard stepped back. He squeezed her hand reassuringly. "In a moment." He turned back to the work table and began clasping the vellum bindings with dizzying speed. The archives, dimly lit from moonlight, began to grow bright, a soft gray permeating the area where Richard worked. The light was there and then everywhere, encasing Fiona and blocking her view of Richard. Of the table. Of the bookshelves and then even of herself. She reached out for him but felt nothing. She tried to make it to a wall, but where she walked was endless gray. As if the color of the world had drained away.

As panic rose, Fiona felt a thrum like a harp cord struck heavily. It rippled through her, and she grabbed her head, dizzy and falling. Before she could hit the ground, strong arms clasped about her waist and held her upright. Color returned, seeping in from the edges of the world and her vision. She took a deep, ragged breath as she had been unbreathing for so long.

A man sat her in a chair, his golden eyes watching her every move.

For a moment Fiona squinted, trying to remember what was happening before her dizzy spell.

He tugged on his beard and sighed.

And then a warmth settled on Fiona like a sun-kissed morning and all the memories of what had happened came rushing back to her. The hideout, the search for the Guardian, the daring rescue, and every moment with Richard that she had over the last ten days.

Richard raised an eyebrow watching her.

She glared at him.

He took a step back.

She rose and poked him in the chest. "Now just what in the name of Larrakane was that?"

Richard's mouth dropped open for a moment, but then he shook his head. A sad accepting smile tugged the corners of his mouth. His next words so at odds with it. "Me protecting against my brother."

If you enjoyed your latest D. Hale Rambo fantasy adventure, spread the word by writing a review! Reviews really help my books get into the right hands, so I'm super grateful for every single one.

The Next Adventure of The Planar Pages

FRAYED EDGES, book 4, releases Spring 2025!
The Book's delicate threads are unraveling, and investigator Fiona Thorne faces her most perilous journey yet. The enigmatic Painted Edge leader weaves an intricate plot, always staying steps ahead. The key to outmaneuvering them might lie with an undercover Travel Guild spy.

With the leaders of the Book anxious and resolute, Fiona and her steadfast ally, Dodger, are tasked with a critical mission. Traversing the sun-baked desert and rolling seas of the Kerus page, they must locate the spy and secure vital intelligence before the Painted Edge springs their next surprise. But the Kerus page holds uncomfortable memories for Dodger and a crumbling Empire that adds to their peril.

Richard's gruff yet caring guidance offers Fiona a lifeline from afar, but can his counsel illuminate the truth amidst the lies? Fiona must decipher cryptic clues and retrieve the spy's crucial information before it's too late. As secrets unravel and alliances fray, Fiona's desires will take her to the brink in this next chapter of The Planar Pages.

Can't wait? Join the adventure at
https://www.dhalerambo.com/fe2025 and get sneak peeks of
FRAYED EDGES before it releases!

Author's Note

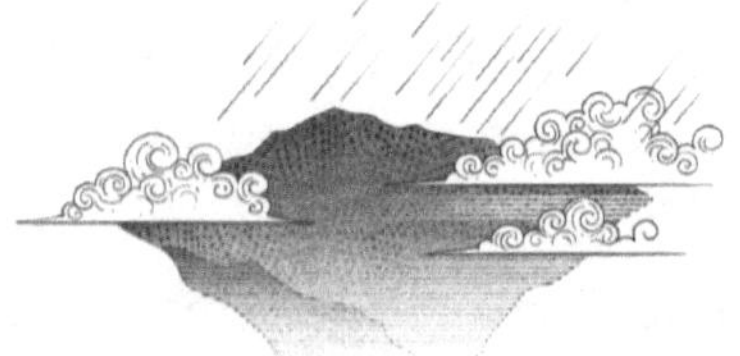

As I sit here and worry about Stella and the dark edge (if I can't see her, I should be worried, as Fiona says), I'm reminded that when writing this story, the characters have made some extraordinary choices. And believe me, it's been their decision. Fiona feeling kinship with a small elemental that throws her into a world of trouble. Gaili taking someone under her wing who could use a kind word and an inquisitive question. Richard deciding to investigate Fiona instead of avoiding her. These choices have really changed The Planar Page series, and for the better I think.

When I concocted this story, I wanted to write about historical periods I love and do a bit of time travel—but my way. I've always loved characters who run through different eras experiencing things firsthand. But I wondered what it would be like if they simply got to do it as part of their waking life. Like feeding themselves or going to the market. They popped over to another realm and did it there. But I had no idea how much history I could get away with without it being too confusing for you, dear reader. What's made up and what is real? As I continue to blur the lines in the upcoming books, I'd love to know what clues you've picked up in the previous books that are facts from our world.

In *Pressed*, of course, there really was a Richard the Lionheart. King of England in the twelfth century and romanticized quite a bit in the Robin Hood stories (and now here!). And though she bears physical resemblance to Queen Elizabeth, Queen Brilliance is a less enlightened version of that famous woman.

Thorn Palace did exist but as the Palace of Westminster. The royal apartments burned down before the sixteenth century and another fire took out the rest in the nineteenth century, leaving behind Westminster Hall, which is still used today. It was situated on the River Thames, which had various other names I've included here. I find palaces and castles extremely fascinating and strived for a balance of historical accuracy (location and names) with fantastical needs (the interior of the palace described here resembles more the Palace of Whitehall, which was used more after the sixteenth-century fire at Westminster).

And of course, I included my rendition of King Henry, or how I imagine he may have been in this particular alternate world. Still vying to keep power over people any way he could. I hope you enjoyed *Pressed*, and I look forward to taking you across the Roman Empire, from my perspective, when we next meet.

Glossary of The Planar Pages series

Find expanded lore, world information and more at
https://go.dhalerambo.com/tpp

Spine: A realm connected to every page in the Book. All page turners live here and can suffer ill effects for being gone too long. Split into over a dozen districts.

Seven Known Pages (as stacked in the Book)

Elemental Chapter

Blaze: page of fire, contains salamanders, flarions, ragnis, and other fire elementals

Depths: page of water, contains water elementals, merfolk, turtles, and more

Mistral: page of air, contains sylphs and other air elementals

Cobbles: page of earth, contains gnomes and other earth elementals

Mortal Chapter

Restless Rise (Rise): page of humans, contains a central mountain with floating islands all round it

Kerus: page of smilodon, elephas, and ursidon

Court of Copper (Court): page of faekin: fairies, fae, fauns, centaurs, and nymphs

<u>Terms</u>

Aer: language from page of air, Mistral

Aguan: language from the Depths

the Binder: leader of the Guild

the Book of Larrakane (the Book): all the known pages of the universe

bookmark: token from a page, used to travel there by a page turner

the Card: a free leaflet by the Travel Guild

the Church of Larrakane: organization devoted to worship of Larrakane

Claire: a language from page of fire, Blaze

Depth's Door: a lake in Spine

diamonnette paper (papers): universal currency

dusty: used to described a page turner who's ready to retire

elephas: like elephants standing on their hind legs, from Kerus

faekin: fauns, fairies, pixies, centaurs, all from the Court of Copper

Fallen Bubble: a cocktail

flarion(s): fire elementals who live in pools of magma from page of fire, Blaze

the Followers: a subset of the Church of Larrakane

format: slang for rumor

the Gilded: six leaders in the Travel Guild, including the Binder

the Hinge: Travel Guild headquarters

inked: blessed by Larrakane with the ability to turn pages

the Inking: historic event that created page turners

jacket(s): slang for officers of the Guild

kora: fish with an oily excretion from page of water, Depths

Larrakane (she/her): bestows the ability to turn pages and creator of the Book

La'mior: a fire forest in Blaze

pagemark(s): safe places where turners can move between pages

page turners (turners): people who can move between pages

Pestles and Mortar: smithy in the Spine

pulp: slang for creatures from various pages who are not page turners

ragnis: metallic-boned quasi-flame creatures from page of fire, Blaze

ripper(s): slang for thieves and smugglers across pages

Schiflan: a language spoken from page of humans, Restless Rise

skimmer(s): slang for tourists visiting other pages

skips: slang for criminals on the run

smilodon(s): catlike people, from Kerus

Sod: language from page of earth, Cobbles

spotter(s): cartographers

sylph: stark white air creatures from page of air, Mistral

the Towers of Calistino (the towers): prison in Copper

the Travel Guild, the Guild: organization that regulates all the comings and goings of page turners in the Book

the Trussadary Inn: hotel in Court of Copper

the Waterfall Palace: hotel in the Depths

unread turner: slang for someone new to being a page turner

ursidon: bearlike people, from Kerus

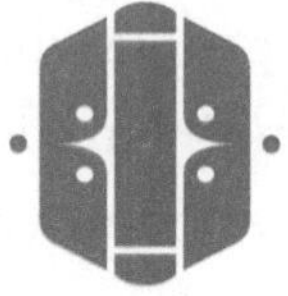

EXPLORE MORE OF THE Planar Pages for FREE by signing up for my <u>newsletter</u>.

Not only will you get me in your inbox with news and giveaways, you'll also receive The Planar Pages prequel HIDDEN WORDS

About *HIDDEN WORDS*

Life flourishes in the Book, a world of stacked realms spanning the ages. Those who can travel between them are page turners, blessed with the power to go from one page to the next.

For investigator Fiona Thorne, turning the page is normal life. Solving mysteries is where the excitement lives. No case is too small to ignite her curiosity, no page too familiar to explore.

Hired by her charming, gossipy neighbor to track down a shipment of rare books, Fiona thinks it'll be easy. She'll search for clues, sort out the issue, and be back in time for her nightly cup of coffee. And her reward? An introduction to one of the most reclusive leaders in Spine, the Druid Elder.

But that dream slips through her fingers as she realizes there's little evidence. She'll have to kick this investigation into high gear if she wants to impress her neighbor and earn her way into a privileged connection.

You can only read HIDDEN WORDS by signing up online for my newsletter at www.dhalerambo.com/newsletter/

Also by D. Hale Rambo

A SERIES OF DECISIONS ON KAIRAS

A COZY HIGH FANTASY trilogy set in the world of Kairas where the deities may be sealed away but their troubles are not.

Book 1, TOOLS OF A THIEF

How do you stop being a thief? Zizy Zakar assumed quitting her job, stealing from her boss, and teleporting hundreds of miles away was one way to give it a go.

Buy it now: teleport yourself to books2read.com/toat

Book 2, COMPONENTS OF A CASTER

Laysa has always vowed to do whatever it took to learn magic. Can Laysa keep her friends alive and survive uncovering the depths of the unknown? Does she have what it takes to be a Caster?

Buy it now: cast your coins at books2read.com/coac

Book 3, ROUTES OF A RANGER

A family under threat. A perilous journey home. Skinny has spent her life running from her past. Now she must achieve the destiny she was denied before she can defeat the enemy at her doorstep.

Buy it now: steer yourself towards go.dhalerambo.com/roar

THE PLANAR PAGES

A secondary world historical fantasy series with investigator Fiona Thorne and her motley crew of friends.

Life flourishes in the Book, a world of stacked realms spanning the ages, like the pages of an epic chronicle. Those who can travel through them are page turners; blessed with the power to go from one page to the next. For investigator Fiona Thorne, being a Turner is normal life. Solving mysteries is where the excitement lives.

Book 0, HIDDEN WORDS (newsletter exclusive prequel)

Cases are ramping up in the Spine and Fiona is in the middle of the action. Hired by her charming, gossipy neighbor to track down a shipment of rare books, Fiona thinks it'll be a piece of work.

Read it for FREE by signing up for my newsletterat go.dhalerambo.com/freestory

Book 1, BETWEEN THE LINES

Blaze, the page of fire, is wasting away. Fire elementals are being smuggled out in waves, but by whom? Fiona is on the job and nothing will hold her, not even the overbearing Travel Guild.

Read BETWEEN THE LINES and buy it now at: go.dhalerambo.com/tppbtl

Book 2, HARD BOUND

Someone has stolen from the Court of Copper, the illustrious fae page nestled within the Book. Is it a member of the fractured counsel, the fabled Order of Seven, or could the thief be much closer to Fiona than she realizes?

The fae realm is only a step away. BUY HARD BOUND at: go.dhalerambo.com/tpphb

Book 3, PRESSED

Between the tangled politics of home and facing her overbearing mother, Fiona counts herself lucky the yearly attendance with Queen Brilliance is only for a few days. But this year, the Queen presses Fiona with an unexpected request—find the mythical Guardian of Restless Rise. Amid schemes and betrayals, Fiona must piece together palace intrigues and myths to discover if the Guardian truly exists.

Join the investigation. BUY PRESSED at go.dhalerambo.com/tpppressed

About the Author

D. HALE RAMBO IS a historical fantasy author whose books transport readers to wondrous worlds filled with magic, mystery, and humor. With compelling and memorable characters at the heart of her stories, Rambo weaves tales to entertain and enthrall.

A lifelong storyteller, she's been writing and creating other worlds since she was old enough to mark them on her bedroom wall.

When she's not writing, you can find her enjoying a stiff cosmopolitan while reading mysteries alongside her favorite pet companion.

Discover more about her wondrous worlds, the versatility of gnomes, and fun fae cocktails at www.dhalerambo.com

www.ingramcontent.com/pod-product-compliance
Lightning Source LLC
Chambersburg PA
CBHW020247010826
48973CB00006B/1690